HIDE & SEEK

An absolutely addictive crime thriller with a huge twist

DI Mike Nash Book 9

BILL KITSON

Revised edition 2020
Joffe Books, London
www.joffebooks.com

© Bill Kitson
First published as *Picture of Innocence*
in Great Britain 2017

**Please join our mailing list for free Kindle
books and new releases.**

ISBN 978-1-78931-438-0

ACKNOWLEDGEMENTS

The plot of *Hide & Seek* demanded a lot of research and background information before I could take up my pen.

My grateful thanks, therefore, to Dr Peter Billingsley for a medical perspective.

To Hannah Outhwaite-Luke and Sarah Trout for their invaluable expert advice on the psychological symptoms and behaviour associated with Narcissistic Personality Disorder.

To Sarah Callego for a virtual tour of the streets and locations of Madrid, and background information about Spanish life and customs.

To Angela Gawthorp, Cath Brockhill and Janette Ozkurt for reading the various drafts and giving their opinion on the merits (and otherwise) of the plot.

And most of all, to my wife, Val, without her hard work and eye for detail, *Hide & Seek* would never have been produced.

CHAPTER ONE

July 1989

She listened, hardly daring to breathe. Although the footsteps were light, the polished wooden floors made them clearly audible. The girl crouched into the farthest, darkest corner of the kneehole beneath the desk, desperate to avoid detection. She heard the footsteps coming closer. Would they enter this room?

They stopped. Silence. Silence, for what seemed an age, as she prayed the footsteps would start again; would go on down the corridor. Then a creaking sound as the study door opened. A shadow cast across the room, someone entered, getting closer. She held her breath. A hand reached out. She gasped and recoiled, but she was hauled from her hiding place — escape was impossible.

'So, there you are. You didn't think there was anywhere you'd be safe, did you? You can't escape me.' He began to laugh, cruelly, wickedly. 'Now you'll have to pay the penalty.'

Lottie began to cry.

Older brothers are hateful — even when you are only playing hide-and-seek.

* * *

The occasion was a double celebration. Timed to coincide with Paul and Bev Davison's tenth wedding anniversary, the event also marked the Davison business empire's successful acquisition of their main rivals, leaving the group a clear leader in their field. What exactly that field comprised was difficult to classify. Several financial journalists had tried, before settling for the ambiguous term, 'industrial conglomerate'.

To do the occasion justice, Paul had organized a party of such proportions that it was sure to make several of the next morning's gossip columns. The venue was the couple's London residence, a mansion with extensive grounds. The lawns had been turned over to the erection of marquees, much to their gardener's despair, while the reception rooms of the house were also set aside for entertaining should the English climate prove fickle.

Paul and Bev Davison were the classic 'golden couple' as one magazine had described them. In addition to Paul's charismatic leadership of the business, Bev had been the most sought-after model to grace the catwalk since the stick-thin clothes horses of the 1960s. In demand from agencies seeking to push the wares of a whole range of products, Bev's image was all but impossible to avoid, whether in the cinema, on TV, in magazines, even in tube stations, on the sides of buses and hoardings worldwide. The term super-model suited her perfectly.

For once, the weather behaved impeccably, so the hordes of business acquaintances, family, friends, celebrities and media representatives who made up the five-hundred-strong guest list were able to throng the grounds in comfort, enjoying the music of the two groups hired for the occasion, and wining and dining on the excellent fare provided by the specialist event catering company.

The party was in full swing, and as the afternoon wore on, Paul and Bev were able to congratulate themselves on another highly successful occasion.

It was 4 p.m. before anyone noticed that their five-year-old daughter Lottie was missing. Lottie's older brother Keith was first to raise the alarm. He spoke to Yvonne, the au pair who acted as their nanny. Together, they searched the house. Then Keith went to find his mother. She was in deep conversation with a man they recognized from the television and it was a few moments before they could attract her attention.

Keith blurted out the news that was to change all their lives. 'Mum, I can't find Lottie. We were playing hide-and-seek.'

At first, it didn't sink in. 'Then you haven't been looking in the right places,' Bev laughed. 'Don't tell me a five-year-old has hidden so well you can't find her?'

'You don't understand, Mummy. I was hiding. It was Lottie who was supposed to be looking for me.'

Bev felt a sudden lurch of fear, a cold grip on her heart. She tried to dismiss it, but the sensation remained. She looked at the au pair. 'Have you searched the house?'

'Yes, Mrs Davison, and there's no sign of her, either inside or out. And there's something else that's weird.'

'What?' Bev's mind couldn't get past her missing daughter.

'One of the paintings is missing from the study.'

Together, the trio sought out Paul. He was giving an interview to a newspaper columnist and Bev felt uncertain whether to interrupt.

'Come on, Keith,' — Bev took her son's hand, signalling Yvonne to accompany them — 'we'll go and have another look. With all three of us searching I'm sure we'll find her soon enough.'

It took them some time to cover the entire house and finding no trace they returned to Paul. He was close to the bar; a glass of wine in one hand as he talked to an attractive woman Bev knew to be a customer of the group. Normally, Bev wouldn't have interrupted. But this was far from normal. She was near hysterical as she grabbed his arm. 'Paul! Paul, we can't find Lottie! We can't find her anywhere!'

After an extensive search of the house and grounds involving both staff and guests, Paul Davison phoned the police.

Within days it would not just be the gossip columns that were reporting the event. By then, it would be front-page news. By then, what should have been the best day in Paul and Bev Davison's married life had turned into a waking nightmare that refused to go away.

* * *

That same evening, a couple took their seats on a flight from Heathrow to Charles de Gaulle airport in Paris. Mr and Mrs Torres had their son with them. The boy seemed subdued for a four-year-old on his first trip to Disneyland. Anyone looking closely at the family would have thought how like his parents the boy was. His close-cropped dark hair, small, neat appearance, all mirrored those of both father and mother. The only difference was his lack of suntan. He was dressed in trainers, denim trousers, polo shirt with a tiny emblem on the pocket, and regulation baseball cap. He looked like millions of other small boys of his age. He did not look in the least like Lottie Davison, whose face, framed by her long, flowing curls would be plastered over the world's press within days.

Later, while detectives were conducting the herculean task of interviewing the mass of people either partying or working at the Davison's house, another aeroplane clawed its way out of Parisian airspace heading for northern Spain. On board, Mrs Torres, now travelling without her partner, held her son's hand in case he cried out with the noise or confusion of take-off. But the boy seemed calm, dozing off even before the seat belt sign went out.

At the same time, a train left Paris for the same destination. One of the passengers, apparently a businessman, was anxious to return to his homeland to get back to his wife and son — or so he would say in the unlikely event that he was asked. When he reached his home town, much later that evening, his wife was at the station to meet him. As they headed into the countryside, they discussed the events of the day. In the child seat specially installed behind them, the effects of the sedative still to wear off, Lottie Davison slept on.

Eventually, they reached the remote farmhouse that had been their home for years. The nearest village was two miles away, their closest neighbour almost as far. That was the reason they'd selected the house. It had taken almost a year to find. When they bought it, the place was a ruin, with no mains services, no roof, and little to recommend it. The locals thought they were mad, and that this madness stemmed from the fact that they were foreigners. By that, the locals meant that they hailed from more than one hundred kilometres away. Nobody knew quite where, and nobody was discourteous enough to enquire, but they knew the couple weren't natives of that region. Their accent was wrong, for one thing. And their way of life. They often disappeared, sometimes for days on end. That was odd, to put it mildly, when there were elderly inhabitants of the village who had never travelled more than fifty kilometres from their birthplace. Not only that, but the couple seemed to have no social life and, when at home, rarely left their own property, save to go shopping. It came as a shock to some residents to discover that the couple had a child. That was a measure of how closely they guarded their privacy. Obviously, the locals concluded, the couple were from the south because it was well known that all southerners were mad.

In both respects the locals were wrong. The couple weren't mad, far from it. Nor were they from the south. This was the fiction they'd allowed to be put about, knowing that all self-respecting northerners believed anyone from the south was either evil or unbalanced, or both. The fiction worked well.

* * *

The ransom demand arrived four days later. The envelope was cheap, one of a type sold by the million every day. The name and address were typewritten as was the note inside.

Neither the typing nor the central London postmark gave any clue as to the identity of the kidnappers. The contents were brutally terse. The first line contained only Lottie's name coupled with the message '£2,000,000 within four days'.

The second line gave the name of a bank in Zurich and an account number. The third and final line contained the threat 'If you attempt to trace her, or try to trap us, the girl will die'. Wary of a hoax, detectives examined the photo attached to the demand. The child pictured still wearing her party frock from the day of her abduction, was undoubtedly Lottie Davison.

Armed with the information from the note, detectives flew to Zurich, where they interviewed the President of the bank. He was concerned, polite, but adamant. 'This bank has made its reputation on guarding the confidentiality of our customers, whatever the circumstances,' he told them. 'Although I sympathize with the missing girl's parents, I cannot comply with your request. Under no circumstances will we reveal any information about that account or the identity of the account holder.'

Swiss police were more cooperative. They set up surveillance close to the bank premises. For the next two weeks, every visitor to the building was followed and identified. In the process, two men and a woman wanted in Germany and Switzerland on forgery charges were arrested, but there was no success in finding those who had abducted Lottie.

On the fifteenth day, a phone call from London caused the two English detectives to check out of their hotel, while their Swiss counterparts returned to other duties. The lead detective put it bluntly to his deputies. 'You'd better come straight home. It's all over. The girl's dead.'

'What? Have you found a body?'

'No, but we've had another note. And a photograph.'

'Oh no! What did it say? What was in the picture?'

'The photo is of the girl. There's no question it's her, and little doubt that she's dead, poor mite. The note said it was Davison's fault, his and ours, for trying to trace them via the bank. Said we'd ignored the warning that they would kill her.'

* * *

The officer heading the investigation into the kidnap and murder of Lottie Davison studied the newspaper report of the press conference held the previous day. The reporter had been impressed by the obvious distress of the policemen, all of whom, he pointed out, were well used to dealing with unpleasant and tragic events.

The detective growled at his assistant. 'Listen to this, "The lead detective was close to being overwhelmed by distress as he outlined some of the more brutal facts of this harrowing case." What the hell did he think I'd be doing, singing and dancing?'

He continued reading aloud what few facts had emerged from the press briefing. '"The original ransom demand was accompanied by a threat that if attempts were made to trace the girl or trap the kidnappers, Lottie would be killed. A second note was received at the Davison family home yesterday. Unfortunately, my officers were unable to intercept the message before it had been seen by both Mr and Mrs Davison. The kidnappers have carried out their threat, despite the fact that the police did not attempt to capture them. In an act of horrific sadism, the like of which I have not seen throughout my career, the perpetrators included a photograph of the bloodstained body of their victim. We will leave no stone unturned in our efforts to bring these evil, cold-blooded killers to justice, no matter how long or what resources it takes."' He tossed the paper on his desk and sighed.

Involvement of the Swiss bank had extended the search Europe-wide. Evidence provided by the photograph turned it into a murder hunt. Despite the involvement of a considerable number of law enforcement agencies in several countries, each following up earlier reported sightings of similar-looking children, ranging, as they found out, from two to fifteen years of age, no trace of Lottie Davison was found.

Eventually, even media interest in what had become known as the 'English Lindbergh Affair' ebbed away only to be rekindled at sporadic intervals. In official circles the file remained open. Although the modus operandi of the crime fitted many other unsolved cases, principally high-value art thefts, the identity of the perpetrators remained as much of a mystery as the whereabouts of Lottie Davison's body.

The detective in charge of the case was reading a memo and winced as he read the final sentence, the instruction from his superiors was brutally clear. With no fresh evidence coming to light, the enquiry was to be scaled back. Unless new information was forthcoming, or a body was found, no additional manpower or resources were to be allocated to the case.

His assistant studied him. 'That's it then. No more we can do?'

'Better tell the rest of the team. Reassign them to other duties.'

He opened the folder for a final time. On impulse, he scrawled a couple of words on the header sheet, a question he'd asked himself throughout the inquiry. He looked at what he'd written, looked at the photo of the child that was pinned to the corner. No matter how hard-bitten his years of dealing with serious crime had made him, the thought of what had happened to this innocent child moved him immeasurably. Tears formed in his eyes. It wouldn't help poor Lottie now. Nothing would. Wearily, he closed the file and put it in his out tray. Soon, it would go into the darkness of the file room. There, unless something dramatic happened, it would lie, gathering dust. Along with that unanswered question: was it an inside job?

CHAPTER TWO

Spring 2013

In the Basque Country, a couple left the hospital consultant's office and walked in silence down the long corridor. The only sound being their footsteps echoing on the marble floor. It was the news they had both dreaded. They had feared that this situation would arise, sooner or later. They had tried to ignore the threat, and as the years passed the chances of it seemed to diminish, but it was always there, lurking like a shadowy figure in the darkness. Now, it was as if the figure had emerged. The fear was thrust to the forefront of their minds, what had been nebulous was now reality, stark unavoidable reality.

After they reached the car and had driven clear of the city the woman spoke. 'It will be expensive, and the consultant told us there is no guarantee of success. Can we afford it?'

Juan Torres manoeuvred round a huge truck laden with vegetables before replying. 'It will take all we have saved plus a lot more besides, but there is no alternative. It must be tried. Anything else is unthinkable.'

'Perhaps we could sell the house.'

His laugh was devoid of humour. 'In the middle of the worst recession for thirty years? With property values so low?

Even if we could find a buyer they would want it for next to nothing. Besides, we need somewhere to live. I have another idea.'

'What is that?'

'A long time ago we had an insurance policy. I suggest we activate it.'

The woman looked aghast. 'That could be terribly dangerous. Is there no other way? The old way, perhaps?'

'No chance. For one thing we are much older now. For another, you are hardly fit enough to work. And along with everything else, prices for what we could obtain would be low, as with house prices. We said the insurance policy was for an emergency. And this is a full blown, lights flashing, sirens blaring emergency.' It was a phrase he'd heard on an American TV cop show. He rather liked it.

'How will you go about it?'

'This evening while you are making supper I will compose a letter.' He paused and thought about it for a moment. 'It will come as a considerable shock when it reaches its destination.'

'Promise me one thing, though.'

He glanced across. He could guess what she was about to say.

'Promise you won't tell anyone about today.'

He nodded agreement. He didn't need to ask who she meant by 'anyone' — he knew.

* * *

Juan Torres was running late. This was almost unheard of. All his life punctuality had been almost an obsession. Timing had been crucial during his professional career. On occasions, split-second timing was essential, not only for success but survival. This was not as critical, but to be late would be unpardonable, especially in such traumatic circumstances.

They had known they could rely on one another, no matter how dangerous or challenging the situation. Without her, there was no teamwork. The routine blown, there was no timing, no sense of the punctual. If he hurried, if he drove a little faster than normal he might be able to make up some of the lost time.

He cast a quick look round the kitchen, ensuring that all was neat and tidy as she would have wanted. His eyes blurred at the thought that she would never see all this again, never stand by the range stirring the contents of a pan, laughing at something he'd said. He rubbed his eyes and his vision cleared.

It was coming up to Christmas; the main roads would be heaving with traffic. He cursed his stupidity for forgetting. There was no way he could get there on time. He'd be more than an hour late, unless he took the mountain road. He'd done it before, many times. Once more couldn't harm. She didn't like him using that road, especially in the winter, but he felt sure she'd forgive him this once. Anyway, he needn't tell her. Even the thought of keeping this small secret from her brought on a twinge of guilt.

His attention was divided between the road ahead and the dashboard clock. It seemed an age before he was able to leave the queue of crawling traffic that filled every lane. Eventually, he turned onto the minor road. Here, although it was narrow and winding, he was able to put his foot down. The road was barely wider than two vehicles in places, but for several miles, as he climbed higher into the mountains, he didn't encounter any other motorists. As he got deeper into the countryside, the hill tops were covered with the first of the winter snow. Steep cliffs rose on one side, while at the other there were sheer drops of several-hundred feet, unprotected by guard rails. The sheep around there had to take their chances.

Another few weeks and this route would become impassable; the only hazard today was the bright winter sunlight, low in the sky. However, for the most part, the sun was behind him, besides which, he had no leisure to look in his rear-view mirror; the road ahead commanded his whole attention. There was little point in looking back anyway, there was unlikely to be anything behind him, and even if there was, no chance of being overtaken.

The first intimation of trouble came with what he thought was a change in the note of his car engine. A moment's panic ensued. What if he should break down out here, miles from anywhere? Almost immediately he felt, rather than saw, a shadow in his peripheral vision. He looked in the mirror, and panic became horror. The view from the rear window was taken up by the bull bar on the front of a pick-up truck.

* * *

At Christmas those staying in the hospital had many visitors. The marble corridors were busy with human traffic as people sought friends and relatives, adding to the normal flow of doctors and nursing staff. No one paid any attention to the dark-haired man who walked briskly towards the private rooms at the end of the passage. He was dressed like a doctor, would have looked like a doctor even without the identity badge and the stethoscope dangling from his neck.

He reached the rooms with the certainty of one familiar with the layout of the building and entered the second door on the left. Inside, he smiled at the solitary occupant, a woman who was looking expectantly towards the opening door. 'A message from your husband,' he told her. 'He apologizes for being late, but there has been a fatal accident on the road. He hopes you will be together soon.'

As he spoke, the man turned the tap on the cylinder providing oxygen to the patient to the off position. Almost simultaneously, he moved the alarm call button beyond reach of her hand. He watched impassively as she struggled for breath, saw her begin to lose the fight. 'Yes, I feel sure you'll be together any moment.'

Minutes later, he turned the oxygen tap back on, although by then it was too late for the woman in the bed.

He left the room and walked back down the corridor. As he turned towards the entrance he almost collided with a young woman who was hurrying towards the reception desk. He glanced round and saw a car approaching with the distinctive insignia of the Guardia Civil on the door panel. Time to leave.

* * *

'The man and woman are dead.'

'And what about the girl?'

'Not yet, they haven't been able to trace her.'

His employer frowned. 'I'm interested in results, not excuses.'

Dermot Black continued as if he hadn't heard. He was well used to his employer's asides by now. 'The woman was dying already. Our man merely helped the process along. That part of it went according to plan. However, when he was dealing with the husband he was seen.'

'What was he doing, strangling him in the middle of a bullring?'

'He was on a mountain road. He tailgated the man's car and shoved it over the edge. It wasn't until too late that he saw a party of climbers watching everything. He had to ditch the pick-up and get out of Spain as fast as he could.'

'The driver knows about our involvement?'

'Yes, and he can't go back to Spain for obvious reasons.'

'Then you'll have to find someone else.'

'That might take a while. It was hard enough finding this one.'

'I don't care; just do it.'

'What about this one? Shall I pay him off?'

'Pay him for a job that's been botched? Pay him when he knows too much? I don't think so. Deal with him, and this time, do it right.'

* * *

17

In the early hours of the morning, motorway service stations are usually deserted apart from trampers, all-night wagon drivers travelling the length and breadth of the country. Although the area close to the facilities is brightly illuminated, the remote parts of the car park are much less well lit. Anyone passing might have been curious as to why not one, but two cars were parked so far from the buildings when there was ample space closer to the services.

However, there were no passers-by.

Both drivers were sitting in the same car. The driver, recently returned from Spain, apologized for his late arrival.

'That's all right,' the man in the passenger seat assured him.

'Have you got something for me?' the driver asked.

'Oh, yes.'

Anyone passing might have heard a couple of dull, plopping sounds and seen a brief flash of flame, almost as if someone had struck a match. They might even have seen the driver slump forward, restrained only by his seat belt.

However, there were no passers-by. A moment later, Dermot Black drove away.

* * *

In Helmsdale police station, DI Mike Nash was bored. It was a rare occurrence and he was thinking how his life had changed. He remembered how, some months ago, his detective sergeant, Clara Mironova, had noticed the brochure on his desk and pointed to it. 'How's the house hunting going?' she'd asked.

'Very well. I found one at last and I'm about to put in an offer for it. Or rather, Daniel found it.' He had passed the paperwork for her to see.

Clara had become accustomed to a situation that at one time had seemed highly improbable with Nash's bachelor lifestyle. Mike Nash, father to a son of whose existence he had been unaware. Daniel, born in France, knew everything about his father. His mother had made sure of that. Unable to live in England, she had returned to her roots. After her death from illness, Daniel was brought to live with Nash and they had slowly got to know each other.

He recalled their subsequent conversation when Clara smiled at the prospect of a house hunting nine-year-old. 'How did Daniel find it?'

'He spotted the photo in the agent's window, decided it met his criteria, and dragged me inside. We went to look at the house on Saturday afternoon.'

Clara had looked at the price and whistled. 'That sounds cheap. Is there something wrong with it? Dry rot, rising damp, or whatever?'

'Nothing so drastic, I hope, but that'll have to await the survey. From what the agent told me, it's been on the market a while and houses aren't exactly selling like hot cakes. The reason it's cheap is that it was let as a holiday home but the firm has gone into liquidation, so the receivers want it off their hands. Added to the fact that the property market round here is on its backside, I reckon I'll be in with a good chance.'

'You're not intending to offer the asking price, then?'

'No way. I thought I'd be cheeky and bid them fifty-thousand pounds less.'

'If you get it for that, you won't be buying it, you'll be stealing it,' Clara commented, as she read the prospectus. 'Smelt Mill Cottage, close to Wintersett village? It is a bit of a way out, unless you work in Helmsdale.'

'Exactly, and that limits the market. However, it's only a twenty-minute ride into the office for me.'

'It's an unusual name. Where does that come from?'

'There's an old lead mine close by. Long abandoned now, but the cottage was occupied by the master smelter, who was in charge of the purification of the ore.' Nash grinned. 'I read up on it, that's how I know.'

'The setting looks superb, but I'd worry about what might be wrong with it. You hear such horror stories about repossessions.'

'I'll be able to deal with any possible problems as long as it's structurally sound. Daniel won't be happy if we don't get it.'

'Why is he so keen?'

'Apart from the fact that we're desperate to get away from the rat-hole we've been forced to rent for the last two years, you mean? I was hoping we could have been out of there long before now but what with the insurance company delays after the explosion at our previous place and trying to find something suitable, it just hasn't happened. I don't know how I'd have coped if Daniel hadn't been away at school. However, the main attraction is that the cottage has a lawn that's big enough for a cricket pitch. Except that at the moment, it's more like a hayfield.'

'You'll have a lot of furniture and so forth to buy.'

'I know, and you've been co-opted to help choose it, and if I'm lucky, I can take advantage of the January sales. Apart from that, I reckon some kitchen units, replacing the bathroom suite and a lick of paint throughout should do the trick.'

Within a week, Nash had learned that his audacious bid had been accepted. On hearing that, he rang his solicitor to start the ball rolling. At first, the man was dubious about the timescale Nash told him he wanted. 'I can't see any hope of completing so quickly,' he told the detective.

'Hang on,' Nash pointed out, 'there's no chain to think about. They haven't a property to buy, and I'm not selling one. Also, don't forget I shall be paying cash.'

'I agree that does make it simpler. However, we still have to get the survey and the searches completed and wait on their solicitor drawing up the documents. I'd say you're looking at ten weeks to three months.'

'Halve that; tell them I intend to move in during February half-term. And if they reckon it can't be completed in that space of time, then the deal's off. That'll get them moving. The house has been for sale for well over twelve months, so the receivers will be desperate to turn it into cash.

Added to which,' he added wickedly, 'neither you nor their solicitors will be overburdened with conveyancing work the way the housing market is at present.'

* * *

Although there was still some work to do, the house was habitable when Nash and Daniel had moved in to Smelt Mill Cottage. Both father and son were eager to see the last of the dingy flat they had rented since they were left with nothing following an attack on Nash's life.

On the morning they collected the keys, they'd arrived at the house minutes before the van delivering furniture was due. The snow of the past weeks had all but melted, much to the relief of Nash. After they entered via the storm-porch, Daniel had dashed off to investigate while Nash opened the large patio doors before the doorbell signalled the arrival of the delivery men. Nash, with the help of Clara and a catalogue for Daniel, had spent a considerable time and a large amount of money, selecting beds, lounge and dining suites and a desk apiece for their new home.

Nash and Daniel had spent the remainder of the half-term holiday with paintbrushes in hand in an attempt to decorate the downstairs rooms. Workmen fitted a new kitchen and bathroom, their amusement apparent as they watched Daniel who had more paint on his clothing than on the walls.

That had been some months ago and now, with Daniel back at school, Nash constricted by a heavy workload, attempted to make a family home for the two of them. He was looking forward to when they could enjoy the fruits of his labour.

He was shaken from his reverie and scowled at the mug of coffee Clara brought in.

'It's OK,' she reassured him, 'It's out of the filter machine. Viv dragged himself away from the computer to make it.'

'What's he doing on there?'

'Searching for cheap flights.' She rolled her eyes. 'This wedding's taking over.'

'It isn't until next year, for goodness' sake. I thought he and Lianne had the honeymoon all booked?'

'They have. This is for the stag weekend.'

'That's got to be months away, surely? Why bother now?'

'He's not booking anything yet, just getting an idea of prices so he can tell both his friends.'

Nash grinned at Clara's sarcasm. DC Viv Pearce, the tall Jamaican, was extremely popular and the guest list for the stag weekend would occupy a fair chunk of the plane.

'He's been told by another friend — so that makes three,' Clara added thoughtfully, 'that if he books for the weekend at the end of August just before the schools go back it will be cheaper.'

'How do you work that out?'

'Everyone is flying back to England then, not going away.'

'Makes sense, I suppose.'

* * *

That evening when he reached home, Nash spotted an unusual stamp on one of the envelopes lying on his doormat. It was addressed simply to The Occupier, Smelt Mill Cottage, Near Stark Ghyll, England. It was fortunate that the Royal Mail had identified the correct destination. Nash was intrigued, his interest caught by the word *España* across the base of the stamp. His curiosity deepened as he began to read.

'Dear Sir or Madam,

I am trying to discover the origin, background, and painter of a landscape that has been in my family since I was a small child, and possibly longer. Sadly, my parents are both dead and the painting is part of my father's estate, so I cannot ask them how they came by it. I am writing this in the hope that you may be able to provide some information, but I am aware that the address, which is all I know, may be insufficient. I have enclosed a photograph of the painting, and if the scene is familiar to you I would be very grateful if you could reply, giving me a more precise location of the setting, even if you have no more knowledge of the work.

The painting bears the inscription *Stark Ghyll from Smelt Mill Cottage*. There is no signature, but the brushwork is of good quality which suggests an artist of some talent. Although I do not think the work is of exceptional value, I would be keen to discover the circumstances in which it was painted, by whom, and how it came into my family's possession.'

The signature at the bottom of the letter was A Torres, with an address in Madrid. Nash stared at the photo comparing it with the view from his window. The evening sun was close to setting, flooding the far side of the valley in soft light. There was no doubt the artist had been positioned very near to the house, possibly even inside it or the garden when he or she had completed the painting.

He decided the letter warranted a reply. He explained that he had only recently bought the house and that he could provide no information about the artist or the painting, save to confirm that it had undoubtedly been completed there. He would enclose a photo that would give a better indication of how well the unknown painter had depicted the scene.

* * *

It was April when the reply came from Spain; Nash had all but forgotten the enquiry about the unknown artist. He had taken Daniel back to boarding school earlier that week following the Easter break.

Nash read the letter discovering that the writer was a woman. Miss Torres was friendly, grateful for the information, and appreciative of his offer to find out what he could about her painting. She added that her curiosity was part professional as well as personal, as she was an artist.

The following morning, when Viv Pearce walked into the CID suite, he was surprised to see Nash crouched over the computer on the corner desk. 'I didn't know you could use one of those,' he commented, a little sarcastically.

'I don't need to when I have you. But I have been learning a few new tricks. I have to try and keep pace with Daniel. Hang on a second.' Nash pressed a key and waited; then smiled, feigning triumph. Almost immediately the printer alongside sprang to life. 'Wow,' he exclaimed, 'looks as if I've managed it — a modern miracle.'

He pointed to the paper beginning to spew from the machine and explained about the letter he'd received from Spain. 'The writer claimed to be an artist, so I thought I'd check out that claim, and it seems to have worked.'

As he was collecting the papers from the printer tray, DS Mironova walked in just in time to hear Pearce say, 'Speaking of Spain, that reminds me, I'm still sorting out a venue for the stag weekend, and yours is the casting vote.'

'I hope you remember I warned you to keep away from Belarus,' Clara said. 'I don't think the old country could handle you lot.'

'There's no fear of that — I wouldn't want to upset your ancestors. So what's it to be, Mike?'

'Why do I have the vote? I'm a bit old for stag nights, let alone a full weekend. And I couldn't go when Daniel's at home. Besides which, if two of us were away who's going to mind the shop? I'd have to clear it with Jackie Fleming.'

'The superintendent wouldn't mind would she? Anyway, Lianne thinks you should go to keep me out of trouble.'

'Fat chance of that,' Clara muttered. 'More like the other way round, with all those senoritas about.'

Nash ignored her. 'When and where are you thinking of?'

'End of August. Madrid or Barcelona? The rest of the gang are split between the two, which do you prefer?'

Guided by the article he'd just been reading, Nash said, 'Madrid, for choice. But Daniel would be at home, so I'm afraid the answer has to be no.'

Pearce looked disappointed. 'OK then, I suppose it can't be helped.'

'Why are you having the stag-do so early?' Nash asked.

'I want to save next year's holiday allowance by going this year, plus it will be cheaper.' He sat at his desk and played with the stapler, his expression one of disappointment.

'Oh for heaven's sake, stop sulking, Viv,' Clara said. 'If Mike can clear it with Jackie then Daniel can stay with me. David should be home on leave then and we all know he dotes on him.'

Viv's face broke into a beam. 'Clara, you're a mate, thank you. That is OK, isn't it, Mike?'

'It doesn't look as though I've got much choice in the matter. Just don't spoil my son too much.'

When he got home that evening Nash read the computer printout. It was a feature article in the arts supplement from one of the English broadsheets, reprinted from the similar section of *El País*. It was no wonder Senorita Torres was able to write about the brushwork of the artist, he thought. She was counted as one of the most up-and-coming landscape painters in Europe. Nash read the article with interest. As he looked across at the long expanse of bare wall in the lounge he had an idea. Perhaps he might be able to put the stag weekend to good use.

He wrote a reply explaining that he hoped to visit Madrid and suggesting they meet. He added that he would bring photos of the area so she could get a better idea of the scenery and in addition, if she had some paintings for sale that might be suitable for his house he'd be interested to view them.

The reply came stating Miss Torres would be happy to meet him, keen to see the photos, and more than willing to show her work to a prospective buyer. She even suggested a possible venue, a bar close to her studio, adding that all he needed to do was tell her when he would be there and as long as she was free she would happily meet him.

* * *

The stag weekend was fast approaching. 'I'll be glad when this wedding's over,' Clara grumbled. 'It's all you can talk about.'

Pearce grinned, a trifle sheepishly. 'It's a big day.'

'What's the problem now?' Nash asked.

'He's worrying over where to base the stag party. Apparently Lianne suggested they need a headquarters, somewhere to go if any of them gets lost. Given the nature of the event I suppose she has a point,' Clara conceded.

'There's a bar on *Calle Huertas* that will do fine, I have the name of it at home. It's right in the centre, between the railway station and the old town,' Nash said without thinking.

Clara stared at him suspiciously. 'You said you've never been to Madrid. How come you know so much about it all of a sudden?'

Nash shrugged. 'Someone told me about it,' he said lamely.

CHAPTER THREE

The stag party landed in Madrid on a Friday afternoon in late August. Having checked in at their hotel they set out to investigate the local bars. Several of Pearce's close friends had thought it would be a good idea for the party to be in fancy dress, and several bar owners, not to mention their customers, were more than a little surprised to see a large group of men dressed in English police uniforms entering their premises. By contrast, Nash and Pearce, the only two in plain clothes, tried in vain to prevent the party getting out of hand. By the time the more enthusiastic members of the group decided that enough was enough, it was almost dawn, and a close encounter with the real thing in the shape of two Spanish police officers, signalled a strategic withdrawal to their hotel so they could begin incubating hangovers.

The following evening, the party was ready for a repeat performance, but when asked about his participation, Nash told them he wanted to look around the city first and would meet them at the bar where they were based. Pearce eyed his boss suspiciously. Admiring the architecture and checking out shop windows had never been obvious hobbies of Nash's.

Shortly before eight o'clock, the time scheduled for his meeting with Senorita Torres, Nash was in *Calle Huertas*. He ambled into the bar and ordered a bottle of *San Miguel*. He glanced round. There was only one young woman sitting alone.

As he wandered over, threading his way between tables, the remainder of the stag party entered the bar. Several of them were wearing the uniforms that had caused much merriment the previous night. Pearce watched in awe as he saw Nash reach the corner. After a brief exchange, the woman made a gesture with her right hand, a clear invitation for him to join her.

'I don't bloody believe it,' Pearce muttered.

'What's up, Viv?' his best man asked.

'How long have we been in Madrid? Twenty-four hours?'

'Thereabouts, why?'

'Mike's pulled already. Not only that, but he's pulled the best-looking female I've seen since the plane touched down. No wonder he didn't want to join us. Looking around the city, my arse. The randy bastard was on the pull.'

'Where? Where are you looking?'

Pearce pointed to the corner.

'Bloody hell! How does he do it?'

'If I knew that, I'd bottle it and sell it.'

* * *

'Senorita Torres?'

She looked up. Nash was struck by her deep brown eyes, eyes that looked sad, sad and wary he thought, and wondered if this had anything to do with the loss of her parents. From her letter he got the impression it had happened recently. 'I am Alejandra Torres, and you must be Mr Nash, yes? Please call me Alondra.' Her gaze wandered to the rest of the English drinkers. 'You are with them? The policemen?'

'Yes, but they're not real policemen,' Nash explained as he sat at her side. 'There are only two real policemen in the party, and we're not in uniform.'

Her eyes widened. 'You are a policeman? Why don't you wear a uniform? Is it because you are not on duty, or because you are in another country?'

'I don't wear one at home. I'm a detective.'

'I see.' She smiled fleetingly. 'So did this enable you find out anything about the painting?'

'Unfortunately, no. The problem is the area is so remote there is nobody to ask.'

'The name of the house is a strange one. I found two definitions for smelt in my dictionary. One is a variant of smell. The other is a small fish.'

'It isn't either of those.' Nash explained the smelting process.

'This is a small house then, Mr Nash? The word cottage suggests that.'

'Mike, please, Mr Nash sounds so formal.' Nash continued, 'Not enormous, but big enough for us.'

'Can you describe it for me?'

'I can do better than that. I took some photos soon after we moved in. I brought them with me.' He reached into his pocket.

'I didn't realize you were married. If it is so remote, isn't it lonely for your wife? You didn't mention her in your letters. What does she think of you meeting a strange woman instead of being with your friends?'

'I'm not married. What made you think . . . ? Oh, I said we, didn't I? I meant my son and me.'

'Oh, I understand. You are divorced, then? Is that difficult for your son? How old is he?'

'No, I'm not divorced either. Daniel is nine years old. His mother died a few years ago.'

'How sad, for you both. Do you miss her?' She suddenly realized how intrusive her questions were. 'Oh, I'm sorry, please forgive me.'

'Don't worry about it. Daniel's mother couldn't live in England.' He explained the circumstances. 'She left before

Daniel was born, before I was even aware she was pregnant. I didn't know about him until after she died a few years ago.'

'I am sorry for making you dredge all that up. But now you are happy?'

'It gets a bit lonely sometimes. Having a small boy restricts the social life somewhat. But I'm used to being alone, and work takes up a lot of my time.'

'It must be difficult doing your job and looking after a child. Who is caring for him this weekend?'

Nash explained, then spread some of the photos on the table. 'I think you can see from these why I need something for the walls. If you have some suitable paintings, they would be ideal, and from what I understand, they would also be a good investment.'

Her eyes widened. 'You have done some research. How did you find out about me?'

'The internet, I read the *El País* article.'

'I put out a selection of my better work ready for you to look at in my studio,' she told him. 'But I warn you, they are not cheap. When would you like to see them?'

'Is tonight OK?'

'I thought you'd prefer daytime so you can see them in natural light.'

'Perhaps both, then I can judge what they would look like at any time.'

She was about to say something else when she saw Pearce approaching. 'I think one of your friends would like to speak to you.'

Nash swung round. 'Did you want me, Viv?'

Pearce looked embarrassed. 'We're moving on, Mike. Will you be coming with us, or . . . ?'

'No, I'll catch you back at the hotel later.'

Pearce waited a second, as if expecting an explanation or an introduction. He frowned. 'Oh, all right — but don't forget why we came to Madrid. Good night, Miss.'

As he walked away, Alondra leaned forward. 'He seemed upset. I think your friends will be gossiping about you all weekend.'

'That's nothing new. The gossip, I mean.' Nash explained about Pearce's stag party.

Her eyes widened at Nash's mention of gossip, but she didn't comment. Instead, she asked, 'Have you eaten?'

'Yes, thanks. I was in desperate need because we'd a lot to drink last night, with nothing to eat beforehand but an airline meal, and you know how bad they are.'

'Actually, I don't. I've never been on an aeroplane — ever. They terrify me, and even the thought makes me feel ill.'

* * *

Her apartment (which was also her home studio) was little more than a hundred metres away from the bar. As they neared the building, Nash admired the architecture.

'I occupy the whole of the second floor. The first floor belongs to a couple who are away, visiting their daughter. The ground floor is a bakery.'

She unlocked the door and stepped into the hallway. In the faint light filtering in from the street, Nash saw a flurry of movement to her right, and a figure emerge from the deep shadow. The assailant's arm moved. A swift blow brought some sort of weapon crashing down on Alondra's head with a sickening thud. As her attacker raised his arm to strike a second time, Nash shouted, 'Hey! What the . . .'

The assailant flinched at Nash's shout, and the swing that was intended to crush Alondra's skull missed. Nash punched hard at the man's midriff. He connected and heard an exhalation of breath, accompanied by a single expletive, 'Fuck!'

The intruder lashed out and before Nash could grab him, squirmed past and was out of the building, hurrying into the throng on the pavement. Nash turned back inside, his main concern being for the girl. He was able to see she was laid face-down on the tiled floor. He found the light switch but the bulb was dead, he heard the sound of smashed glass underfoot. Nash felt her neck, seeking a pulse, and was reassured to feel a gentle throb under his fingers. He looked around but realized there was nothing he could do in the darkness of the hallway. Nor dare he leave Alondra to summon help, for fear that her assailant would return.

Nash took his mobile from his pocket, but then paused for a couple of seconds, his finger hovering over the keypad. He dialled 112, praying that the emergency operator would understand him.

* * *

Nash spent the next few hours at the hospital waiting anxiously for news of Alondra's condition. His vigil was broken by an interview with the local police, whose attitude changed markedly when they learned that the English tourist who had reported the assault was a senior police officer. They informed him that Alondra's apartment had not been entered and examination of the crime scene had produced no forensic evidence. Nash sympathized, there seemed little to be learned from the stygian gloom of the hallway.

He was relieved to be told that Alondra had recovered consciousness. 'We will keep her here at least overnight,' the doctor informed him, 'because we must determine if she has the concussion. However, the X-ray results show no fracture, which is positive.'

It was almost four in the morning when Nash returned to the hotel. One or two of the stag party were still in the bar but there was no sign of Pearce.

Shortly after 9 a.m. Nash was down for breakfast and helped himself to a selection from the central carousel, realizing suddenly that he was extremely hungry. He was just tucking into a croissant when the prospective bridegroom joined him. He looked in good shape, a fact that Nash commented on.

'I paced myself,' Pearce told him. 'It's a long weekend, so I decided not to overdo things. I was in bed before two o'clock. Much the same as you I expect. When you weren't in the bar I assumed you got to bed early. Elsewhere,' he said, a little cynically.

'Look, Viv, I know I was supposed to meet you back here. I'm sorry, but I got caught up in something.' Nash smiled ruefully and explained what had happened. Viv's eyes widened with surprise as Nash described the attack and the aftermath.

'Sounds like you had fun — although not the sort of fun I thought you had in mind,' he remarked.

'Fun is about the last word I'd use to describe last night. And it isn't over with yet. The local police gave me Miss Torres' keys, so I've to go to the hospital to return them and see how she is. I'm sorry to have put a bit of a damper on the weekend, but it wasn't my doing. What have you got planned for today?'

'Those of us who can face daylight are going sightseeing. I suspect for most of them that means shopping for presents to apologize for their absence this weekend. I understand that things haven't gone to plan, but if you can make it, we'll be meeting up in that bar again tonight.'

'I'll do my best,' Nash told him. 'But after last night I think it would be better if I don't make any promises.'

* * *

Alondra was sitting up in bed, and looking rather pale and forlorn. She admitted to having a severe headache and told Nash, 'Thank you for all you have done. But I have spoiled your weekend and you wanted to look at the paintings.'

'That doesn't matter, it's far more important that you're OK. Anyway, I can always look at the paintings tomorrow. Our flight to England isn't until the evening. Today, I can take you home and make sure there are no bad men lurking in the shadows,' he said with a smile. 'This time I'll be ready for them.'

'You are very kind to go to so much trouble.' Alondra smiled as she spoke, putting her hand on Nash's to reinforce her message. It was only a fleeting gesture, but it set Nash's pulse racing.

Sometime later, Alondra was home, sitting resting on her bed, her head supported by pillows Nash had arranged for her. He had taken up position in an armchair alongside the bed, having first removed several items of skimpy feminine underwear from the seat. 'Feel like talking?' he asked.

'I want to thank you. For saving me from injury, and for taking care of me.'

'No problem. What puzzles me is why someone from England tried to kill you. Have you any idea why?'

Alondra looked puzzled. 'How do you know he was English?'

'He swore in English,' he explained.

'I know nothing about England. I have never been there. The only connection with England that I can think of is that painting. And you, of course.'

'Your English is so good, and you have almost no accent, that I thought you must have spent time there.'

'No, my mother taught me. She and my father spoke English as often as Spanish at home. I didn't go to school as such, not until I came to Madrid for college. My mother was my teacher. She said it was the only way to be sure I got a decent education.'

'That makes the attack even more senseless. Are you sure you can't think of anything that would cause you to be attacked?'

She was about to say no, but hesitated. 'There is something, but I don't understand it. It might be connected with what happened to my father.'

'How do you mean?'

'Last December I had been in France, attending an exhibition of my paintings. When I phoned home, my father told me that my mother was in hospital terminally ill. He said that she had forbidden him to say anything before because she didn't want to spoil the occasion for me. It was my first international showing,' she explained. 'I came straight home. My father arranged to meet me at the hospital next day. Then they told me' — she sobbed with distress — 'that mother had died before I got there. By that time I was worried about my father too, because he was always punctual. I waited, but he never showed up.' She paused, fighting for control over her emotions.

'Take your time,' Nash said gently.

'He and my mother were so close, I was afraid things might have been too much for him, so I left the hospital and drove to Onati, to the farmhouse where we live,' she explained. 'The house was deserted and his car had gone. I waited, but it was the *Ertzaintza* that arrived.'

'The what?'

'That's the name for the police in the Basque Region. Like the *Guardia Civil* in the rest of Spain. They told me why he didn't get to the hospital. There is a road my father often took to bypass the local town. I don't use it, because it is narrow, winding, and there are some treacherous bends. In the winter it is far worse when the snow comes. If you go off the road it is certain death. And that's what happened. At first I wasn't sure whether if it was an accident, or whether he had done it intentionally. That was until the next day, after the eyewitnesses came forward.'

The distress was etched in her face, but she continued with barely a pause. 'A party of climbers told the *Ertzaintza* that there was a pick-up truck. It came up behind my father's car and pushed him over the cliff. There was no way he could escape. The witnesses were close enough to see the driver clearly. They gave police a description of the vehicle and the man. The truck was found abandoned, burnt-out, in some remote spot. When they checked they found it had been rented, and the hire company had all the driver's details, including his licence. They found out these were forged, but they had a photograph. That was circulated on TV and in the newspapers, as well as all police stations. They managed to trace the man as far as the French border. He'd been using various names, but after he entered France they lost track of him. As far as I know he's still out there.'

'You're saying that your father was murdered, but that you've no more idea of a motive for that than the attack on you?'

She began to shiver, although the room was warm enough for Nash to be sweating slightly. Shock and the reminder of what had happened to her father were taking their toll. 'I . . . Mr Nash, I want . . . Will you stay here tonight? I'm frightened. I don't want to be here alone. I would feel safer if I knew you were here.' She remembered the reason for his visit to Madrid. 'No, no, I am sorry, that is selfish of me. You must rejoin your friends.'

'They'll probably be too drunk to miss me. Of course I'll stay, on one condition.' He saw the wary look return to her face. 'The condition is that you call me Mike.'

She smiled, and he realized it was almost the first time he'd seen that. 'Tell me where to find a blanket, and I'll kip here.'

'Kip?'

'Sleep,' he explained.

The armchair was comfortable enough as a seat, but as a bed, much less so. Sometime in the early hours something disturbed his sleep. He waited, listening and watching. The apartment was in darkness, the night air still and warm. The only sound he could hear was Alondra's breathing, even and relaxed, from the bed only a few feet away. He was almost convinced he'd dreamed or imagined it, when he heard a scraping sound, slow and steady, like a cutter across glass. Nash discarded the blanket and got out of the chair. As he moved, he took his mobile phone from his pocket. He heard the girl's breathing change and knew she had woken up. 'Alondra,' he whispered. As he spoke he fumbled with the mobile, before finding the torch application. He switched it on.

She sat up, blinking in the light. 'What is it?' her whisper matched his tone.

'I think someone is trying to break into the apartment. Is there a door or window they could access easily?'

'In the kitchen,' she replied instantly. 'The fire escape.'

'Go into the bathroom and lock yourself inside. I'm going to try and scare them away.'

Nash waited until he heard the bolt on the bathroom door slide softly home before tiptoeing into the lounge. He memorized the position of each item of furniture before switching the torch off. He crept towards the kitchen and stopped by the partially open door, listening. The scraping sound had ceased, to be replaced by the click of a door being opened.

Nash stepped forward and raised the mobile to eye level. He turned his head slightly to one side and pressed a button on the phone. After a brief delay there was a sudden explosion of light. Nash had a vague impression of a man's silhouette against the wall before the outer door slammed shut. He switched the kitchen light on, darted across the room, and opened the door in time to hear the clatter of footsteps on the steel rungs of the fire escape, accompanied by a rich variety of swear words. Again the language was pure Anglo-Saxon.

Nash inspected the scene. He placed a couple of pans on the floor against the foot of the door, and for good measure leant their lids against the lower panel. If anyone tried to come in that way again, they'd make a noise comparable to the average brass band.

He tapped on the bathroom door. 'It's safe to come out now.'

She opened the door cautiously, an inch at a time.

'They've gone, and I don't think they'll be back.'

'How can you be so sure?'

'Because of this,' Nash held up his mobile. 'I took their photo. It's a bit blurred, but they won't know that. And if they do return . . .' He explained the warning alarm he'd set up.

Reaction set in, she began to tremble, and before he could say anything to comfort her she broke into tears. He put an arm around her shoulder, to console her. She clung to him as he guided her back to her bedroom, turned the lamp on, and helped her back into bed.

'Thank you again, Mike. That is twice you've saved my life.'

He returned to the armchair and pulled the cover over him. After the feel of her body against his, the chair seemed colder, even more uncomfortable than before. As he listened to her breathing ease into the regular pattern of sleep, he wondered what was behind the determined attacks. Was it, as she suggested, connected to her father's murder? Surely it must be, thought Nash. The coincidence was too strong for it to be otherwise.

When Nash awoke, he was alone. He leapt out of the chair and reached the kitchen door. He sighed with relief. Alondra was standing by the worktop watching the coffee machine. 'You scared me,' he told her. 'I thought something had happened to you.'

'I'm sorry. You were sleeping and I didn't want to wake you.'

'How's your head this morning?'

'Oddly enough, it's fine. A little tender, but nothing more.'

They sat on the balcony outside her lounge drinking coffee. 'I think we ought to call the police again,' Nash told her.

'Why? I mean, it's over now.'

'No it isn't. I'd say it's far from over. Especially if this is linked to what happened to your father. Look at it this way. There have been two attempts on your life. I'd say it's fairly certain they won't give up unless they can be scared off. For the time being I think I've done that. They probably believe I have a clear image of the intruder on my phone. If they see the *Guardia Civil* here, that should forestall them. Especially if the police can be persuaded to have a small piece about the break-in inserted in the paper or on the radio stating they are confident of making an arrest.'

'I'm not sure I could persuade the police to do that.'

'Maybe not, but I might be able to.'

'You would do that? To wait with me until the police arrive? But what of your friends? Shouldn't you be with them? Won't they miss you?'

'They'll manage without me. Besides, if I'm given the choice of going around with them or staying here with you, I'm afraid it's no contest.'

Alondra made the call.

Nash returned to the subject of the attacks. 'Is there anything in your past or that of your parents, no matter how trivial or insignificant, that could be a link to England?'

'Nothing that I know of, but then I really know very little about my parents.'

'You said they spoke English a lot. Might they have been from England originally? What were there full names?'

'Boringly Spanish. She was called Juanita, he was Juan.'

Nash stared at her then smiled.

'What is it? What is so funny?'

'Juanita and Juan. Turn them into English and you have *Janet and John*. It's a famous series of children's stories. So now we've established a possible English connection. At a guess, I'd say they were hiding-out in Spain and that their past has caught up with them. What baffles me is why you're being targeted. Unless they think you have something they want. That painting, for example.'

'I think you must be a good detective to work out so much from so little information.'

'It's all guesswork, but if I'm right, it might be sensible for you to come to England.'

'But surely, if you are right, the danger would be greater there?'

'Your father was murdered. There have been two attempts on your life. How much more dangerous can it be?

Besides, if you came to England, it might give us chance to find out what's behind all this.'

'I can't leave everything and run away. I have to deal with my father's estate. Also I have some paintings to finish and I must return to France for ones that have been commissioned since my exhibition.'

* * *

The *Guardia Civil* officer in charge spoke good English, which helped. What helped more was Nash's production of his warrant card. The officer agreed to make a big show of investigating the break-in, even to the extent of trying to get the item on the radio. 'May I say that the attacks were foiled by the intervention of a visiting police officer? That would carry a lot of weight, as there are many English people here.'

Nash agreed with some reluctance. After the forensic work was completed and the officers had departed, Nash and Alondra stood uncertainly in the lounge. 'How about dealing with what I came for?' he asked.

'The paintings? I'd forgotten about them.'

Although Nash appreciated the paintings in her studio he only found one that appealed to him. A short while later, he was the owner of a small landscape he knew would go in his study. 'I still need one for the dining room and one for my sitting room. Something bigger. Perhaps like that huge one in the bar where we met. At a guess, I'd say you painted that too.'

She smiled. 'Very observant, Mr Detective. But that one is really expensive.'

'And these aren't?' he said, pointing to the canvases.

'Only moderately so.'

'Go on, shock me. Tell me the price?'

She did. And it did shock him.

'I have others but they are at the farmhouse in Onati. Perhaps you could visit me there to see them,' she suggested with a smile.

'Maybe,' Nash said. 'I will be in France myself in October.'

'Will you be there on holiday?'

'I have to take Daniel to visit his aunt. He usually spends time with her during the summer holidays but we were too busy decorating the new house.'

'So, Daniel is also a painter?' Alondra laughed at her joke. 'Then perhaps I could come to meet you there.'

'I'd like that. I'll see what can be arranged.'

Before he left, they exchanged phone numbers. As Nash wrote his down he joked, 'You don't need the address, you already have that. If you need help, or if you change your mind and decide to come to England, call me.'

CHAPTER FOUR

Nash collected Daniel. He hugged his son and, having thanked David and established how they had occupied their time while he was away, Nash said, 'Come on, Daniel, we've lots to do. It's only a few days before you're due back at school.'

On arriving home, he carried the parcel containing the painting into the house; unwrapped and inspected it. Thankfully, it had survived the hold of the aircraft undamaged. He stared at it for a while.

'That's a nice painting, Papa,' Daniel said, peering over Nash's arm. 'Where did you get it?'

'From a lady I met in Spain,' he replied, absentmindedly. There was no doubt Alondra was a talented artist. He wondered if this would be the only reminder of her. He hoped not and thought he would like to meet her again in the future, if only to buy more paintings. He remembered helping her load her belongings into her car ready for the journey to France.

'When I return next month, I shall go straight to Onati, not here to Madrid,' she told him. 'It will be safer there. Then I can finish clearing the house of all my parents' effects. I might find something that will give a clue as to what this is about. I was going to sell the house' — she looked round the apartment — 'but now I think I'll keep it. Hopefully, I can make some sense of what has happened.'

He wondered how she would cope, alone in a big old house. For many people the solitude would be unbearable, but she seemed content to be alone. Maybe that was part of what attracted him to her, the fact that she was a loner, as he had been most of his life. Nash grinned self-mockingly. No, that wasn't what had attracted him. He remembered the way she had embraced him as they said their farewells. Now he would have to ready himself for the stream of salacious sarcasm Clara would direct at him after she had spoken to Pearce. For once this would be totally unjustified, but he doubted whether that would stop her.

* * *

It was obvious Pearce had already told Clara something of what had happened in Madrid. Nash had only been in his office a few minutes when Clara entered with a mug of coffee. 'Viv made you this. I suggested he put an extra spoonful of sugar in, because by the sound of it, you might need the energy.'

'Don't start!' Nash indicated a chair. 'Sit down and I'll explain. It wasn't at all what you think. Do you remember that letter I got, the one about the house and the painting, the woman who was asking about Stark Ghyll?'

'Oh, yes, you found out she was an artist, didn't you? Don't tell me she wanted you to pose for her, because you're no oil painting.'

'Thank you, but if you could manage to listen for two minutes together without either a sarcastic comment or an insult, I'll explain.'

Clara folded her arms and assumed an expression of bored tolerance. That vanished as Nash narrated what had happened. 'Blimey!' she said when he'd finished. 'I know things have been quiet around here, but going to Madrid to search for crime is a bit extreme, even for you, Mike. What do you think it was all about? A jealous lover? Dispute over a painting? Or something to do with her family?'

'Certainly not the first two. It could be connected to her family. She doesn't know much about them, even her parents, which I find extremely odd. Whatever it is, I think the motive lies in England.'

'Why on earth do you think that?'

'Because Alondra's attacker was English. He swore in English. But everything about her life seems shrouded in mystery. For example, how did an original painting of a Yorkshire mountain scene end up in a remote farmhouse in the Basque Country? I tried to persuade Alondra to come to England so I could try to find out more, but she's stubborn and a real loner.'

'You were quite taken with her, weren't you?'

Nash smiled; a trifle sadly, she thought.

'I suppose I must have been.'

'Let's hope she changes her mind.'

As Mironova got up to leave, Nash looked after her. 'What, no sarcastic punch-line?'

'Don't worry, I'll think of something.'

When Clara went into the outer office, Pearce was sipping tentatively at his coffee. 'Sore head?' she asked.

Pearce nodded, then regretted it.

'Mike was explaining about the artist he met, and the attacks on her. What was she like?'

'An absolute stunner.' Pearce described Alondra as best he could remember from the one brief glimpse he'd had of her. 'She is slim, beautiful, with very short dark hair, typically Spanish. I don't know how Mike does it. He didn't say much on the return flight, but there again, the rest of us slept for much of the way.'

'Looking at you I can't say I'm surprised, but the full story is even more fascinating.' Clara repeated what Nash had told her. 'I get the impression that this is different from his usual romantic misadventures. I wouldn't be surprised if we haven't heard the last of Senorita Torres.'

* * *

The letter from Alondra arrived at Smelt Mill Cottage at the beginning of October. She explained that she was now back in Onati and had experienced no further problems. She enclosed photographs of several paintings she thought might be of interest, enquiring if he still intended to visit.

Nash was impressed by the photos but was unsure how Daniel would react to being left with his aunt. The problem was solved later that evening when Daniel rang him from school. 'Papa, when we go to visit *tante* Mirabelle in the October break can we go on Eurostar instead of the ferry? Please, Papa.'

'Why do you want to do that?'

'Some of my friends have been on it and they didn't get seasick.'

'I see,' Nash said, grateful that Daniel couldn't see the smile on his face. 'But you don't get seasick on the ferry, Daniel.'

'I do when it's windy and it could be windy this time,' he added a little hopefully.

'I'll see what I can do.' Nash thought for a moment. 'Here's what I suggest. If I can arrange things would you mind staying with your aunt for a couple of days without me? There's a call I'd like to make while we're there.'

'That's OK, Papa,' Daniel said excitedly. 'Does that mean—?'

'I said I'll see what I can do.' Nash laughed as he finished the call.

With that, he phoned Alondra. She suggested they meet in the town of Bayonne where she had a commission to deliver, halving the journey time for him.

'That sounds fine,' Nash said. 'I'll have to find somewhere to stay overnight.'

'Don't worry about that. Leave all the arrangements to me. I am so looking forward to seeing you again.'

* * *

Nash arrived in Bayonne and found the hotel Alondra had booked, checked in to the luxurious room, and wandered down to the bar. He gazed out of the window at the Adour River flowing gently under the neighbouring bridge.

'Hello, Mike.'

He turned to find Alondra standing behind him. She reached up and gave him the customary greeting of a kiss on each cheek. Her eyes sparkled as she smiled at him. 'Mike, it's lovely to see you again. Thank you for coming.'

'Not at all, I'm very pleased to see you too and relieved that you're safe and well. Have you been here long?'

'I arrived this morning and delivered the painting for the client, so now my time is free. Would you like to take a walk? It is a lovely afternoon and the town is so beautiful. Besides, I guess you must be tired of sitting behind the steering wheel.'

As they headed out of the hotel, Alondra slipped her hand into the crook of his elbow and smiled up at him as she snuggled closer. 'Do you mind?'

He looked at her, drinking in her beauty as he shook his head. The smile she gave him set his pulse beating a little faster.

By the time they headed back towards the hotel, it was early evening. 'Are you hungry, Mike?' Alondra asked.

'Yes, I am.'

'Good, because I've booked us a table to thank you for rescuing me and keeping me safe.'

Nash began to protest, but Alondra placed her finger tips gently against his mouth. 'No argument, please, Mike, I insist.' With that, she steered him round a corner into a small cobbled street towards a bistro.

The touch of her slim fingers against his lips set his pulse racing again. 'What about the paintings?' he asked.

She smiled. 'They can wait until after dinner.'

Nash couldn't resist teasing her a little. 'I see, you plan to get me tipsy so I'll pay more for them.'

'Tipsy?' The word baffled her.

'It means intoxicated.'

'I wouldn't do that, Mike. Not to you. And not to sell paintings.'

After the meal, eaten by candlelight in the romantic setting, Alondra took his arm and snuggled against him as they strolled slowly back to the hotel. As they crossed the car park she said, 'I think we should take the paintings out of my car and inside, please, Mike.'

She opened the boot and they unloaded the canvases, together with a small holdall.

'I thought you'd already booked in,' Nash said.

'I have, but I didn't bring the bag in earlier.'

As they re-entered the hotel, Nash asked, 'Where do you want to put the paintings?'

'Why don't we take them to your room?'

Once inside the bedroom, Nash walked across to the sofa and placed the paintings down carefully. 'There's plenty of space, that's for sure. Did you think Daniel might be with me? Or didn't they have a single available?'

She smiled once more and replied, 'No, it seemed the most appropriate.'

As he began to unwrap the top painting, Alondra placed a restraining hand on his arm. 'Mike, they can wait.'

Across the room he noticed her holdall on the chair alongside the bed. She smiled a trifle nervously. 'I only booked one room.' As she spoke, she began to unbutton his shirt. 'You don't mind, do you, Mike? Do you?'

* * *

Nash woke late. He stretched out, luxuriating in the king-sized bed. He turned to look to his left. Alondra was still asleep. He felt a great surge of tenderness and leaned across to kiss her. As he moved, her eyes opened and she smiled. Seconds later, as they kissed, tenderness was forgotten.

'We're going to be late for breakfast,' Nash said later.

'Why don't we order room service? Then we can take a shower, and you can look at the paintings.'

'Oh, yes, the paintings, I'd all but forgotten them. They were the reason you brought me here.'

'No, Mike, they weren't the reason. They were the excuse.'

Clad in the luxurious robes provided by the hotel, they took breakfast in front of the window overlooking the river. 'How soon do you have to return?' Alondra asked him. As she spoke her foot was gently caressing his shin.

'I'm in France all week, but I have to spend time with Daniel. I don't see as much of him as I'd like with him being away at school.'

'Do you think he would allow you one more night? I booked the room and it would be a shame to waste it.'

'I'll have to phone and let them know. His aunt is quite elderly and I don't want her worrying.'

'Make the phone call. Then you can look at those paintings.' Alondra stood up and stretched, and as she did so the robe parted, revealing her superb figure. 'And after that, Mike, our time is our own, what little there is. It isn't enough, so let's make the most of what we have.'

A day later than expected Nash headed back to collect Daniel. In the boot of the Range Rover lay two paintings which he knew would always remind him of the past two days with Alondra.

CHAPTER FIVE

On the slopes of one of the biggest, most testing climbs in North Yorkshire, the walker stared at the young woman. She didn't look right. Her clothing for one thing, no way was she dressed for the outdoor life. And her footwear was all wrong. Young, quite pretty, what was she doing out? He walked over to her. Jeans would have offered better protection against the weather than the cheap cotton skirt. And with nothing but that blouse covering her, she must be half-frozen. Who on earth ventured out without an overcoat at this time of year? 'Excuse me, are you all right?' There was no answer, so he tried again. 'Are you all right? Not lost, are you? Only this isn't the easiest walk around. Not for beginners, anyway.'

His persistence was rewarded. She looked up, her expression troubled. 'Sorry? What did you say?'

He tried to place her accent but failed. 'Do you need help? Directions?'

'No.'

The monosyllable and the tone of delivery discouraged further conversation. He shrugged. 'As long as you're certain. Enjoy your walk.' He continued on his way. He'd gone a further mile when he looked back. The woman was still seated in the same position. The walker shook his head despairingly. People! He'd never understand some of them.

Her eyes were fixed on the hillside. It was exactly as she remembered from within her room at that place. Even the sunlight piercing the broken cloud and dappling the meadow was exactly like the image in her memory. That was why she'd come here. It was the hill. The name was as firmly implanted in her brain as the day she'd first heard it. Stark Ghyll, the name made her shiver. Because Stark Ghyll represented her misery. Stark Ghyll had witnessed her suffering. Stark Ghyll was synonymous with her darkest moments. Now her decision had been made it seemed only fitting that she should come to Stark Ghyll.

It took more than an hour for her to reach the summit. Once there, she perched on a large boulder. After a while, without looking left or right she walked slowly, deliberately to the edge of the sheer cliff face. Away in the distance, sunlight reflected on the water of Lamentation Tarn, its surface ruffled by the same breeze that pushed through her long, dark hair. Her gaze shifted as she looked down. The rocks below appeared hard; hard and sharp. She let go a long, weary sigh and stepped forward into oblivion.

* * *

Mike Nash had only been back from France a couple of days when he got a phone call from Professor Ramirez, the pathologist, known throughout the force as Mexican Pete, despite the fact that he was of Spanish origin. 'I've been conducting a post-mortem on the body of a young woman who was found at the foot of Stark Ghyll. It happened while you were on leave.'

'Yes, I've read the file, and Clara has filled me in on the details. Although, to be fair, we have no idea who she is, or whether she fell, jumped, or was pushed. A walker who saw her beforehand came forward and he said she was alone, so our guess would be either an accident or suicide, but it is a guess. It's all a mystery.'

There was a pause before the pathologist replied. 'Not as much of a mystery as the one I've got for you. Before I commit it to paper, I'd like to talk to you about it. I appreciate the fact that you're a brilliant detective, but I think even you might struggle to find an explanation for this.'

'I'm due in Netherdale early this afternoon, for a meeting with Superintendent Fleming about staffing. I could come along to see you after that, if you like?'

'That'll do fine. I'm not going anywhere.' The pathologist added with dark humour, 'And neither is she.'

When Nash reached the mortuary, Ramirez was seated behind his desk. 'The young woman was in her mid-twenties,' the pathologist began. 'She was in reasonable health before her death. The only remarkable thing I could find was that she was pregnant. The pregnancy was fairly advanced, certainly far too late for an abortion. Although it wasn't easy because of the extensive damage caused by the fall, I noticed certain deformities in the foetus. In view of those, I believe there would have been little chance of the child surviving. It may well have been stillborn, might even have died in the womb, in which case there could have been severe complications for the mother.'

'Are you suggesting that the woman knew this? Do you believe she had been told such dreadful news and that was why she jumped — if she did jump?'

'Possibly,' Ramirez agreed, 'but when I said it was remarkable that the woman was pregnant I wasn't referring to what I've just told you.' He gestured towards the file on his desk. 'What I cannot understand is how the dead woman became pregnant — because I believe she wasn't sexually active!'

* * *

At the farmhouse in Onati Alondra stared at the *bombero*; his fire-officer's uniform soot-blackened. The visor of his helmet raised, now the emergency had passed, revealing that the grime from the fire had also streaked his face.

'You were lucky in two ways,' he said.

'How am I lucky?' Her voice was hoarse, little more than a croak, her throat dry and parched from the smoke.

'First of all you were lucky that the fire was spotted by the field party from the university who were returning to their campsite. They had been to a local bar. Otherwise,' the fireman sighed, 'it is often the case that victims die from the suffocating effects of smoke rather than the fire itself.'

'And the other piece of luck?' She sipped from the water bottle the fireman had given her.

The *bombero* lifted a gauntleted hand and waved at the nearby building. 'This farmhouse is old. They knew how to build properly in those days. The walls are almost half a metre thick and of solid stone. Stone does not burn. Whoever set the fire didn't take that into account.'

She lowered the bottle and stared at him. 'The fire was deliberate?'

'For sure it was. Could you not smell the gasoline? How do you think so much damage was achieved? But no matter how hot the fire, like I said, you cannot burn stone. That, and the vigilance of the campers, saved your life. However, I must report this. The *Ertzaintza* must carry out an investigation. They will class this as attempted murder.'

She shivered. The night air was cold, but the thermal blanket provided by the fire service protected her. The shiver was from fear. First, her mother had died. Then her father had been killed, murdered, as she now knew. Now, another attempt on her life. And the worst of it was she still had absolutely no idea who was doing this. Or why.

The officer assigned to her case, while sympathetic, failed to find any reason for the arson attack. He could see no political motive, no crime for gain, or of passion, although that was always a possibility in the Basque Country. The last suggestion had been the only moment in the series of interviews that had made her smile. After the firemen and police officers left, Alondra went back inside the farmhouse. The place stank of smoke and gasoline. She hurried over to the stairs and up to her bedroom. Fortunately, the end of the house containing her room had escaped with no more than the smell that clung to clothes, bedding; to everything. She sat down on the bed and tried to assess her situation.

It was as the *bombero* had said; the fabric of the building had saved her life. That was all well and good, but what was she to do now? She had fled there to escape the danger that had beset her in Madrid. The capital was certainly unsafe and now Onati was no longer safe.

Alondra swallowed, miserably aware that Mike Nash had been right. She should have listened to him. And if he was right about one thing he could have been right about everything. Thought of what Mike had said made her sit up straight. The painting! She stood up and strode swiftly across to the door and went to the head of the stairs. The landing was open plan, so she could see down to the sitting room wall below. That side of the room had suffered little damage, certainly not enough to destroy both painting and frame. Alondra could see the picture hooks on the wall. But the depiction of Stark Ghyll had gone!

She walked slowly, thoughtfully, back into her bedroom. Now she knew she had to travel to England. Perhaps there she could find out why she was the target of so much malignant hatred. Her major problem was going to be how to get there in one piece. Once there, perhaps Mike would protect her. Her thoughts dwelt on the detective, his kindness, and the care he'd taken over a complete stranger, plus their two nights in Bayonne.

Mind on the job, she cautioned herself. If you're going to reach England, you've got to think as Mike would do. Try and plan. A strategy that would outwit those threatening her, as Mike had done with the intruder in Madrid with no more than a mobile phone. Before leaving there were a couple of jobs that remained to be done. But she could do them en route. That was simple enough. It was the rest she needed to work on. The idea didn't spring into her mind fully formed. Rather it grew piece by piece in the quiet of her room. By the time she was ready to leave, Alondra had her action plan worked out to the last detail. All that remained was for her to carry it out. Having packed only essentials, she paused for a word with the bored-looking police officer who had been left to guard her and the house. 'I am going away,' she told him. 'I will be gone for some time. If anyone should ask, tell them I have gone to Ibiza.'

He stared after her as she climbed into her car. Ibiza, he thought, who visits La Isla Blanca at this time of year?

The first part was straightforward. For this, it didn't matter whether she was being followed. Having called at the bank in the nearest town, Alondra started her journey to the capital sticking to the main roads and keeping a wary eye on the traffic around her.

Had circumstances been different, she might not have decided to demand a copy of her mother's medical records from the hospital. Alondra didn't for one moment think there would be anything untoward in the contents, but the attack on her home convinced her she'd made the right decision. She produced the documents she needed to prove her identity, and signed a form confirming safe receipt of the file.

When she returned to her car she walked round it, checking. Only when she was absolutely certain it was safe did she get in. She was undecided whether her actions were paranoia or sensible precautions. Once she reached safety she would examine the file carefully. She would be content when she was satisfied that all was in order, and not before.

* * *

El Corte Ingles had grown from a tailor's shop to become one of the largest, most successful department stores in Europe. Along the way the group had diversified by either establishing or acquiring a travel agency, supermarkets, DIY stores and IT services, plus lots more. The flagship store in Madrid city centre, where the original building had gobbled up its neighbours, now stretched over a huge, sprawling location.

Alondra's first stop was at the travel agency. Choosing a desk where she was in plain sight, she explained to the assistant that she was hard of hearing, and asked that she spoke slowly and clearly. Her theory that most people's idea of slowly and clearly is a muted bellow was soon proved correct, and the details of the journey Alondra was booking were broadcast to those within range clearer than if they'd been put out over the public address system.

As the transaction was nearing completion, Alondra was interested in the movements of a man she could see in her peripheral vision. He seemed to be inspecting every centimetre of a vast range of suitcases on display only a few feet away. For good measure, she repeated everything the assistant had told her. The time her flight would take off from Madrid airport, the time she would need to check in, and the scheduled landing time at Heathrow. Having done this, she thanked the assistant and left. As she did so, she noticed that the man's interest in luggage seemed to have ceased abruptly.

She moved from floor to floor, from department to department. She glimpsed 'suitcase man' as she had begun to think of him, on several occasions. Eventually, after several pauses to inspect electrical goods, furniture, clothing, and shoes, she ended up in the lingerie department.

Alondra saw a mature-looking member of staff, who appeared to have some seniority, and asked her assistance. 'I don't want to make a fuss,' she began hesitantly, 'but there is this man. He was following me earlier, when I wanted to try a dress on I found him loitering by the entrance to the fitting rooms. I had to leave — I was so upset. Now, he's followed me in here. I want to buy a new set of underwear, but I can't. The thought that he might see me even choosing anything like that would put me off.'

Fifteen minutes later, aware that 'suitcase man' was undergoing an uncomfortable interview with the store's security team, Alondra emerged into the street and headed for the car park. The knowledge that she was no longer being followed heartened her considerably. The set of expensive underwear in the carrier swinging from her hand merely enhanced her wellbeing. Pausing only to collect her suitcase from the car boot, she headed for the railway station.

Next morning, as 'suitcase man' paced the departures hall of Madrid airport watching passengers assemble at the check-in desk designated for the Heathrow flight, Alondra was seated on the bunk of her cabin on the ferry from Santander to Portsmouth. The crossing would take twenty-four hours. Still reluctant to be seen on deck or in the public lounges, Alondra decided to start reading the hospital file regarding her mother's final illness and treatment.

She had been reading for a while when she saw something she didn't at first comprehend. She stared at the page. That was wrong. It had to be. Was it a typing error? She turned to the next page. No, there it was again. She read the entry over and over, taking in words and figures but unable to process the information into anything that made sense. Another turn of the page brought another shock. Her brain reeled at this assault on her understanding. She closed the file, but sat nursing it, arms wrapped around it like a lover clutching her sweetheart. After a long time she opened it again, perhaps hoping she'd read it wrong, or misunderstood the meaning. All it brought was confirmation of the unbelievable.

For the remainder of the voyage she remained locked inside her cabin, unwilling to face a world that had suddenly been turned on its head, a world full of danger; a world that she could no longer comprehend. Her feeling of disorientation was enhanced by seasickness, and it seemed an age before the ship reached port. Even then she had a long journey ahead of her. She found her way to the railway station and booked a ticket for the first leg of her journey. She wanted it to be over, wanted to see Mike again. Perhaps he could make sense of the barrage of seemingly unanswerable questions flooding her mind.

She had completed all but the last leg of the journey before her nerve failed. She had hired a car in York and with the aid of a road map set off towards Netherdale. At first, the drive had been difficult, demanding all her concentration. Finding the correct road out of the city was one problem. Accustoming herself to driving on the left was a far greater one. When she was clear of the built-up areas and had crossed the busy ring road, the traffic levels lessened as her confidence grew. She reached Netherdale, bypassed the town, and took the road signposted for Helmsdale.

She was halfway there when she pulled off into a lay-by and consulted her map. Doubts flooded her mind. What if Mike didn't want to see her? Suppose their time together in Bayonne had meant nothing to him — a fling. Men could be like that. She dismissed the idea; after all it had been he who suggested she came to England. But the doubt persisted strong enough to prevent her dialling his number.

Her doubt and insecurity prevailed. She wouldn't take a rapturous welcome for granted. Rather than suffer the humiliation of rejection, she would book into a hotel somewhere and call to see him. Where was the nearest place? She tried to remember the name of the village he'd told her of. Failing in this, she consulted her map. There it was: an insignificant dot with little in the way of a road network nearby. She started the car and set off for Wintersett village. From what little she knew about English villages, most of them had a pub. Hopefully Wintersett might have one with rooms.

* * *

The caller gave the identification code they'd agreed on.

'What have you to tell me?'

The report took some time. When it was over, Dermot Black gave brief instructions, before ending the call. Now he would have the task of reporting the news to his boss. He reached the office, knocked on the door and waited to be summoned.

'I hope you haven't come to report another failure?'

'Not exactly. Not a failure, but no success yet. The girl seems to have more lives than a cat. I've just spoken to our man. He sent one of his best operatives as a replacement to Spain. The girl has survived three attempts on her life.'

'Four,' his employer corrected him.

'Yes, well, three recently. The first two were thwarted because she had an Englishman in tow, and he got in the way.'

'Why didn't he deal with the meddler as well?'

'I'll come to that in a minute. He traced her to her flat in Madrid and made two attempts; then he lost her. It was weeks before he tracked her down again. He followed her and torched the farmhouse where the family lived. Someone called the fire brigade and they rescued her. Before he set the fire he removed some photos and the painting.'

'He should have disposed of her before he set the fire.'

'He wanted it to look like an accident; given what happened to her father, which I think makes sense.'

'What was that about the Englishman?'

'That's the unsettling bit. Our man attacked the girl but the English bloke got in the way. She ended up in hospital, and after she was released he went back to finish her off, but the bloke was staying the night. Next day the police arrived. Our man followed the bloke back to his hotel and found out who he is. Apparently, he's a copper, name of Nash, a DI working in Yorkshire.'

'Why should we worry about a country copper?'

'He checked him out and it appears Nash is a bit different to the average: ex-Met, and bloody devious. After the farmhouse fire she gave our man the slip in Madrid, but he's caught up with her again in this country. She's hired a car and is in Yorkshire.'

'How did he find that out?'

'Don't ask; it'll be on the expenses he submits. He reckons she's on her way to meet up with Nash. That might be nothing more than the usual. Apparently, Nash has a bit of a reputation that way, but his involvement with the girl is making me uneasy.'

'That's easily remedied. Instruct our man that we will double his fee if he takes out both the girl and Nash. And tell him to make sure it's done soon, I'm a little tired of waiting for results.'

CHAPTER SIX

The landlord of the Miners Arms in Wintersett watched his wife chatting to their only resident as the guest sipped her coffee. He was firmly of the opinion that all foreigners were mad, and what he had just overheard reinforced that viewpoint. Acknowledging that the visitor was a painter by profession, he could see no rhyme or reason for her plan to drive her hire car up the dale simply to complete a few sketches.

No matter how well the commission promised to pay, the landlord wouldn't have ventured forth, risking life and limb in a little tin box in sub-zero temperatures merely to do a bit of drawing. And if he had been forced to drive anywhere, he certainly wouldn't have left the warmth and comfort of the vehicle to sit in a snow-covered field. But then, he wasn't Italian, and he wasn't insane.

Having eaten her breakfast, Alondra returned to her room and added an extra sweater, hoping the clothing she had brought would be sufficient against the cold. The morning was frosty, but the sky was cloudless, which encouraged her. As she left, she failed to notice that she had missed one crucial item; her mobile phone plugged into its charger on the dressing table. She reached the car, started the ignition, and eased cautiously down the hard-packed ice of the pub car park.

* * *

When Nash had turned onto the minor road leading to Wintersett the previous evening, he was glad he'd the Range Rover to rely on. The main roads were clear enough, but he needed the weight of the vehicle and the four-wheel drive to cope with the snow, which had been compressed into hard-packed ice. He'd reached the cottage and carefully steered the car into the parking space alongside.

Although the outside temperature was well below freezing, the house itself was warm, courtesy of the Aga that powered the central heating. He'd pondered whether to light the log fire in the lounge but decided against it. That could wait until he returned with Daniel. Once lit, the fire could be kept burning for days, weeks on end, even. He'd allowed himself the luxury of a glass of wine before he ate. It had been a strange year, he thought. He'd be glad when Daniel was home. Although he wouldn't admit it to anyone else, he missed his son, but recognized the need for Daniel to be away. It had proved tricky balancing his unexpected responsibility as a single parent with his duty as a police inspector.

Before going to bed, Nash had made a point of checking the local weather forecast on television. He liked the forecaster, a youthful-looking professional who, like Nash, hailed from the West Riding. The region's weather was far from easy to predict, but Paul Hudson had a reputation for accuracy. On this occasion, however, the weatherman refused to be specific. There would be snow, he told viewers, but as to where and how much, it was impossible to gauge.

Not that Nash had any choice. He had to drive. If he'd been able, he would have opted not to travel, except perhaps as far as Helmsdale. The trip to Harrogate and back wasn't one he relished. He thanked providence that he'd chosen to buy the Range Rover. Although he'd questioned the extravagance at the time, he knew that if any vehicle was capable of tackling such adverse weather conditions, his would be the one.

The morning sun streamed through the large picture window in the lounge as Nash sipped his coffee. The sky was a brilliant blue, without a cloud to be seen. It was cold, admittedly, which would mean icy road surfaces, but at least there had been no fresh snow overnight. Nash finished his coffee and checked that he'd put his shopping list in his pocket. The previous evening, he'd prowled the kitchen, and the larder, checking cupboards, fridges, and freezers. He wasn't prepared to be caught out, should they be stranded by the snow. He would ensure they had sufficient supplies to withstand a siege. He had already bought and secreted Daniel's Christmas presents. One of the advantages of the boy being at boarding school was that Nash didn't have to worry about smuggling parcels into the house or wrapping them late at night. Chances of them being discovered before Christmas Day were minimal too.

Nash set off early, passing through Wintersett village before picking up the Helmsdale road. As he passed the Miners Arms he saw a small car pull out of the car park and turn in the opposite direction. He wondered fleetingly where the driver was headed. Rather them than me, Nash thought, doubly grateful for the Range Rover. On reaching Helmsdale, he was fortunate to get a parking space close to the entrance to Good Buys supermarket, his first call. After completing his shopping, Nash was busy transferring bags from the trolley to the boot when he heard a familiar voice.

'Ayup, Mr Nash. How's tricks? Surviving life amongst the corrugated Methodists?'

Nash looked up and smiled at Jonas Turner. The old man's term was one used locally for those of the Wesleyan persuasion who attended the tiny wayside chapels made from the utility material. 'Not many of them out our way, Jonas,' he replied.

Turner thought for a moment. 'Aye, your reet,' he agreed, 'any road, it ain't Wesleyans you ought ter fret about 'avin for neighbours, it's that weird lot from over t' other side o' Stark Ghyll. The Church of the One-Way Street or whatever fancy name they give it. About as straight as nine-bob notes, I reckon they are. Met any of 'em yet?'

Nash shook his head. 'I think it's a closed community. They certainly don't encourage visitors. I've seen high security prisons that were less well guarded. What do you know about them?'

'Not much, 'cept for the senior brother, or whatever they call 'im. The 'oly Brother J. Malachi Entwistle.' Turner spat the title out scornfully. 'Malachi, I ask yer. I remember 'im from way back, only 'e weren't Malachi then; 'e were Malcolm. And I were fair teken that 'e didn't finish up as a lazy, idle good fer nowt same as 'is father. Mind you, I'm not surprised 'e got religious bug. 'is father were allus claimin' 'e saw visions. Visions! I reckon that were usually on account of t' eight pints of Old Peculier 'e'd supped afore.'

'Strong stuff, Old Peculier,' Nash pointed out. 'I reckon eight pints might make anybody see visions.'

Turner sniffed. 'Never does it to me. Any road, Malcolm went off ter Bristol University and got a degree in chemistry or summat. We thought we'd seen last of 'im. Then up 'e pops as t'oly Brother J. Malachi Entwistle. Seen the light and started spoutin' to any fool as was daft enough to listen. Not the sort of weirdoes I'd want as neighbours, but I suppose they're 'armless enough, unless they're trying to force them Come-To-Jesus pamphlets or car stickers on you. Anyroad, they're well out er your way over yon side o' t' dale. So, 'ow's that young man o' yours? Young Daniel, I mean? Settled in at that fancy school all right?'

'He's fine. I'm on my way to collect him. Term finishes today.'

'Well you take extra care o' young Daniel, Mr Nash. 'Cos he's most precious thing tha's got. Aye, and tek it steady on roads. It's fair slape wi' frost and I reckon we're due another dumpin' o' snow afore day's out.'

* * *

Had Alondra been more familiar with the area, she might have known that the wispy clouds beginning to form over Stark Ghyll were the forerunner of trouble to come. As it was, her mind was preoccupied with whether to put them in the sketch. They would break up the relentless, unbroken blue of the rest of the sky, which threatened to take the prospective viewers' attention from what the focal point should be. Her mind made up, she set about adding them, but found it problematical, as they were moving faster than she could record them.

Before she realized how quickly the weather had changed, something soft brushed against her cheek. As she glanced up, she saw that the outline of Black Fell had begun to blur. Stark Ghyll summit, further in the distance, had vanished in low cloud. A big, fat snowflake landed on the middle of her pad. She scooped up pad, easel, and stool and started towards the car. By the time she reached the roadside, snow was falling heavily. By the time she climbed into the driving seat, the windscreen was covered. By the time she'd switched her lights on and started the ignition, she was staring into a whiteout, the wipers barely able to cope with the accumulation of snow on the glass. She was thankful that she had only a short journey to reach the safety and comfort of the pub.

Neither the small car not its driver were a match for the snow. She managed quite well for a couple of miles, easing the car round bends where the driving line was all but invisible, before a slight miscalculation led to disaster.

The blurring of the road and the verge caused her nearside wheel to mount the snow-covered grass bank. Even then she might have been able to rectify the mistake, had the wheel not struck a large obstacle, a stone. The steering wheel bucked violently, wrenching itself from her grasp and she felt the rear end of the vehicle slide remorselessly towards the wall.

The soft snowdrift failed to protect the vehicle from the effects of two hard objects colliding: one at speed, the other, immovable. Unable to prevent or lessen the impact, she listened in horror to the rending, grating sound of metal self-destructing. Even had she known what she'd hit the irony might not have been appreciated. Invisible in the snow, the painted white milestone inscribed *Wintersett 2 miles* was intended to aid motorists.

As the din died away to an eerie silence she realized the trouble she in. The silence was broken by a tiny sound, the gentle drip, drip, drip of escaping liquid. At first she thought the radiator must have been punctured by the impact. Then her nose told her different. Petrol! She had to get out. What's more she had to do it immediately. At any moment the vapour could ignite.

At this point, her luck, which up to then had all been bad, improved slightly. Her seat belt unfastened easily. By some miracle the driver's door was undamaged. It took all her strength to push it open. She scrambled out, rolled and pitched headlong into a snowdrift that all but buried her. She was instantly chilled to the marrow, but as she fought to recover her balance, the car which had threatened to become her coffin, shifted and slid fractionally sideways, a sharp edge of torn metal striking and scraping along a stone from the wall.

The spark was sufficient to ignite the petrol fumes. She heard a dull whoosh of sound that turned instantly into a roar. The explosion that destroyed her car was accompanied by a vivid flash of light and a thunderous report. At once deafened and blinded, she buried her face into the snowdrift. As the backdraught from the inferno washed over her, she waited for the miniature hell she had created to subside.

She eased herself upright. What remained of her car was little more than a mangled, twisted heap of flaming scrap metal. But that was the least of her worries. She knew she had to move quickly. Cold was already attacking her extremities. She clawed her way out of the drift and cast a glance back at the carnage, before turning to walk towards the village. Wearily, stiffly, every muscle protesting, she began to plod through the ever-deepening snow; snow that was now being driven horizontally by the freshening wind directly into her face.

She had already made one calamitous mistake in attempting to drive in impossible conditions. She had been lucky to escape with her life. At no point had she considered the possibility of hypothermia. If she was unable to find shelter soon, that mistake was likely to prove fatal. Before she had travelled a mile she was all but wading through the snow, her concentration focused on avoiding falling, on being able to stay on the road. Focused on not wandering off the margins, which were being rapidly obliterated, and in searching with increasing desperation for some dwelling or barn where she could seek refuge.

The strain of walking was sapping what little energy she had left. This was compounded by the drop in her body temperature, which she was powerless to counter. She wiped her face for the umpteenth time, to clear her vision as much as to dry it. So blinding was the snow that she had chosen to walk alongside a wall that marked the low side of the road, to ensure she was still on course.

Suddenly, the wall vanished. She half turned, away from the driving pellets of snow, blinking and rubbing her eyes with the sleeves of her coat. At first she thought her eyes were playing tricks, or that she was hallucinating. She squinted through the fast gathering darkness. No, she wasn't seeing things. It was a house. She waded down the drive, the wind and snow obscuring her footprints almost as soon as she had made them. She reached the slight shelter provided by the open fronted storm-porch in front of the door and leaned thankfully on the wall. To her left was an oval plaque, the inscription covered in snow. She rubbed it off and read the words. Smelt Mill Cottage. She realized that chance had brought her to Mike's door. She leaned on the bell. The sound echoed through the building but brought no response. 'Mike,' she wailed, 'Mike, where are you?'

* * *

Nash stored Daniel's trunk and the rest of his belongings in the car and spent a few minutes chatting with the headmaster of the junior school as he watched his son bidding farewell to some of his classmates.

For most of the journey to Helmsdale he listened to Daniel's gossip about the school, the masters, his friends, and everything that had happened during the autumn term. Nash wondered, with some amusement, if his parents had been subjected to the same level of gossip when he'd been at school.

'I'm top of my class,' Daniel suddenly announced.

'You are? For everything?' Nash asked a little surprised.

'No, Papa.' Daniel giggled.

'Well what then?' Nash smiled at Daniel's obvious amusement.

'French, of course!'

They had almost reached Helmsdale when snow began to fall. Nash kept his foot firmly on the accelerator. So far the main roads were clear, and there was little chance of him being stopped for speeding. Apart from the fact that the traffic officers knew his car, Nash reckoned they'd probably be engaged elsewhere. His aim was to get home before the weather deteriorated too far.

Once they turned onto the minor road leading to Wintersett, the effects of the snow were far more obvious. Nash was confident they would reach home without any problem, but even with the traction provided by the four-wheel drive there were one or two tricky moments on the final stretch from Wintersett to the cottage. Dusk was delayed by the snow's reflected light, nevertheless it was almost dark by the time Nash inched the car carefully into the driveway. He went to switch off the ignition but paused as he spotted something in the beam of the headlights. He glanced sideways; it was obvious by his expression that Daniel had also seen it. Father and son exchanged looks of complete astonishment before turning their eyes back to the vision in front of them.

CHAPTER SEVEN

Just as Alondra thought she could get no colder, she heard something. In the silence created by the snow, she thought it was an engine. As she convinced herself that her imagination wasn't playing tricks, she saw the slanting flakes of snow illuminated by powerful beams of light. She struggled upright. If she could reach the road, she might get the approaching vehicle to stop.

Before she had chance to move, the engine sound died back to a whisper. The vehicle was approaching at little more than walking pace, its driver ultra-cautious. She was about to step out of the shelter of the porch, when she saw the headlight beams turn towards her. The car was about to enter the drive. 'Mike!' she exclaimed. The effort of moving, small though it had been, was sufficient to sap her remaining strength. A nauseous sensation was swiftly followed by one of lightheaded dizziness, before the car, the snow, and the hillside beyond began revolving in a disoriented kaleidoscope. Her vision blurred to blackness, her knees crumpled, and she tumbled onto the snow-covered drive in an untidy heap.

'Daniel, stay there!' Nash killed the ignition and thrust the car door open. He stepped cautiously onto the drive. Outside the vehicle, the cold was piercing. How long, he wondered, had the figure been exposed to the savagery of the storm?

Nash was aware of the danger of hypothermia. As he went forwards, he tried to remember a first aid course he'd attended long ago. The first priority was to remove the sufferer from the cold.

He got his hands under the victim's armpits and lifted them to a sitting position, realizing that this imitation of a snowman was actually a woman.

He signalled to Daniel. As his son joined him, he passed him his bunch of keys. 'Unlock the door and I'll get her inside.'

He braced her against his knee, hauled her upright, and with the body across his shoulder made his way cautiously over the few yards to the porch where Daniel was holding the door open.

Nash followed him inside, turning left into the kitchen. As he deposited his burden on a carver chair alongside the table, only then did Nash recognize Alondra.

Daniel rejoined his father in time to see Nash unzip her jacket. 'Can I help, Papa?'

'Yes please, Daniel. We need to get her warm as quickly as possible. Run upstairs to the airing cupboard. I need a couple of bath sheets and as many hand towels as you can find.'

As Daniel darted away on his errand, Nash removed Alondra's boots. She was still not conscious, lolling sideways in the chair. Fortunately, the chair arm prevented her nose-diving onto the tiles. He removed her jacket and unfastened the drawstring at her waistband, hoisted her to her feet and rolled her trousers down. He discarded the sodden garments and removed her socks. Her feet were small and slender, he noticed. More important, they were extremely cold. He wondered how low her body temperature had dropped.

Daniel returned half-submerged under a pile of towels. Nash was grateful they had bought a job lot in a summer sale. 'Leave one of the bath towels and four hand towels,' he told the boy. 'Take the rest into the cloakroom and put them into the tumble drier. You know how to work it, don't you?'

Daniel nodded, listening to his father as he continued to issue instructions. 'Put it on the highest heat and turn the big knob to ten minutes, then come back. And, Daniel, thanks. You're a great help.'

Nash removed the rest of her clothes, dropping them on the floor. As soon as they were off, he wrapped her in the bath sheet. Daniel returned in time to see his father lift the woman out of the chair towards the range. Guessing what he needed, the youngster moved forward and pushed the chair close to the Aga. Nash seated her back down and opened the oven door. He reached over and turned the thermostat as high as it would go. Pausing only to scoop the hand towels from the table, he placed these on the Aga and switched on the kettle.

As he waited for it to boil, Nash told Daniel, 'There's some chocolate in the pantry, I think. It's only cooking chocolate, but it'll have to do. This is the lady who did those paintings I bought. She was obviously coming to see us and must have had an accident.'

'I've got a better idea.' Daniel ran to the hall and returned with his small rucksack, the only item he'd brought from the car. He produced a large chocolate Santa, which he held up for inspection.

'Brilliant, son.' Nash beamed at him. 'As soon as she's awake, you can feed that to her, a little at a time. That's going to be your job. She needs sugar from the chocolate to make her better.'

As he spoke, Nash brewed a mug of tea, added three spoonfuls of sugar and cold milk, then tested the temperature with his little finger. Not hygienic, but this was no time to be finicky.

Daniel dashed from the room. 'Back in a minute,' he yelled.

Momentarily puzzled, Nash moved over to the Aga and took the towels off the top. They were warm enough for what he had in mind. He draped one over her neck, and parting the bath towel for a moment, placed another over her groin and the remaining two under her armpits.

The warmth and movement caused her eyelids to flutter, then open in time to see the man holding a mug in front of her. 'Alondra, it's Mike. Do you feel able to hold this without spilling it?'

She nodded, stretched out her hands and cupped them round the mug, luxuriating in the warmth. 'Sip it slowly,' Nash told her as Daniel returned at full-pelt.

He held out a large furry rabbit, wearing pyjamas. 'My hot water bottle, the lady can put her feet on it.'

'Brilliant idea.' Nash filled it and gently placed it beneath Alondra's feet. 'When you've finished your tea, I want you to eat the chocolate Daniel will give you.' He turned to his son. 'Watch her, please, Daniel. I'll be back in a second.'

He scooped up her wet clothing and walked down the corridor to the utility room that housed the washer and tumble drier. After removing the hot towels from within, he pushed the bundle of sodden garments inside and reset the timer. He hurried back into the kitchen just as Daniel was taking the empty mug from their visitor. 'I need to put some warmer towels on,' he told her. 'While I'm doing that, Daniel, I want you to nip upstairs and bring me a blanket and a duvet. Let's get our guest as warm as we can.'

Mike began substituting the bath towel. As he did so, she looked down and saw for the first time that she was naked. Nash rewrapped her in a warmer bath sheet. 'I had to get your wet clothes off,' he explained.

'Oh, Mike, I'm so glad you found me. I think you've saved my life again.'

He set about filling the coffee machine. 'It'll take a few minutes,' he told her. As he spoke, Daniel returned, clutching a blanket and dragging the duvet behind him in the manner of Father Christmas and his sack. He helped his father wrap Alondra, first in the blanket, ensuring her feet were covered, and then in the duvet. 'Start feeding her the chocolate,' Nash told him. 'I'm going to get the shopping and your school stuff out of the car.'

He returned several minutes later and removed his outer coat and flat cap, both of which were covered in snow. 'I'll leave your school things in the conservatory for tonight; we can deal with them tomorrow. How are we doing with the feeding?'

'She's already eaten half of it, Papa.'

'Good. I'll make her a mug of coffee. While she's drinking that, will you give me a hand putting the shopping away?'

Alondra sipped her coffee as she watched them in action. Their teamwork was excellent. Nash brought a collection of carrier bags into the kitchen which he placed on the worktop and began to empty. He passed the contents to his son with instructions where to put each item.

'At least we won't starve, unless it snows until March. Now' — he turned to their guest — 'how are you feeling? Warmed up enough?'

'Yes,' she told him, 'much warmer now.'

'Daniel will show you the utility room. Your clothes are in the tumble drier. They should be dry now.'

When Daniel returned, Nash smiled at him. 'You like our guest, don't you?'

'Yes, Papa, how did you know?'

'You wouldn't give your chocolate Santa up for just anyone.'

Daniel considered the matter thoughtfully. 'She has a nice smile, and she doesn't talk to me as if I'm a little boy. She's pretty, too.'

'Yes, she is, very pretty. I'm glad you like her. While I'm cooking dinner you can show her round. We should make the bed up in the room next to yours, do you agree?'

Daniel's chest puffed with pride at being consulted. 'That sounds good.'

When Alondra reappeared, Nash explained their plan.

Daniel showed her the ground floor first. She looked round approvingly at the boy's den, his father's study and the lounge and dining room. As they went upstairs she asked, 'What made you choose this house in so remote a place?'

'It's safer,' Daniel told her. 'We used to live in Helmsdale, but some bad men blew up our flat with a bomb. Papa was almost killed. We thought it would be safer here.'

She stared at Daniel, uncertain whether to believe him, or if this was a youngster's fantasy. 'A bomb? I thought your father was a policeman, not a spy?'

'He is a policeman. A detective. *Maman* used to find all the press reports about his cases and read them to me. She said he was a brilliant detective.'

'But weren't you hurt?'

'Oh, no. I wasn't there. I was visiting tante Mirabelle. She's in France, you know,' he added in a matter of fact tone, as only a nine-year-old would.

When they returned to the ground floor, she was still doubtful if what she had heard was the truth or a fairy story.

After Nash phoned the pub and explained the position, they settled down to eat. There was little conversation over the meal. Once they had finished, Nash asked Daniel to clear the plates. He turned to Alondra, 'I'll go and make up the bed in the spare room, if that's OK with you?' his eyes signalling Daniel's presence.

'Of course, Mike. I wouldn't intrude.'

He returned as Daniel was wishing Alondra goodnight; in time to see her kiss the boy, who smiled with delight as he set off to go upstairs.

Nash turned to look at Alondra. She was standing in the middle of the lounge, her expression troubled.

'I'm glad to see you, but what changed your mind about coming to England? Why didn't you phone me?' he asked.

'I was worried you might not want me here,' she confessed.

'I said all along you should come. You'll be safer here,' he reminded her.

'I wasn't sure you meant it, or whether it was just, well, you know; just talk. Even after our time in Bayonne.' She coloured slightly and hurriedly began to explain what had happened in Onati. 'I knew nowhere in Spain was safe, so I decided to make a run for it.'

'I thought you wouldn't fly.'

'I didn't.'

'And how did you make sure you weren't followed?'

He looked at her admiringly after she described how she'd foiled her pursuer in Madrid. 'That was clever.'

There was more she had to tell him. But that could wait. She was too tired. The central heating was on full blast. She was having difficulty remaining awake.

'Time you were in bed. You need some rest.' He watched her climb the staircase, saw her pause at the top and smile down at him. He stayed there for a few seconds after she'd gone. Weariness and the knowledge that she was safe would ensure she slept soundly.

* * *

Next morning the grey light filtering round the edges of the curtains in Nash's bedroom warned him that the snow hadn't abated. He parted them an inch and peered out. Snow was still falling heavily, still being driven horizontally by the strong wind. What he could see of the landscape was featureless. Even the walls had disappeared under the drifts they had trapped, which in turn had engulfed them. There would be no chance of him getting to work or Daniel to the childminder. Nash smiled. Normally, that would concern him. Today, however, he was more than happy to stay home.

As the coffee was brewing he went through to the lounge. With no prospect of leaving the house for the next few days, it was time to light the fire. The inglenook contained a huge fireplace. The hearth was of solid stone, about a foot deep. The opening was almost tall enough for Nash to stand upright inside, and certainly wide enough for him to lie down. The grate, which filled the aperture, was a masterpiece of architectural ironmongery that would hold a substantial section of tree trunk. There was a stack of these in the wood-shed, lengths that would burn for days at a time. He set about the task, stacked a series of short logs around the burgeoning fire and placed the guard in front of it.

He glanced across at his watch. It was almost eight o'clock. He rang Helmsdale station.

It was the uniformed sergeant, Jack Binns, who answered. 'You'll be snowed in, I guess,' he greeted Nash. 'That's what you get for living in the wilds. Mind you, it's no better here. I don't think we'll be seeing Viv today, and two of my men have already rung in to claim a duvet day. Skivers, the lot of you.'

'What about Clara? I doubt she'll make it.'

'Actually, she didn't even go home last night, that's how bad it is. As we've no residents at present, she slept in one of the cells. She's making breakfast at the moment. Toast and coffee.'

'You're a brave man, Jack.'

The sergeant laughed, but said, 'Seriously, it's a right mess. Helmsdale is cut-off, all the roads are impassable. Only Netherdale is functioning, and the traffic-lads are having a hell of a time, rescuing stranded motorists and dealing with shunts. Fortunately nobody's driving fast enough to do any serious damage.'

'There shouldn't be much crime then.'

'No, the villains have more sense and stay indoors. It's only us that are mad enough to go out. Here's Clara now, I'll put her on.'

Nash explained the situation before adding, 'Not only that, but Alondra was here yesterday afternoon when we got back from Harrogate. She had to make a run for it from Spain. They had another go at her.' He passed on what Alondra had told him. 'There's obviously more to it, though, but she was so weary last night I didn't press her.'

'The poor girl must be exhausted and terrified. One thing's for sure, with the weather as it is she's quite safe with you and Daniel.'

'I'm not sure how long this weather's going to last, I looked at the forecast last night and it wasn't very encouraging.'

'I shouldn't worry, there's bugger all happening here. I'll tell Jackie for you, shall I?'

'If you would, please. Tell her she can phone if it's urgent. And you can too, of course.' He knew Superintendent Fleming would handle things in his absence.

'I won't call you unless it's necessary.'

He had just reached the kitchen when Alondra appeared. She stifled a yawn and smiled at him. 'I think that was the best night's sleep I've had in months.'

'You obviously needed it. Coffee?'

'Please, it smells gorgeous. When I was talking to Daniel last night, he said you bought this house because your previous home was destroyed by a bomb. Is that true? Or was it his imagination?'

'It was true enough. We spent two years living in a grotty rented flat until we could find something suitable. The bomb was principally a diversion while the villains robbed a bank. However I think there was an element of personal hatred involved too.'

'Did you catch them?'

'For the robbery, yes; some of them. Not the one who planted the bomb, though.'

'Isn't it strange? If you hadn't escaped, I might have been dead too.'

Nash looked up, in time to greet Daniel who had wandered in. 'Good morning, sleepyhead.'

Daniel smiled shyly at Alondra as he wished her good morning.

'Right, breakfast,' Nash told them. 'Anyone for bacon butties?'

'What are we going to do today, Papa? Am I going to the minder?' Daniel asked.

'No, we'll have to stay here. Too much snow. So, a spot of work for all three of us.'

'What's that, Papa?'

Nash only had to say two words to bring an air of excitement. 'Christmas tree.'

'Have we enough stuff?' Daniel asked excitedly.

His father laughed. 'I hope so. I bought everything I could find in the shops in Helmsdale, Netherdale and the market stalls. It'll keep us busy for most of the day, I reckon.'

Looking back, Alondra thought of it as one of the happiest days she could remember.

CHAPTER EIGHT

That evening, once they had eaten, Daniel retired to his den. Nash and Alondra went through to the lounge, where the log fire was burning brightly, complementing the lights on the Christmas tree.

Alondra stared at the reflection of the fire in her wine glass. 'Mike, remember you told me how you looked me up on the internet after I wrote to you?'

Nash nodded.

'The facts you discovered,' Alondra continued, 'refer to a person who doesn't exist.'

Nash blinked, sleepily. 'Sorry, I don't follow?'

'Your research was accurate, as far as it went. You found out that I live in Madrid, and that I am a landscape painter, that is also correct. But when you said that my name is Alondra Torres, and that I am thirty years old, that is not correct, or at least I cannot vouch for it being correct. I am not entirely certain who I am, how old I am, where I come from, and I am not at all sure that such a person actually exists. Maybe she never did.'

'You're going to have to explain that.'

'I told you my father was murdered, but I also told you my mother was terminally ill. She died the same day as he did.' Alondra's face twisted with distress. 'Many years ago, several years before I was born, she had been treated for cancer,' she gestured towards her abdomen, paused, and sipped at her wine. She stared into the flickering flames of the fire before she spoke again. 'I was in Madrid when she died: I wasn't even aware that she had been ill. And because of what had happened to my father I demanded to see the case notes from the hospital and read them on the way to England. I wasn't going to be happy until I was satisfied that everything possible had been done for her. Bear in mind I had lost both parents. One had been murdered, I wanted to be sure everything was above board with the other. This was when I learned all this.'

'You can do that in Spain? Get records, I mean.' Nash pictured the queues outside NHS hospital managers' offices if that facility was available in Britain.

'Certainly you can, if you're not happy with the way the case has been handled. As I was reading the notes, one fact leapt from the page at me. Well, two, to be strictly accurate. The first was the description of the operation she had undergone to stave off the cancer in the first place. The other, was the date that procedure was conducted. It was two years before I was born.'

She paused and looked at Nash, her eyes sparkling with unshed tears. 'Mike, the operation was a hysterectomy.'

'So that means—'

'She could not have been my mother. At first I thought there was a mistake, and that someone had got the dates wrong; a typing error, something as simple as that. But when I checked further back in the notes, to the time before she had the hysterectomy, the prognosis was that she would never bear children.'

'That suggests you were adopted.'

'That would be the simple solution. But I don't . . . I'm not sure. It may be so. But when I returned to Onati, I could find absolutely no paperwork. All I found was a key in one of the desk drawers. It had a fob on it from *Banco Santander*.

I went into the branch in the nearest town armed with my father's death certificate and they confirmed that it was the key to a safety-deposit box. When I looked inside, I found some money, another key, and some papers. One was my birth certificate, which gave my date of birth as 1984. It listed them as my parents, but now I know this cannot be true. It has to be a forgery.

'Also inside were photographs of me. My mother had insisted one be taken every year on my birthday but I never saw them. There were no photographs on display at our house. So what was the point of taking them, if only to secrete them in a bank vault?'

'That's certainly odd. Was there anything else in the papers?'

'Only an address, together with a number.'

'A telephone number?'

Alondra shook her head. 'No, definitely not a telephone number. The address is in Switzerland, in Zurich to be precise. I checked it and found that the premises are those of a bank. My guess is that the number is that of a bank account and that the other key is for another safe-deposit box.'

'You haven't been there to test your theory?'

'No. There was no time.'

'And there was nothing else in the house that could be a clue?'

Her smile was devoid of humour. 'If there was, I never had chance to find it. That night there was the fire.'

'You think the fire was raised to destroy evidence? Or as another attempt on your life?'

'No, if there was evidence there, they removed it first. But I don't believe there was anything. I'd already searched, bear in mind. And there is one other thing . . .'

Nash looked at Alondra, who was staring into her glass as she swirled the wine gently around. She looked up. 'The painting of Stark Ghyll was displayed on the wall below my room. That part of the house was undamaged. However, when I went back into the house, the painting had gone.

Whoever torched the building wasn't trying to destroy evidence. They could have removed that like they removed the painting. They were trying to kill me.'

She was deeply upset, naturally, Nash thought. He tried to concentrate on the practical side of things. 'Let's see if we can make any sense of all this. Tell me about your supposed parents. Might there be something about them that would provide a clue as to why someone tried to kill you? What they did for a living, relatives or friends — especially in Britain. What was it that resulted in a painting of a remote Yorkshire landscape ending up in an equally remote farmhouse in northern Spain?'

'Don't think I haven't asked these questions, Mike, over and over again. It was then that I realized I knew absolutely nothing about them, their background, anything. That sounds absurd, but it's true.'

'What about people close to where you lived? Somebody usually knows something, in my experience.'

'I asked. All the locals said was they thought they were from the south. But their accent wasn't from the south. I'm beginning to believe they weren't even Spanish, although they were both fluent Spanish speakers.'

'Might they have been English?' Nash guessed.

'It is possible. Not purely because of the painting. I told you before; they spoke English to each other as often as they spoke Spanish.'

'What about your father? Where did he work?'

Alondra shrugged helplessly. 'I have no idea. When I asked them, they told me he was retired. From what, I haven't a clue. Mother told me they didn't need to work as father had been lucky on *ONCE*.' She saw Nash's puzzled frown and explained. '*ONCE* is the Spanish national lottery. Sometimes the jackpot is huge.'

'That could be true. Some lottery winners try to avoid publicity at all costs. But that doesn't explain either your father's death or the attempts on your life. Something about their past must have a bearing on it. That's one problem. The other is trying to discover your true identity.'

'If you can find that out, then I'll believe you're as great a detective as Daniel makes out.'

'That sounds a bit like the opening of an episode of *Mission Impossible*. However, we're stuck here with nothing to do, so why not give it a try. I have the laptop. We might be able to find something. The problem is, knowing what questions to ask in order to come up with meaningful answers.'

'Where would you start?'

'With your parents, and then with you. And if we don't discover anything via the computer, we could always try the bank in Switzerland, OK?'

She nodded agreement.

'Right, what were they like? Physically, I mean. Try and give me a mental picture of them. Unless you have photographs?'

'No I don't.' Alondra stared at him. 'I've never given it a thought, but there were no photos in the house at all, ever. Why is that, do you think?'

Nash shrugged. He could think of a couple of reasons, but now wasn't the right time to share them. 'All right, you'll have to give me a description.'

'They were both strong, father in particular. Not he-man, Mr Universe type strength, but lean and muscular, without an ounce of fat. Even when I was fully grown he could lift me with one hand. Mother too was very strong, especially in her arms and wrists. And they were both graceful movers. I used to imagine they were dancers, or gymnasts. Or athletes, even.'

'OK, so that gives me an idea about them. Now, let's think about you. Start by telling me anything about yourself that you haven't already mentioned. Anything, no matter how trivial, could be vital.'

'There is nothing.' Alondra paused. 'Oh, just a weird thing, if you're concentrating on physical appearance.'

'And that is?'

'My mother would never allow me to grow my hair. I have always had the short elfin style. I've got used to it, it's easily managed and saves time. The point is that I can't remember it ever having been any other length.'

'You mean your hair was this short, even when you were a child?'

Alondra nodded. 'Ever since I was little I wanted to grow my hair like other girls, but my mother wouldn't listen; what's more, she made me promise to always keep it this short.'

'Did she give any reason?'

'I think she said it was a superstition, something like that. When I was tiny, I used to dream that I had long wavy hair — at least I believed it to be a dream. Now I can't be certain, everything is so confused, I can't make out whether it was a dream or a memory.'

'That could be significant. Let's consider the few facts we know and try making some suppositions from them.' Nash recapped all they knew. Then he added, 'When an adult changes their appearance, it is either because they want to improve it, or because they wish to disguise their identity. Given that you have become a remarkably beautiful young woman, I refuse to believe you were anything but a very pretty child. So I think we can discount the idea that it was done to improve your appearance. The superstition idea is also a non-starter. Which leaves only the fact that they wanted to disguise you. But why, and from whom?'

Alondra watched as he refilled her glass. 'I would never have thought of that,' she admitted. 'But why?'

'Look at it this way. If they were in hiding, if they were hiding you, that would suggest they acquired you by other means than legal adoption. That opens up other unpleasant possibilities. However, there is more to it.'

Alondra frowned. 'I don't understand.'

'None of what might have happened when you were a baby explains why your father was murdered. Nor does it explain the arson attack on the farmhouse, the disappearance of that painting, and the attempts on your life. The possibilities are that you know incriminating facts about someone, or that Swiss bank contains something these people don't want you to see. Or that it contains money they want to get their hands on. Any one of those would be reason enough. Or,' he added reflectively, 'it could be a combination of all those. Tomorrow, I suggest we set to work trying to find out who Alondra Torres really is.' He smiled at her. 'But whatever the outcome, I am glad you're here.'

She raised her glass. 'And I'm glad too, Mike, I'm happy to be here with you and Daniel. You have made me so welcome, and I feel safer than I have done since all this started.'

'Better than the Miners Arms then,' he teased.

'No contest.'

* * *

It was some time before Nash fell asleep that night. He thought about the young woman who was only yards away down the landing. Although his sleep was dreamless, when he awoke, a question had already formed in his mind. When he went downstairs, he found Daniel and Alondra already in the kitchen. Daniel was instructing her on how to use the coffee machine. 'Good morning, sleepyhead,' he greeted his father.

Nash smiled at the dig. 'Alondra, I've a question for you. Did your parents ever take you to Switzerland?'

Her response was instant. 'No, they never took me abroad. In fact they never took me anywhere, apart from the local town when they went shopping. The first big city I went to was Madrid, where I studied art.'

'Then how did you go about obtaining a passport?'

'Father sorted it out. I didn't need one until a couple of years ago when I began exhibiting my work. He filled the forms in. All I did was sign them.'

'I see. Did either of them ever disappear without taking you? I'm thinking two or more days at least. I'm intrigued as to why they had a Swiss bank account, if they never used it.'

'My father occasionally went away for a few days at a time,' Alondra conceded. 'He told me he had business to attend to.'

Nash saw Daniel's puzzled expression. 'Alondra has asked me to find something out,' he explained. As he spoke, he glanced outside. At last the snow had stopped. The sky was a deep, cloudless blue, although it felt bitterly cold, even in the kitchen in close proximity to the Aga. 'I'm going to attend to the fire in the lounge. After that we'll have breakfast and then,' he paused. 'I think we should wrap up warm and try out one of Daniel's Christmas presents. I know we're early, but this is too good a chance to miss.'

As they ate, Alondra questioned Nash about the possibility of prolonged isolation, and the effect. 'How will you cope if the house is cut off for two weeks or more?'

'That shouldn't be a problem. I've plenty of food in. I even have several cartons of milk in the freezer. I've all the ingredients to make bread, and the Aga's ideal for that. There's ample wood and coal for the fire, and the oil company delivered a thousand litres last week, so I think we'll survive. The first thing to run out will be fresh vegetables, but there again I've a lot of frozen stuff. My only concern is if the freeze hits our water supply. Judging by the reading on the thermometer in the conservatory, that's a possibility.'

'You are on mains water, though, aren't you? We weren't at the farm, but we didn't get extremes of weather like this.'

'Yes, but the mains supply was only installed recently, three or four years ago, I believe.'

'Did the water company decide to provide the supply, or had it to be paid for? I wouldn't have thought it would be worth their while, given that there are so few properties around here.'

'There's a big place a few miles away that belongs to one of those weird religious sects. I believe they paid for it; a sort of goodwill gesture to the rest of the community.'

CHAPTER NINE

When they were muffled in sufficient clothing to counter the piercing cold, Nash opened the back door. Drifting snow had piled up waist-high, giving the entrance the appearance of a half-open stable door. After a few minutes shovelling they had cleared a path sufficient for their needs.

Once the others were in position, Nash went to the wood store. Daniel's eyes went wide with surprise and delight when he saw what his father was carrying. Alondra too gasped in admiration.

'Wow, that's a super toboggan.' Daniel stared at the masterpiece of polished wood and shining metal. 'Thank you, Papa.'

Although Daniel got the lion's share of the action, by the time they returned indoors all three of them had taken several turns and had several tumbles in the snow.

As a treat to follow their outing, Nash served toasted crumpets dripping with melted butter to accompany their hot drinks. Alondra, who had never tasted them before, agreed with Daniel's confidently voiced opinion, 'They're scrummy! You'll love them.' He continued by saying, 'If we're not going out again this afternoon, how about we play a game of hide-and-seek?'

The crash of breaking china that followed Daniel's innocent question caused Nash to turn sharply. Alondra's mug had been the victim, dropping from her nerveless fingers onto the tiled floor. Her wail of distress had accompanied the breaking mug. At first he thought it was the damage that had upset her. But he saw how pale she was, almost as white as the snow outside. Added to that she was trembling, and for a second Nash thought she was about to collapse. He hurried across the kitchen. 'Are you all right? What's wrong?'

She shook her head, as if trying to clear it. The trembling had ceased, but she looked distressed. Along with her obvious discomfort and embarrassment was a look of puzzlement. 'I don't know,' she replied. Her words came slowly, as if the thought process was difficult. 'I'm not sure, but I felt such a horrid sensation. It was fear as I've never felt before in my whole life. I don't understand it.'

'Come into the lounge and sit quietly by the fire. Daniel will make you another coffee, won't you?'

'Yes, Papa.'

Alondra went slowly through into the lounge and Nash watched her carefully. Was it coincidence that she had reacted at the precise moment Daniel spoke? Or had the boy's words evoked a bad memory? There was no doubt Alondra didn't understand what had caused her distress. Could the explanation be more prosaic?

'You're not on any medication, are you? I know that sometimes people suffer attacks and withdrawal symptoms when they have to go without their medicines.'

Alondra shook her head. 'No, nothing.'

'I'm going to clear the mess up. Daniel will stay with you to make sure you're all right.'

'Mike, I'm truly sorry about the mug.'

'Don't worry, we've plenty more to go at.'

Daniel thought to distract Alondra by putting on the television. Now that the schools had broken up for the Christmas holiday, TV stations were showing scores of films during the day, many of them old classics. When Nash wandered back into the lounge he smiled approvingly at his son's consideration. 'If you two are going to watch that, I'll go prepare tonight's meal. Beef casserole,' he informed them.

That night after dinner, Nash tried searching the internet for some clue as to Alondra's true identity while she and Daniel remained in the lounge. Although he sat in front of the computer screen for over two hours he could find nothing remotely connected to her. Many of the websites he visited were in Spanish, so rather than disturb Alondra he used the translation tool. Eventually, he conceded defeat.

Once he'd switched the computer off, Nash poured them both a small whisky. 'I think you'll be all right drinking this,' he said as he handed her a glass. 'I was a bit doubtful about offering you alcohol after what happened at lunchtime, but you seem fine now.'

'Thanks, Mike, I feel OK.' She sipped at her drink. 'That was totally weird,' she admitted. 'I didn't want to scare Daniel by saying so at the time, but it was what he said that did it. Suddenly, I had this horrid sensation of foreboding that something truly awful was about to happen.'

'Any idea what it was?' Nash kept his tone light.

'Absolutely none. All I can say is that as he spoke, it didn't seem to me as if it was Daniel saying those words but that he had become someone else.'

'An adult, you mean?' The spectre of child abuse hovered in Nash's mind.

'No,' Alondra said firmly. 'Of that I am sure. It was as if Daniel had become another child, a boy, but don't ask me who they were or what they looked like, or anything like that, because I don't know. But it was so vivid that I find it hard to think it was simply my imagination.'

'Maybe, maybe not. Have you ever experienced anything similar?'

'Definitely not. I'm sure I would have . . .' Alondra's sentence trailed off.

'What is it?'

'Nothing like as bad as what happened today,' Alondra spoke as if reluctant to admit the occurrence. 'It was a couple of years ago. I was considering visiting Italy to do some painting. The obvious way was to fly there. I'd never been on a plane before, but the thought of flying brought on a horrendous panic attack. I broke out in an uncontrollable sweat and I had difficulty breathing.' She looked across at Nash. 'Mike, what on earth is wrong with me? I have this dreadful fear of flying, and even the mention of a child's game is enough to bring me to the point of collapse. To make matters worse, I have no idea of my true identity or even my nationality.'

Nash saw how close she was to tears. He moved closer and put his arm around her shoulder to console her. Her clean scent, unmasked by perfume, was faint but distinct. He felt her warm breath on his cheek. With difficulty, he repressed the excitement of this as he held her close and kissed her gently. 'Cheer up, Alondra. We'll sort this out, don't you worry.'

'Mike, the one thing that is keeping me sane at present is that you and Daniel have taken me into your home like this.'

'Why not do some drawing tomorrow? That might be therapeutic.'

'I could do that, I suppose.' She paused. 'When do you think the roads might be clear?'

'Not for a few days at the earliest. The forecast is for more snow and ice, and there's little or no chance of a plough coming along here. Why? Do you want to get away?'

'No, I feel safe and secure. Nobody can get at me here. I'm warm, well fed; I know I'm cared for. You've treated me as was part of your family. In fact I've felt more content in the last couple of days than at any time I can remember. My only regret is that sooner or later the snow will melt, and with it, it will take away my reason for staying.'

'Then I'll have to try and think of another excuse to keep you here.'

* * *

Dr Anna Nixon hurried along the corridor from the laboratory to her colleague's office, keen to share her discovery with him. He listened to Anna with growing interest, and when she had finished, examined her report carefully.

'Have you checked all these figures? Are they accurate?'

'Of course,' she replied. 'You know me well enough by now not to ask that question.'

He smiled. 'I should do, especially if you're using "know" in the Biblical sense of the word.'

Anna shook her head despairingly. 'I think the work we're doing is having a bad effect on you. Either that or you're secretly taking Viagra. Anyway, what are you going to do? Show them to the boss?'

'I'll have to tell him, but I've no idea how he'll react. He's getting more and more unpredictable. If it wasn't for the fact I believe what we're doing here will be of great benefit to society, I think I'd have resigned long since. Anyway, I'd better go tell him.' He looked up at the clock and headed for the door.

The scientist looked at his boss dubiously, wary of the reaction his news would bring. 'Mr Davison, I have to report that Dr Nixon and I have analyzed the results from our latest subject and I'm afraid she's totally unsuitable.'

'Very well, pay her off and send her on her way. Usual conditions.' There was a pause. 'Have you been able to identify the cause? More important, can anything be done to rectify the problem?'

'There is no way of being absolutely certain. You have to bear in mind that we are breaking new ground. Everything we do is, by nature, research, and to be honest as there are no case histories to compare notes with, only our own findings, much of it is little better than trial and error — so far,' the scientist admitted ruefully, 'mostly error. However, I have one suggestion, but it does have some serious drawbacks, both from an ethical and scientific point of view. It's a result of Dr Nixon's analysis of the DNA structure of our subjects.'

'Tell me what it is, and let's see what the snags are.'

The scientist cleared his throat, a sure sign of nerves. 'You know genetics is still in its infancy, I believe we need someone with as similar a genetic construction to the original as possible. Having studied results from all the tests since the programme commenced, the only near-satisfactory one came from earlier this year, but we were unable to complete our work.' Davison looked at him sharply as the scientist continued, 'I'm speaking of the unfortunate young woman who fell to her death.'

'I know exactly who you're referring to. What was so different about her?'

'Analysis of her genetic structure showed that her DNA was far more similar to the template than any of the earlier failures. I believe that is the reason we were closer to success with her. I'm convinced that we stand a far greater chance of succeeding if we are able to obtain the use of another subject whose DNA is close to that model. A family member, for example, would be ideal.'

'But surely there are great risks involved in using such a subject? Problems that have been known for centuries — nothing to do with what we're trying to achieve.'

'That is a possibility. But having studied the matter at great length, Dr Nixon and I believe the chances of that happening are remote, and the problems you refer to stem from the different methods used.'

'Stem? I take it that pun is so bad it was unintentional.'

'The point is,' the scientist ignored the barb, 'that with the technology we are applying, such a risk is vastly reduced. I strongly believe this to be our best way forward, but of course it depends on the availability of a subject. That, I leave up to you.'

'Very well, I'll give the matter some thought. You can go.'

The scientist left and Davison walked across to a desk in the corner of the room, opened a drawer and took out a photo. After studying the image of Alondra Torres for some moments, he pressed a button on his desk. He waited until the door opened. 'I've a job for your friends,' he told the newcomer. 'The target remains the same, but the objective has changed. I want her brought here, alive and well.'

Kidnapping had worked well once, even though in the long-term, he had been let down by those he had trusted. There was no reason why it shouldn't work again. And after that, there was a certain poetic justice in the use her body would be put to. It was ironical that if his instructions had been obeyed in the first instance, her body would not have been available for the task he required her to perform. Once that had been completed, providing the result was all he hoped it would be, she would be as disposable as before, if not more so. This time round, her death would not merely be desirable, it would be absolutely essential.

* * *

Dermot Black had worked for Davison for a long number of years, done things for him that he would prefer not to dwell on, and yet sometimes he realized he was little closer to understanding him than he had been the day they met. This sudden change from wanting the young woman dead to being desperate to capture her unharmed was just another instance of his unpredictability.

The contact he phoned was more than a little surprised by Dermot's opening remarks. 'It's a good job that you haven't killed the girl because that would have caused a problem, to put it mildly. Let's just say that plans have been changed. Now, instead of disposing of her, your new task is to bring her to me, and,' he paused for emphasis, 'in perfect condition, not even a bruise or scratch on her. Got it?'

He barely waited for the man to agree before continuing, 'I want it done so there is no chance of her whereabouts being discovered. Let me know if there is anything you need, and when you're ready I'll tell you where to take her. That information is for you and you alone. Understood?' Dermot concluded, 'There will of course be a bonus on top of the original fee — a large bonus.'

The man who had been hired to kill Alejandra Torres put his phone down and stared at it in disbelief. He looked up as the door opened and relaxed when he saw it was his colleague. 'We've a change of plan,' he told the man, going on to explain their new mission.

'There's only one problem with that,' his colleague told him. 'I've located the girl. She's staying at a pub in Yorkshire, in a little village called Wintersett, to be exact.'

'What's wrong with that?'

'Only that the area is buried under a foot or more of snow. I hope they don't want us to do the job in the next couple of days, because there's no chance of us getting anywhere near her.'

CHAPTER TEN

The following morning brought yet another change in the weather. No further snow had fallen, but the piercing cold had intensified, accompanied by a blanket of thick, impenetrable fog. After breakfast, Daniel, disappointed that a further session of tobogganing was off the menu, departed for his den to wrestle with one of his computer games.

'I'm going to take your advice and try some sketches,' Alondra told him. 'It will be unusual for me, because I don't often work with pencils. I use charcoal normally.'

'Why is that?'

'Because I prefer oils to water colour.'

Nash returned a few minutes later bearing pencils and a large quantity of printer paper. 'I won't need all that,' Alondra protested.

'Use what you want,' Nash told her. 'I've another three packets to go at. I've pulled a chair in front of the lounge window where you'll have good light, and stoked the fire so you'll be warm and comfortable. I'll be in my study if you need anything else. I'll have to ring my office and check how things are.'

'Thank you, Mike.'

In fact, Nash made two phone calls. His first, to Helmsdale, found Clara Mironova in a philosophical frame of mind. 'The main roads are mostly clear,' his DS told him, 'but the minor roads are a total no-go area. Gritters and ploughs are working flat out but they're struggling with the low temperatures. And now this fog is causing extra problems. Fortunately, most of the criminals seem to have ceased working, probably gone abroad if they've any sense. How are things there? Have you discovered more about your guest?'

'Yes and no. She's a real mystery woman.'

He explained everything Alondra had told him. 'I've tried any number of internet searches, but without any luck so far. What I need is a stroke of luck or brilliance. I feel sure if I only type in the right search criteria I might get a result. The problem is there are so many options, and they throw up literally millions of results. Knowing which might be pertinent is proving quite a headache.'

'Why not ask Viv?'

'I thought he was on leave until Monday?'

'He's changed his plans. He and Lianne were going through to Bradford to see his parents and do some Christmas shopping, but in view of the weather that's all cancelled.'

'Is he about?'

'Not at the moment. He's gone to check out a break-in on the Westlea.'

'Ask him to give me a ring when he's free, will you? There's no rush. It's waited this long; another day won't harm. It doesn't look as if we'll be going anywhere in the near future, unless there's a dramatic change in the weather. And the forecast isn't promising.'

'Are you well stocked-up?'

'Yes, I went shopping before I collected Daniel. We've plenty of fuel too.'

'Sounds as if you're equipped to withstand a siege.'

'Hopefully it won't come to that. However, I'd better let Jackie know the situation.'

His conversation with Jackie Fleming followed broadly the same lines as that with Clara.

'It's eerily quiet here, Mike,' Jackie told him. 'If I was you, I'd stay warm and cosy and spend your time looking for a transfer to somewhere like Barbados.'

'Not likely, they get hurricanes there.'

'Another plan ruined,' Fleming sighed. 'Clara told me you have an unexpected guest.'

Nash related Alondra's story again.

'Sounds intriguing. You can do some detection during your layoff.'

'I'm already trying that,' he said as he ended the call.

He collected two mugs of coffee and wandered through to the lounge. He was just in time to see Alondra slide a sheet of paper under the rest of the stack.

As he set her mug down he glanced at the top sheet of the pile. It was a sketch of Black Fell, the summit crowned with snow but the lower slopes clear. Even with a pencil sketch, the effect was spectacular.

'I like that,' Nash told her. 'I reckon you've reproduced it perfectly. But how did you manage that with all this fog?'

She smiled and tapped the side of her head with the pencil. 'Memory!'

'I see, now are you going to show me the other sketch?'

Alondra looked confused.

'The one you hid so carefully when I came in,' Nash persisted.

'You're too observant. I suppose that comes with your job. Please don't laugh though. I'm not a portrait artist.'

She held the paper up, somewhat reluctantly. It was a drawing of Nash and Daniel, laughing and excited. She must have captured it from their tobogganing session. 'Wow!' Nash exclaimed. 'You've got Daniel off to perfection, but I think you've flattered me almost beyond recognition.'

'The artist can only draw what they see,' she told him severely.

He looked down the sheets and saw the tiny caricature in the bottom left corner; the same as on the paintings he had bought. 'Do you always draw a cat on your pictures?'

Alondra glanced down at the pencil impression of the animal. 'Yes, it's a sort of trademark. I've always been reluctant to sign my name. My mother wouldn't have it at any price. She said she regretted giving me the name but by then it had been registered. She refused to use it and preferred the cat, my initials.'

'Your initials? But that doesn't make sense.'

'Yes, it does C A T, Carlota Alejandra Torres.'

'But your name's Alondra. I've been searching for information on Alondra Torres.'

'Oh, I'm sorry; it never occurred to me. Alondra is short for Alejandra; I have always been called that.'

'It doesn't matter. I can try again. But Carlota, that's a lovely name.'

'Yes, I quite like it, but my mother banned me from calling myself Carlota. That is what is stated on my birth certificate. Although, as everything else is a lie I've no reason to believe that to be true.'

Armed with this new information and with nothing else to distract him Nash returned to his study. He switched on his computer. If they were able to track down Alondra's real identity, Nash was concerned that the revelation, if it contained unwelcome news, might prove too devastating for her. Alondra's state of mind might be even more fragile than was apparent. He wanted to protect her from anything that might damage her emotionally.

He met with no success, and was about to give up, when the phone rang. 'You wanted a word, Boss?'

'Thanks for phoning back, Viv.' Nash explained the problem.

When he finished, the DC asked what searches he had tried, then told him, 'OK, leave it with me. I'll call you back when I've had a go.'

Pearce's greater familiarity with computers enabled the search to be completed much faster, but when he rang back, he was able to report no more success than Nash had achieved. 'However, I've just had an idea. I'm trying it now,' Viv told him.

Erasing her name from the search box, Pearce substituted the phrase 'people born' and followed this with the date. After clicking the search icon, he watched the screen load. Halfway down the page he saw an entry that looked promising. He scrolled down to it and stopped, his finger poised over the keyboard. He sat motionless, his expression one of stony-faced disbelief. 'Hell's bloody bells,' he muttered, forgetting that Nash was still on the phone.

'What is it, Viv? What have you found?'

'Mike, I think you should enter the same search parameters and see if you come up with what I've found.' He gave Nash the details and waited.

Nash looked at the result, his astonishment as complete as Pearce's. 'Good God!' he muttered. 'Are you looking at the same screen as me?'

'I think I must be, judging by your reaction,' Pearce replied.

Nash read the few words that formed the title of the article, then clicked on the file name. He read it through once. 'There can't be any doubt, Viv. There are too many coincidences for there to be any mistake.' He read it over again, his mood swung now to one of suppressed excitement. He returned to the main search and clicked on another file. This one contained a photograph.

Seeing the photo gave him an idea. 'Viv, you see the other article. The one with the photo?'

'Yes, got it, Mike.'

'Can you do me a favour?' Nash explained what he had in mind.

'Yes, I'll give it a go. Fortunately this computer has some fairly sophisticated software. What do you want me to do when I've finished? Shall I e-mail it to you?'

'Please. But before you go, put me through to Clara. I think we ought to act on this, even without more evidence.'

He explained to Clara what he wanted, and why.

There was a stunned silence as she digested the news. 'Bloody Hell, Mike!' she exclaimed after a long pause. 'You sure about this?'

'I'm not absolutely certain and there's no way we can be at this stage. It'll take a lot of work to prove it one way or the other. But I'm prepared to bet I'm right.'

'You don't bet,' Clara pointed out.

'No, but I think I'd chance a tenner on this one.'

'OK, I'll get on with it,' Clara paused, 'or should I ask Jackie to do it? A request like that would carry far more weight coming from someone of her rank.'

'Good thinking,' Nash approved. 'If she has any questions ask her to phone me.'

As he switched the computer off, Nash murmured cheerfully, 'Well, Senorita Carlota Alejandra Torres, have I got news for you.'

* * *

Over dinner that evening, Nash was unnaturally quiet. His worries over the possible effect of revealing Alondra's true identity had increased rather than lessened now he thought he knew the full story. How would she react when she learned of the traumas surrounding her early life? And what long-term damage might he be causing merely by telling her? Despite these concerns, he was certain that telling her was the right, the only, thing to do. Maybe the effect would be lessened given their unnaturally monastic existence. By the time Alondra got to meet with people en masse she would have had time to adapt to the news.

'Mike,' her voice interrupted his thoughts. He looked up. 'Mike, Daniel was talking to you.'

'Sorry, Daniel, what were you saying?'

'Is it all right if I watch a DVD after dinner?'

'Of course it is. Maybe Alondra will watch it with you while I stack the dishwasher and clear the kitchen.'

'I thought we were going to have a look at your computer again?'

'That'll wait.'

By the time Nash had finished his chores, the cartoon Daniel had selected was almost over. Nash sat in his armchair and watched his son and their guest as they laughed at the antics of *Wallace and Gromit*. Daniel carefully replaced the DVD in its sleeve and switched off the set. He then kissed his father goodnight, and, much to Nash's surprise, asked Alondra if she would accompany him upstairs. Although he could almost always gauge what his son was thinking, on this occasion Daniel's behaviour baffled him. After a term at boarding school Daniel didn't normally require someone to take him up to bed, or tuck him in.

'I'll be in the study when you come back down,' he told Alondra.

It was almost ten minutes later when she returned, by which time Nash had read the e-mail from Pearce, printed off the attachments, and closed his laptop down.

'What was that about?' Nash asked her.

She smiled enigmatically. 'Oh, I think Daniel just needed some reassurance, someone to talk to.'

Alondra's statement didn't enlighten Nash at all. He was about to press her for details when she asked, 'Aren't you going to switch your computer on?'

'I don't need to.' Nash reached across his desk and picked up file cover containing a sheaf of papers. 'It's all here. Are you ready for it?'

'You've found something out? About me?'

'I think you should sit down,' Nash didn't answer her directly. He gestured to the chair alongside his. 'I've quite a bit of news for you, and it's going to come as something of a shock, I'm afraid.'

She sat down.

'This wasn't my doing. Viv Pearce, our detective constable, is far more computer literate than I am. However, I believe we've found out who you really are. Your true identity, I mean.'

'Who? How did you find out?'

'Before we get too excited, I want to make sure, so be patient while I ask you a couple of questions. Firstly, those photos you found in the bank safety-deposit box; what's happened to them? Do you still have them?'

'I'm not sure where they are. I took them back to the farmhouse, but . . .' She frowned as she tried to recall. 'They might have been destroyed in the fire. I certainly didn't see them afterwards. If it hadn't been for what happened to the painting, I'd have sworn the photos had gone up in smoke. But now I'm not sure.'

'I'd suggest we keep an open mind on that subject. Now, can you remember how old you were when the first photo was taken? Were you a baby?'

Alondra stared at him blankly. 'No,' she said slowly. 'No, I wasn't. I'd be five-years-old, maybe six. Yes, I'm sure that was the first photo of me. I know that because I remember the dress I had on in the photo. It was my favourite.'

'Don't you think it was odd? That they didn't have any photos of you when you were a baby? Most parents fill their house with baby photos. They would put more up if they hadn't run out of wall space.'

'You don't have photos of Daniel as a baby,' Alondra said without thinking. She saw the look on Nash's face and stammered, 'I'm sorry, Mike. I didn't mean . . . I wasn't thinking. I realize you couldn't have; you didn't know about him until he was older.'

'Not to worry,' he reassured her. 'But you agree, don't you? First of all they don't photograph you until you're five—'

'Or six,' she interrupted.

'I think you'll find the first photo was taken on your sixth birthday,' Nash stated emphatically. 'I'll explain why I'm so certain later. So, not only didn't they start snapping you for several years, but when they did, instead of putting them on show they secreted them in a bank vault.'

'It sounds crazy when you put it like that.'

'I agree, but I think you'll find there's a logical and practical reason for their behaviour, it fits with everything else we've discovered.'

Nash reached across and took the top piece of paper from the file on his desk. He handed it to her. 'Does that look familiar?'

Alondra looked down at the photo. She studied it for a few seconds, her mouth worked, but no sound came out. Eventually, she stammered, 'That's me . . . the hair is different but . . . it is me, when I was tiny, isn't it? Where did you get it?'

He didn't answer but reached over and passed her a second photo. It was identical to the first in all but one detail. Both photos were of little girls. They were around the same age: no more than four years old. They were dressed identically; their features were identical. The only difference was the style of their hair. In the first, the one Alondra was so sure was of her, the hair was very short. The other little girl had long hair in ringlets.

'I don't understand. Do I have a sister? Is she my twin?'

Nash shook his head. 'No,' he told her gently. 'I don't think you have a twin. In fact I don't think you have a sister. I do think you have an older brother, but that's part of the story.'

Alondra started at him, thoroughly confused.

'Both those photos are of the same girl,' Nash smiled reassuringly at Alondra's stupefied expression. 'DC Pearce downloaded one photo from the internet and used the software on the police computer to change the hair. That photo' — Nash gestured to the first image — 'is as you remember yourself. The other is what you would have looked like had your hair not been cropped. The one with long hair is the original. The reason your hair was cut, and the reason your mother insisted it remained so, was to avoid the slightest chance that someone would recognize you.'

Alondra frowned. 'Why would anyone recognize me? I was only a small child.'

'Oh yes they would. Twenty-five years ago, that photograph' — Nash pointed to the second image again — 'was on the front page of every newspaper in Europe and a lot from further afield. It was shown on TV news bulletins worldwide and you were referred to on every radio news broadcast.'

She stared at Nash, wondering if he had lost his sanity. 'Why? Were my parents famous? Did they really win the lottery?'

'Not really. I'll explain the reason in a few moments, Lottie.' Nash slipped the name into the conversation so naturally that it was a second or two before it registered.

'Then why . . . What did you call me? Did you say Lottie? That's not my name. But—'

'But it sounds familiar?' Nash suggested.

'I think . . . Oh, I don't know.' She shook her head in confusion. 'Who is this Lottie? Not me.'

'Let me tell you the full name.' Nash watched her face as he intoned it, 'Charlotte Alexandra Davison, who was known to her family and friends as Lottie.'

'Charlotte Alexandra, but that's—'

'The Anglicized version of your name,' Nash agreed. 'They didn't change your name. They simply used the Spanish equivalent.'

'If I am the person you're talking about, why all the secrecy? Why all this cloak-and-dagger stuff?'

'Lottie Davison came from what I would call a privileged background. Her parents were wealthy, extremely so. Her father ran a huge industrial conglomerate. Her mother was a former fashion model.' Nash went on to explain the events of the day of the party.

'You think these people are my real parents?'

'Your birth parents, but not the parents who raised you.' He could see she was struggling with what he was saying but pressed on. 'During the party, Lottie's elder brother suggested they play a game of hide-and-seek in the house.'

Nash was watching Alondra carefully as he spoke. She had been staring at the photo, but at the mention of hide-and-seek, her head jerked up as if obeying the command of an invisible puppeteer. Her mouth parted in astonishment as he continued, 'At some point during their game Lottie disappeared. When she didn't reappear, she was reported missing. Worry must have turned to panic when Lottie's parents received a ransom demand.'

Nash could see Alondra was in a state of shock. He leaned forward and took her hand in both of his, massaging the back of it gently. 'The note demanded a large ransom — to be paid into a Swiss bank account.' He felt her hand quiver under his and pressed it comfortingly. 'Along with the demand came the usual threat. If any effort is made to try and trace the girl or trap the kidnappers, Lottie would be killed.'

'What happened?' Alondra's voice was calm, detached, almost as if she was listening to a news bulletin.

Was she too calm? Nash wondered.

'To be fair to the police officers handling the case, they were in a terrible position. On the one hand there was this threat, which had to be taken seriously. However, they would have been aware that threats of this nature are invariably made along with a ransom demand. On the other hand they had to make every effort to rescue the girl, which they could only do by setting a trap for the kidnappers, which in turn put the girl at risk.'

Alondra maintained the dreadful calm. Sooner or later the dam would burst, of that, Nash was certain.

'What did they do?'

'They set up surveillance outside the bank. Two weeks later it was called off. The Davison family had received another note, accompanied by a photo.'

Alondra's tone was one of curiosity, no more. 'What did the note say?'

'It acknowledged that they had paid the ransom but that they had disobeyed instructions and knew what the consequences would be. The photo was of a child's body; her head covered in blood. The likeness was too strong for there to be any doubt that the victim was the missing girl.'

'But that's absurd,' Alondra exclaimed. 'If the poor girl was dead, how can you possibly think I am her? All you've done is take the similar names and made it fit.' She pulled her hand away from Nash. 'You're making all this up. Leave me alone.' She ran from the study leaving Nash biting his bottom lip wondering if perhaps all this had been too much, too soon.

CHAPTER ELEVEN

Alondra was sitting in the lounge staring into the log fire. Nash poured two whiskies, walked to the sofa, and handed her a glass. He saw her shiver momentarily. 'I'm sorry, Mike. It's just all this is so . . .'

'I know it's hard to believe but we can prove it all. Do you want me to go on?'

She sipped her drink, took a deep breath and nodded.

Nash sat beside her and smiled. 'Photos are easy to fake you know. Look what Viv did with those.' Nash gestured to the papers Alondra was still clutching. 'Admittedly technology is a lot better nowadays, but he told me that only took ten minutes' work. At the time, detectives had every reason to believe the photo was genuine. They started the biggest manhunt for years, convinced they were now handling a murder inquiry. Despite the expenditure of a huge amount of time and effort, no trace was ever found of the kidnappers. Significantly, the child's body was also never found. Eventually, Lottie was presumed dead, although the case was never officially closed. And that's how things have remained, until today.'

A host of questions whirled round in Alondra's brain, questions she knew even Nash was unable to answer.

'Alondra,' his tone was gentle as he continued, 'I believe we have an explanation for a lot of things that have puzzled and upset you, and about the way you were brought up.' He tapped her hand with his finger to emphasize each of them as he again went through all they had discussed about her background. Nash frowned as he spoke, at a stray thought that had crossed his mind. 'There's your reaction to Daniel's suggestion of a game of hide-and-seek. Somewhere in your subconscious mind there must be a repressed memory of what happened to you when you played that game before. Finally, and this is only speculation, there's your fear of flying.'

'Why do you think that might be significant? Surely lots of people are afraid of flying.'

'At a guess, I'd say the kidnappers, let's call them Mr and Mrs Torres, would want to get you out of sight as fast as possible. They could have got on the first available flight out of the country.'

'Surely they would have needed papers for me.'

'If your current passport was arranged by your father, I've no doubt he knew who to ask back then.'

'But I've no memory of flying.'

'You've obviously no other memory from that time either. However, your subconscious might know, as it knew about hide-and-seek, and associated both with something terrible.'

'Mike, oh, Mike, this is all too horrid. I don't want to be this Lottie girl. Can't I still be Alondra?'

The dam was close to bursting, Nash realized. 'I think you'll have to remain Alondra, at least for the time being, for your own safety.' He tried to reassure her. 'I think we should keep this knowledge to ourselves.'

'I don't understand. I'd have thought you'd be anxious for it all to come out in the open. Surely finding all this out would be considered a great achievement, do wonders for your career?'

Nash was surprised; she seemed to have accepted the situation so calmly. He'd forgotten how, in many cases, reaction to shock can be delayed. It encouraged him to reveal the last part of his analysis of the situation.

'All I've done so far is request a copy of the original file. I'm not interested in making a name for myself. My only concern is for you, and keeping you safe. My career counts for nothing compared to your safety.'

'You think this is why I might be in danger? Because of all this?'

'You told me so yourself. What other reason could there be behind those attempts to kill you? You said at the time, you couldn't think why anybody might want you dead. Well, I can think of a reason now.'

Nash could tell Alondra hadn't followed his train of thought. 'If I'm right, the couple who we believe abducted you are dead. All right, one of them died of natural causes but the other was murdered. Add that to the attempts to kill you, and the fact that the kidnappers took photos of you every year. Why do you think all that happened?'

'I can't think. My brain won't accept any more.'

Nash spoke slowly, patiently, as if to a small child, or a very elderly person. 'OK, we're going to play a game called "let's suppose". I make a statement and you accept it. Right, here goes; let's suppose the original message and the fake photo were a smokescreen. Let's suppose the Torres couple had been paid to kidnap you. A commission, if you like. And, to take it one step further, let's suppose they were then instructed to kill you. Are you with me so far?'

Alondra nodded. She held Nash's hand tightly as he continued, 'However, although kidnapping is a very serious offence, it pales into insignificance alongside murder; even more so when the victim is a child. Maybe the abductors were afraid to take that extra step. It takes a particularly sick mind to kill a child in cold blood. Alternatively, being mercenary, as we know they were, maybe they decided to keep you as an insurance policy, to give them a hold over their client. Or it might just possibly be that they had grown attached to you. From what you told me about the way they raised you and protected you, I'd like to think it was the latter. It makes sense, especially with what we know about the woman and the fact that she couldn't have children of her own.

'I've had a chance to think about them since we discovered all this' — Nash gestured to the papers still clutched in her hand — 'My guess would be that they were career criminals. Something is ringing a bell at the back of my mind to do with the way these two operated, but I can follow that up later. You told me they didn't work, that they had no obvious means of support, but that they were reasonably well off. Perhaps the kidnapping was their curtain call and they reckoned they had made enough to retire. They would have concerns that one day the money would run out, or they might be faced with an emergency, such as a life-threatening illness requiring expensive treatment. If that happened, they would have to utilize the one remaining asset they had. They resort to blackmail. Perhaps they would take copies of those photos from the vault and send them to their client along with a demand for pension rights.' Nash smiled. 'Or child support. Receiving those photos after all these years would have come as a hell of a shock. However, the client isn't prepared to pay again, and decides instead to clean the stables. They have to go, and now that he knows you're still alive, so do you. Fear that incriminating evidence exists must be making the client desperate to put an end to you before your identity, or theirs, is revealed.' He felt her hand tremble under his and knew he had got his point across.

Alondra's eyes were brimming with unshed tears. 'I said I wanted to find out who I really am. Can I undo that please?'

'I don't think that's an option anymore,' Nash told her gently. 'Not because of anything I've done or anything I've found out; but because of the attempts on your life. They won't stop. They won't be deflected. All we can do is try and find out who they are before they find out where you are.'

Alondra's smile was one of deep sadness. 'I don't see how you can keep me safe and find out who is behind all this, not in time.'

'At least you're safe for the present. That gives us a chance to investigate.'

'At one point I thought it was one of the worst decisions I'd ever made; setting out that day and ending up here, half-dead. Now, I'm beginning to hope it might have been one of the best.'

Nash glanced at his watch. 'I suggest a hot drink and bed for you. It's late, and you've had a big shock. A good night's sleep will make things seem much better.'

* * *

Sometime during the early hours a noise woke Nash. He reached over and flicked the lamp on. Alondra was standing by the door. She was wearing the T-shirt Nash had lent her. It never looked that good on me, he thought. As his vision cleared, he saw that her face was a mixture of emotions. Distress was uppermost, and it was clear that she had been crying. There was also anxiety, as if she was unsure of her reception.

'I couldn't sleep . . . I didn't want to be alone . . . Do you mind?' she stammered nervously.

'Of course not.' He extended one hand, pointing to the edge of the bed. 'Come and sit here.'

It appeared that was not exactly what Alondra had in mind. She reached behind her and closed the door. She stood alongside the bed for a brief second, lifted the duvet and slipped into the bed. 'Hold me, please, Mike. Hold me so tightly that I can't feel or hear or see anything else in the world but you and me.'

He put his arm round her as she sobbed quietly against his shoulder. Eventually, she stopped crying and he could sense her breathing become easier, more regular. He became aware of her hand, pressed into the small of his back, caressing him gently. Suddenly, she sat upright and removed the T-shirt in one smooth, swift movement, dropping the garment on the floor.

* * *

Alondra was half-awake. She was aware that something had caused her to surface from the depth of a contented sleep. She turned to gaze at her companion. Nash was still sleeping. She blinked for a moment taking in her unfamiliar surroundings. The gentle sound of breathing alongside her brought memory flooding back in a joyous sensation of wellbeing that swept through her entire body. She stretched lazily, sensuously, careful not to wake him; a temptation she found difficult to resist.

Along with the satisfaction the night had brought; there was another, deeper, more gratifying emotion. It took a while before she identified it. For the first time since she could remember, she felt a sense of being wanted, of belonging. She'd been reckless in France, but now a tiny part of her urged caution. Why should things change simply because this man makes you feel more alive? Could she take a chance?

She decided it would be discreet to return to her own room. Suppose Daniel came in early to see his father, this morning of all mornings, and found them together? She slipped quietly out of bed and stood for a moment looking down at the detective, the man who had given her identity. Her saviour, her lover. How quickly he had come to mean so much to her.

Alondra picked up the T-shirt and wriggled it on over her head. She tiptoed to the door and opened it quietly, praying that it didn't creak. She took a cautious step into the landing and turned to close the door behind her; then stopped, rooted to the spot, her hand on the doorknob.

Seconds later, she re-entered the bedroom and walked slowly, thoughtfully, across to the bed.

Nash stirred, opened his eyes, and smiled at her. 'You're up early,' he said, stretching out his hand.

She took it, but stood looking down at him, her expression grave.

'What's the matter?' he asked. 'Is something wrong?'

'No, of course not. How could there be?' Alondra saw the look of surprise on Nash's face and smiled. 'When I came into your room last night I wanted the comfort of feeling needed, loved, even if it was only pretence, even if it was only for a fleeting moment; more of what we had in Bayonne. However, I think you should have a talk to Daniel this morning.'

'It's a bit early for that, don't you think?'

'Err . . . no, actually, I think it's a bit late. I just bumped into him. He had to know I was coming out of your room.'

'He's only nine,' Nash protested. 'He probably thought you just popped in to ask me something.'

'He's nearly ten. And not if the wicked grin and the thumbs-up sign he gave me are anything to go by.' Alondra paused for a second. 'Come to think of it, I've never seen him look so much like you as he did then.'

'Cheeky bitch,' Nash muttered. He flung the duvet back. 'I'd better go have a word with him though.'

'I'll go for a shower,' Alondra said. 'That will allow you time to be alone with him.'

Whatever doubts Nash had about Daniel's reaction to what had happened were soon dispelled. Daniel was in the kitchen helping himself to a bowlful of cereal. He turned when he heard his father approaching and set the packet down on the work surface, put his arms around his waist and hugged him. 'Papa, is Alondra going to stay with us? Is she going to be my new *maman*?'

Nash returned the embrace, smoothing the youngster's unruly mop of fair hair with one hand. 'I don't know, son. Would you mind awfully if she did agree to stay with us?'

He felt Daniel's hug tighten. 'I'd like her to, Papa.'

'Why would you like it?'

'Because she's nice to me. Not only because you're about; when we're alone as well. And I think she makes you happy too, doesn't she?'

Daniel's growing up in front of me and I've hardly noticed, Nash thought. 'I think she's nice too,' he replied weakly.

'All the other boys at school have got mothers and fathers. Some even have two of each. I'm the only one in my year who hasn't got a mother. It would be terrific if you came to school and I was able to show Alondra off. She's much prettier than the mothers I've seen, so all the other boys would be really jealous. And when I'm away at school she'd be company for you, so you wouldn't be lonely or sad.'

'Oh, Daniel, Daniel.' Nash hugged the boy tight. 'Do you still miss your mama as much as ever?'

'Sometimes I think she will come back; that it was all a dream. But then I know she won't. That makes me sad.' He sat quietly for a moment and then suddenly announced, '*Maman* would be proud. I had a fight.'

'A fight? Where? Who with?'

'It was the first week of term. One of the boys in my dorm heard me crying. It was after lights out and I remembered how *Maman* used to tuck me in, then talk to me before she kissed me goodnight. That was what made me cry. He called me a cry-baby and a Mummy's Boy. Then he pushed me down some steps. Only four,' Daniel added hastily, seeing the look of horror on his father's face.

'What did you do?'

'I hit him in the belly. Then he hit me on the nose. That made my eyes water. So we had a fight.'

'Who won?'

'I did,' Daniel said. 'Or I was winning until one of the house prefects stepped in and gave us both a detention. Nobody called me names after that.'

Nash was in a fix. He knew he should advise Daniel against taking the law into his own hands, but the boy had to learn to stick up for himself. 'Try to avoid fighting,' he said. 'But don't let others push you around. And whatever happens with Alondra, I'll be sure to tell you.'

'Maman told me this would happen. And tante Mirabelle told me, too.'

'They did?'

'It upset me when *Maman* said it, but she told me it would be all right, because whoever it was, it would be someone nice; someone I'd like. I asked how she knew that. She told me that you wouldn't choose anyone that wasn't nice.' Daniel paused before adding, 'It will be nice if Alondra stays. Then we can be like a family.'

CHAPTER TWELVE

'What happened to the number and key for the Swiss bank? Did you leave them in Spain?' Nash had been thinking.

'No, they're in my bag in the bedroom at the pub. Why?'

'Because that safe-deposit box could contain information about you and what happened years ago. It might even tell us why it all kicked off again, and who is trying to kill you. I want you to ask the landlady to get that paper and read out that number to you. Then ask her to keep it and the key safe, no matter what happens, until we can collect them. I don't want them disappearing.'

Alondra's call to the pub provided disturbing evidence that she hadn't left the danger behind. The landlady promised to keep the items safe. Alondra began writing the number down, but as she did so, the cap of the pen dropped off and rolled over the edge of Nash's desk, hit her knee and rebounded under the kneehole. Alondra was about to end the call, when the landlady asked, 'Did your cousin get hold of you?'

'Sorry, what did you say?'

'Your cousin? He phoned yesterday to say your auntie's been taken ill.'

Alondra felt a chill of fear run up her spine. 'Oh, yes, yes of course, my cousin. He did, thanks. Apparently, she's a lot better today.' She replaced the phone and stared at Nash, her eyes wide.

'What's wrong?'

'The landlady told me that a cousin I wasn't aware of, phoned the pub to tell me an aunt I didn't know existed has been taken ill. Wasn't that kind of him? Oh, Mike, they've followed me. They know where I am. They're going to try again.' There was a note of rising hysteria in her voice.

'Take it easy, they don't know we're onto them. We can give you protection and scare them off.'

She smiled, a little tremulously. 'It's strange; I keep forgetting you're a police officer.'

Alondra went to replace the pen on the desk; then remembered the cap. She thrust the swivel chair back and bent to retrieve it. Suddenly, the simple act became fraught with terror. 'I can't,' she gasped. 'I can't,' she repeated, her voice high-pitched with dread.

'What's wrong?' Nash asked. He was shocked by the change. Her face was white, she was trembling.

'It isn't safe. Under there. It isn't good enough. You'll find me.'

Her voice was now little short of a scream. Attracted by the sound, Daniel appeared from his den and stood in the doorway. 'So there you are,' he said.

Her cries and sobbing intensified. Nash, who had witnessed everything without understanding it, hurried to console her. He put his arms round her, feeling her shivering uncontrollably as she stared in wide-eyed terror over his shoulder. Across the room, the small boy who had inspired such a hysteric reaction stared back and smiled encouragingly. His smile broke the spell. Suddenly, he was Daniel again. Suddenly she was grown up again, and this was Mike's study, not some other room, in some other house.

Nash could feel her quivering lessen and her breathing returned to normal, she looked at Daniel and gave him a weak, watery smile. 'I'm sorry, Daniel,' she told him. 'It was just that you startled me, and for a minute I thought you were someone else.'

Nash let go of her, but Alondra held on to his hand. 'Mike, I don't know what that was about. Everything got confused. I thought I was somewhere else, then I thought Daniel was . . . Well, I'm not sure who I thought he was.'

'It seemed to kick off when you were going to pick something up from under the desk,' Nash commented neutrally. 'Maybe that sparked off a memory. Was there a desk in the farmhouse in Spain?'

Alondra shook her head. 'Nothing like that.'

Nash's intention had been to distract her from what he guessed was the root cause of her upset. It was possible that she was remembering an incident from Spain, but in the moments of extreme panic her voice had become shrill; high-pitched. Like that of a small child.

Nash was anxious to let Alondra see he wasn't concerned about their safety, so Daniel's suggestion of another session of tobogganing came as a welcome distraction.

As they watched the boy careering down the field with ever-increasing expertise, Alondra joked, 'I think you've got the makings of a potential Winter Olympics competitor there. This area is ideal for tobogganing and skiing.'

Nash smiled. 'You've just given me an idea for his next birthday present.'

* * *

Nash rang Mironova and explained the development. 'I need to reassure Alondra,' he told her. 'She's petrified that they're going to have another go at her. We need to put a stop to it. With all that's gone on and the revelation about her identity, she's in a terrible state.'

'Poor girl,' Clara sympathized. 'It must be terrible for her. But no doubt you're doing what you can to console her,' she added wickedly. 'Leave it with me. I'll see what we can organize.'

Clara rang back within an hour. 'I got Jackie to deal with it. Helmsdale Council have put a snowplough at our disposal after lunch tomorrow. It's the earliest they could promise it for, and they said it depends on whether it snows again or not.'

'We're in their hands, I suppose. What about the driver?'

'Jackie told them there was an element of risk involved, although she couldn't be too specific for operational reasons. The manager said he has a bloke who sounds ideal; a former paratrooper. David will be in the passenger seat on the outward journey,' Clara explained, 'He's bored and looking for some excitement.'

Nash wondered why Clara's fiancé, a tough army officer, was lending a hand. Her statement gave Nash chance for payback. 'Not getting enough excitement at home, then?'

She ignored the innuendo. 'David will stay with you after we smuggle Miss Torres and Daniel out. Is there anything we haven't thought of?'

'I think you've covered all the angles. What happens once they get clear?'

'I'll meet them at Wintersett with plenty of protection. I thought Miss Torres should collect her stuff from the pub, but what about accommodation?'

'Talk to the manager of the Golden Bear at Netherdale. They've a big family suite that would be ideal, if it's available.'

'Is that everything?'

'Yes, unless you have any news for me.'

'Hang on. I knew there was something else. Jackie had a bit of a to-do with the Met. They weren't keen on sending the files on the Davison kidnapping. In the end she'd get God to intervene. Apparently they're still sensitive about that case. Anyway, the chief prevailed. The files should be here tomorrow.'

'Thank her for me, will you.' Nash smiled at how easily the nickname for the chief constable had become commonplace and wondered if Gloria O'Donnell actually objected.

* * *

That evening, Nash told Alondra and Daniel of the planned evacuation. He explained the details and for Daniel's benefit, gave the reason behind it. 'We think some nasty men are threatening to hurt Alondra. We don't know why, but we can't allow that to happen, can we? Auntie Clara will be waiting for you at Wintersett.'

He fielded the boy's questions easily but was intrigued when Daniel again asked Alondra to escort him to his room. She returned a few minutes later, her expression thoughtful.

'What was that about?' Nash asked.

She smiled. 'Daniel was trying to reassure me. He told me not to worry because his Papa wouldn't let anyone harm me. And there I was, concerned that I was putting you in danger. He's a lovely boy, Mike, and a real credit to you.'

'I don't think I'm in any danger. Nor should you be with the protection you'll have around you now.' He paused. 'I want you to give thought to an idea I've had. I know you have a fear of flying, but now that we've identified the probable cause, do you think you might be able to overcome it?'

He saw the alarm in her eyes. 'What have you in mind?' she attempted to keep her voice calm.

'I was thinking about Zurich. If we can get confirmation that the account exists, we need to see what's in that safe-deposit. If you agree to go, I'd be in the next seat to you. However, if you don't think you'd be up to it, we can always go by train. The thing is, there's only a few days left before Christmas, and this is urgent. I'd rather be back in time to spend Christmas here with Daniel. It's our first one in this house so I want to make it special. Don't worry, though, we might be able to get there and back in time, even by train.'

Alondra fought against the nausea in the pit of her stomach and failed. She ran for the bathroom and was violently sick. When she returned, she resumed her seat. 'I'll think about it.'

Nash chose to ignore her absence and told her, 'Good, and by the way, as Daniel seems happy with the arrangement,

I see no reason for you to continue using the spare room, do you?'

The change of subject took her by surprise. She looked up. 'No, I suppose not.' She smiled as she saw the look in his eyes. It was obvious that he wanted her, and she loved the feeling of being wanted.

* * *

Overnight, the thaw started, and by next morning the effect was apparent. With no likelihood of further snow, it seemed nothing could prevent the evacuation. By lunchtime Alondra and Daniel were ready, and the air of tension in the household was markedly increased.

Shortly after two o'clock, Daniel was on watch at the window and reported that the snowplough was in sight. To avoid attracting suspicion, the driver would travel the full length of the road. On the return leg he would stop outside the house where he and his co-driver would disembark, ostensibly for a tea break. This would be made apparent by them standing outside the conservatory with mugs in hand.

Nash stood by the dining room window with Alondra and Daniel to watch the plough pass. It was an impressive sight as the blade pushed large drifts of snow aside, tackling even the deeper drifts with ease. Even through the double glazing they could hear the sibilant hiss as the spinner scattered grit-salt to complete the work.

It was a tense fifteen-minute wait before the wagon came back. As the driver pulled to a halt Nash hugged his son. 'Don't forget, do as Auntie Clara says and I'll see you tomorrow, OK?'

'Yes, Papa. And don't worry, I'll take care of Alondra,' he stated, the excitement of the adventure gleaming in his eyes.

For good measure, despite knowing that David Sutton was watching, Nash then embraced Alondra.

Once the two men were supplied and sipping tea from their mugs, Nash greeted the driver who he recognized as the one who usually operated the recycling wagon that collected from the cottage. 'Not much different from your normal work, still clearing rubbish away.'

The driver laughed. 'I prefer this. The overtime is far better; all those midnight call-outs.'

'A bit more risky than emptying wheelie bins though.' Nash thought for a moment, 'Mind you, I suppose this road is a lot less hazardous than driving half way up Stark Ghyll for the bins.' He pointed across the valley.

The driver sniffed derisively. 'Are you talking about that so-called religious lot over there? I wouldn't know. They've consistently declined our services. Told our manager they're a "closed house" and don't want any intrusion on their property. Mind you, I had to go up there yesterday with that,' he jerked his thumb towards the vehicle. 'You got off luckier on this side of the dale. Across there, the snow brought all the power lines down. I had to clear a way through for the engineers to fix it.'

'Somebody else described them as weird.' Nash's curiosity was roused. 'Why did you say "so-called" religious lot?'

The driver added to the gossip Nash had already heard from Jonas Turner at the supermarket, explaining that his brother-in-law, a driver for a pharmaceutical company, delivered there regularly and had never got through the gates. 'He reckons he goes there more often than to the cottage hospital.' He shrugged his shoulders and laughed. 'I suppose as long as they keep themselves to themselves and don't try thrusting their strange ideas down other peoples' throats they can't be doing much harm.' He drained his mug. 'Now, I think we should get this show on the road. Are my passengers ready?'

Daniel, following David's instructions, dashed swiftly up the drive, head bowed so as to be invisible behind the high, snow-capped hedge. Once he reached the wagon, the boy slipped into the cab via the passenger door that the co-driver had obligingly left open, then crouched in the footwell.

All that remained was for Alondra, now wearing David's donkey jacket and bobble hat, to make her way to the cab.

She accomplished this, appearing to be chatting nonchalantly to the driver as they ambled up the drive.

Nash watched the snowplough leave, his guts churning with worry. Although he had dismissed the danger in front of the others, he knew the next part was the riskiest of the whole operation. Being stuck inside the house, helpless to intervene should anything go wrong, merely heightened his anxiety. His last sight of the vehicle carrying his son and their guest into possible danger was the orange flash of the hazard lights mounted on top of the cab.

David was watching him. 'Don't worry, Clara will make sure they're safe.'

'I appreciate you helping,' Nash said. 'How come you're involved?'

'Actually, it was your boss. Clara knew we were putting together a hostage rescue and protection programme. She told your superintendent, who phoned our CO and explained the situation. We have to keep updating our methods to meet the needs of new technology and so forth, so he volunteered me. I have one or two items with me that might give any potential raiders a nasty shock.'

The wait until Clara phoned was a kind of torture Nash would never want to endure again. The relaxed tone of her voice soothed his nerves immediately. 'It was a complete success,' she told him. 'We met them in the pub car park, round the back, so they couldn't be seen from the road. I'd posted a couple of men on the roadside anyway, and they reported there was nobody within sight. As soon as Miss Torres collected her things we set off in convoy. I left my mobile number with the landlord, and told him if anyone came asking for Miss Torres, he'd to tell them she'd checked out and he believed she was heading for Scotland. Then he was to let me know. We got them in here via the goods entrance.'

'How are they both?'

'Daniel's fine, but I think your girlfriend is worrying about you, especially after I explained to Daniel that you'd stayed there as a decoy.'

From the way Clara phrased it, Nash guessed the others were out of earshot. 'They're having afternoon tea, courtesy of room service. Unfortunately, Daniel found the menu. Lisa Andrews will be here from headquarters to relieve me soon and will stay overnight. Apparently Netherdale is as quiet as we are at the moment. By the way, the file's arrived from London. Jackie says she thinks the chief's bought into your theory big time and can see the kudos for the force if we solve a twenty-five-year-old case.'

'There's a long way to go before we do that,' Nash said. 'But as soon as I can get out of here, we can at least make a start.'

After they ate dinner, Sutton briefed him. 'I'll be on watch tonight. If anyone comes near the place, I'll wake you. Otherwise, we set off for town first thing in the morning. But if anything untoward happens, I want you to stay close to me.'

'Any particular reason?'

Sutton smiled. 'Orders! Clara told me if anyone harms a hair on your head my life won't be worth living. Must be nice to know your staff care so much for you.'

'Really? She used to try and poison me with coffee on a daily basis.'

'Thankfully, I prefer tea.'

* * *

Next morning Nash and Sutton were on the road early. As they approached Netherdale, neither of them noticed the four-wheel drive car travelling in the opposite direction. The driver stared in his rear-view mirror. Was he too late? Surely not. The road through Wintersett was still closed; he'd heard it reported on the local radio. Besides, in that area, Range Rovers were fairly common.

CHAPTER THIRTEEN

Nash opened the outer door of the suite and put his bag down, a split second before he was engulfed by two embraces, one around his shoulders, the other round his waist. He returned both before he went to put his bag in the nearest bedroom. It already contained Alondra's suitcase. He wandered back out into the sitting room as Alondra and Daniel were joined by DS Mironova, struggling with a large file box.

'Morning, Mike, I've brought some of the files on the Lottie Davison kidnap. The rest is at the station.' She dumped the heavy box on the desk. 'And I asked Mexican Pete to come here as requested. He should be with you later this afternoon.'

'Thanks, Clara.' Nash looked across at the others. 'Have you eaten yet?'

'No, we waited for you,' Daniel told him. 'Can we eat now? I'm starving.'

'Me too,' Alondra said.

'Use the bedroom phone. Order the works for me and whatever you two want while I speak to Clara.'

'She seems very nice,' Clara said once they were alone. 'I hope you're behaving yourself?'

'It's not me you should be asking that.' Nash smiled enigmatically.

Clara raised her eyebrows. Fortunately, the risk of Daniel's return prevented any possible demands for explanation or potential number of sarcastic comments. Instead she said, 'I did what you asked. The details are in the top of box. Where do you intend to go with this? How will you move the investigation forward?'

Nash explained his idea of visiting Zurich. 'Before I do anything though, I want to study these files. Someone knows or has guessed Alondra's true identity. I need to work out why they wanted Lottie Davison dead back then, and why this has suddenly kicked off.'

* * *

After breakfast Nash installed his son in front of the TV. Daniel put a DVD into the player and settled back to watch cartoons. 'Clara got the details of that Swiss bank,' he told Alondra. 'I suggest we ring them. She got a contact name for us. The man is expecting our call. At a guess, I'd say he won't reveal much, if anything, over an open phone line. All we can hope is that he will be prepared to confirm that they do hold that account and that there is a safe-deposit box.'

As Nash predicted, the contact was extremely guarded.

'This will only take a few moments, Miss Torres,' he began. 'I have several questions to ask. Some will be straightforward, others less so. They are designed to confirm your identity. We must avoid disclosure of information to an imposter. If you fail to answer correctly, this conversation will terminate immediately.'

'Very well,' Alondra agreed weakly.

The first few questions concerned her full name, date of birth, home addresses in Madrid and Onati. Next, the banker asked, 'Please tell me what happened on your tenth birthday?'

'My tenth birthday?' Alondra echoed. 'I don't know . . . I can't remember . . . Oh, yes, I fell off my new bike and cut my knee. Is that what you wanted to know?'

The banker's reply was in the form of another question, 'And what was the name of your English teacher?'

'I didn't have one.' Nash saw Alondra smile. 'My mother taught me at home. You're trying to catch me out.'

She detected a hint of a smile in the banker's voice as he moved on. 'What was the title of the first painting you sold?'

'It didn't have a title,' Alondra replied. 'I can describe it for you though.'

'Please do.'

'It was a sunset scene. The sun was sinking behind two mountain peaks. I captured it as it was trapped by the cleft between them.'

'And what did the art critic of *El País* write about it?'

'He thought it showed raw talent, and that he looked forward to seeing more work by the same artist.'

'Very good, and finally, what nickname did he bestow on you?'

'He called me Cat-woman, because of the logo I use.'

'Excellent, now please read the number you believe might be one of our accounts.'

Alondra began reciting it, but after five digits the banker interrupted. 'That's enough. Now please describe the key in your possession.'

'It is about five centimetres in length, and is of brass, I believe. It has a number engraved on it. The number is—'

'Don't read that number out, please,' he cut in sharply. 'If you visit our premises you will need your passport, a valid driving licence containing a photograph, your parents' death certificates and you will be required to answer more security questions. You will be allowed one person to accompany you, and they must provide similar identification. Before entering our building you will need to make an appointment.'

Before she had chance to reply, the dialling tone informed Alondra that the call had been terminated. She replaced the receiver and repeated what the banker had said.

'Only to be expected,' Nash responded. 'Do you have all that information, or is it back in Madrid?'

'No, because of what had happened to the farmhouse, I brought it with me. It's all here.'

'Good, that saves one leg of the journey. Now we must decide whether we go by air or on trains.'

'What if there's nothing in that safety-deposit box? What if there is no box? The banker didn't confirm it.'

'That key has to open something,' Nash pointed out, 'and by the nature of those questions it's obvious the bank was primed what to ask. Who else would know all those details, especially that business of the cut knee? However, before we consider dashing off to Switzerland I need to make arrangements for Daniel.'

'Where will he stay? Do you have relatives he could go to?'

Nash shook his head. 'Only an aunt and uncle but they're far too old to cope with a youngster. I think Clara and David would be happy to have him for a few days. The other thing I must do beforehand is study that file, but above all else I need to get a friend of mine to help tighten our security.'

Nash picked up the phone and rang Jimmy Johnson. Jimmy had been a burglar until Nash saved him from a prison sentence and made him promise to go straight. Johnson now ran a successful locksmiths and security firm in Helmsdale.

'What dae you need?' the Scotsman enquired.

'I think we should go for the best available, Jimmy.'

'CCTV an' the works? That'll cost ye. Mind you,' Johnson sniffed, 'being in the polis, you'll have plenty of money, no doubt.'

Nash grinned. 'Whatever it costs, Jimmy. It'll be worth it.'

'I'll order the equipment. It'll tak' a few days tae get it installed, though.'

'That doesn't matter. I'm going to be away. If I'm not back before you're ready to start, call Sergeant Mironova. She'll have a spare set of keys.'

Johnson snorted in disgust. 'Time was when I'd never think of phoning a polis station. An' I wouldnae 'ave needed a set of keys either.'

Nash was still smiling when he ended the call. The smile faded though when he opened one of the folders on the desk and began reading about the abduction of Lottie Davison.

* * *

Alondra studied the detective as he was reading. If his theory was correct, the contents were all about her and her natural family. She realized that in addition to everything he had already done, that he was prepared to travel halfway across Europe on her behalf. She felt a sudden swell of emotion, not merely gratitude but affection for the man who was prepared to do so much, go to so much trouble, all for her. Was this love? Was that how it started?

If Mike was right, why was she not more eager to return to what he believed to be her own family? How come she felt so ambivalent about them? She realized with something of a shock that the only time she had felt totally secure, comfortable and relaxed, had been the few days she'd spent at Smelt Mill Cottage. The fact that she considered her stay to be too short should have told her something, had she been able to reason matters out more rationally.

As she watched Nash, she wondered about him. She guessed he had been involved with a number of women besides Daniel's mother. Yet it seemed there was no one in his life at present. Indeed, Daniel, with disarming innocence, had intimated as much. Why? If Mike was ready to go to so much trouble for her, the very least she could do was to agree to attempt the flight. The idea terrified her, and she felt nausea rising, the acid taste of bile in her throat. She slipped quietly out of the room, unnoticed, reached the bathroom and retched.

* * *

The reports from the Lottie Davison enquiry showed it to have been a thorough, well conducted investigation. Witness statements and background checks had been meticulously carried out on everyone at the house. The catering staff and the security firm employed to prevent gatecrashers had been questioned longest and hardest, but nothing suspicious had emerged.

In addition, there were contacts derived from Paul Davison's business activities and it was obvious that he and his wife led an active social life. Bev Davison's public and charitable events allowed many people regular access. In all there were over a thousand names in the separate, neatly tabulated and indexed lists.

Nash was convinced of two things. First, that the kidnappers had displayed such a high-level of expertise, they must have had considerable experience in carrying out such crimes, or at least ones of a similar nature. Equally, he felt certain that no matter how great their prowess they could not have carried out the abduction without the help of someone either within the household or closely connected to the family.

On the header sheet, in the corner was a scrawl. Written by the lead detective, Nash guessed. The man obviously suspected what Nash had surmised; otherwise, he would not have written the words 'inside job?'

Nash pushed the file away, distancing himself from it mentally as well as physically. Ploughing through all the paperwork was likely to bring more confusion than clarification. He needed a fresh approach.

He picked up another folder which contained reports on the Davison family and their business. The file had been updated regularly, even after the abduction enquiry ended.

The background information on the family made fascinating reading.

The business empire DMG, founded by Lottie's grand-father, was reckoned to be worth billions of pounds when she was kidnapped. The group was involved in the manufacture of chemicals and had expanded nationwide before diversifying into other products.

Paul Davison, Lottie's father, had entered straight from school and eventually assumed responsibility for sales, marketing, and financial operations. His brother Matthew had gone to Bristol University and obtained a degree in bio-chemistry and was in charge of production, quality control and development. There was a third brother, Nash learned, named Luke. A footnote reported that sadly, Luke Davison had been killed in a climbing accident two years prior to his niece's abduction. Money doesn't necessarily bring good fortune, Nash thought.

At the age of twenty-three, Paul Davison, now managing director, had married Beverley Slater, the renowned model. She had forsaken the catwalk after her marriage, to concentrate on her new role. Six months into the marriage, Lottie's elder brother Keith was born, and five years later, Lottie appeared.

Nash did a rapid calculation. By his reckoning, Paul Davison would now be sixty-four years old, his wife sixty-one. Ex-wife, it seemed, according to an update, for Paul and Bev had divorced less than three years after Lottie disappeared. Nash wondered if the abduction had been responsible for the break-up.

On a further update the latter history of the family made for depressing reading. Paul had remained at the helm of DMG for five more years before handing control to Matthew and was now believed to be living in seclusion in the West Country. He had reportedly sold his extensive art collection and used his fortune to found a religious community. The file had been meticulously collated. There was even a copy of the press release announcing Paul Davison's retirement.

After Lottie disappeared, Bev Davison began a downward spiral of alcohol and drug dependency that increased sharply following her divorce. She was last reported as seeking treatment at a rehab clinic near London. The cost of that had been met, not by her ex-husband, but by Matthew Davison. 'Well, well, well,' Nash muttered. 'I wonder why? Was Matthew taking brotherly love to extremes, perhaps?'

Nor did the tale of family misfortunes end with Bev. Lottie's brother, Keith, had been in trouble several times as a teenager and been excluded from private school. Despite this, he had been accepted by a university. Nash wondered, a trifle cynically, how large a donation his father had made to the college. After two years as an undergraduate, Keith had been forced to take a year out, the report citing a complete mental breakdown. Eventually, he completed his course getting an acceptable degree and subsequently obtaining a teaching post. However, he still seemed unable to settle and when last reported on, was believed to be teaching children with learning difficulties in southern Africa. The story of a family disintegrating, Nash thought.

The next page contained an interview that, if accurate, shed more light on the troubles of Lottie's parents. It was the account of a Swedish girl, Yvonne Marcinczak, who had been employed as an au pair. She had left the Davison house soon after Lottie vanished, having married a farmer, and was living in Norfolk. She described the Davison brothers' relationship as tempestuous, that there was never any love lost between them. The next part of the interview was even more enlightening. According to the au pair's allegation, Paul and Bev's marriage had been in trouble long before the divorce, long before Lottie's abduction. Nash studied the interview transcript carefully.

'They were always fighting. I remember one that went on for days, weeks even. It was when Lottie was only a little baby. Paul called Bev a drunken whore, a slut and a nymphomaniac. She said he couldn't keep his dick in his pants long enough for it to cool down and he shouldn't be surprised she wouldn't sleep with him as she didn't know from day to day whose bed he'd crawled out of, and what diseases he'd brought with him.'

'Did you see any evidence that these accusations might have been true?'

'Mrs Davison did drink quite a lot, but that is all. Mr Davison was away quite often, so what he did then, I have no idea. If either of them was sleeping with other people they certainly didn't do it at home.'

Nash read the detective's final comment with interest. 'I feel certain this witness knows more but is unwilling to share that information.'

* * *

Nash closed the folder and sat for a few minutes staring at the cover, without really seeing it.

'Have you discovered anything?'

Nash looked up, startled. He'd been so engrossed that he'd forgotten his surroundings, or that Alondra was in the room. He certainly wasn't going to tell her what he'd just read. He glanced at Daniel before replying. 'I've only looked at the first few pages. It'll take days to go through the rest. Sadly, it seems that the abduction led to the break-up of the marriage, and the disintegration of the family, but that could have happened anyway. As to a suspect or motive for the kidnap, I've no idea.'

Alondra was about to ask him what he meant by the term family disintegration when there was a loud knock on the room door.

Nash greeted the visitor, 'Professor Ramirez, it was good of you to come.' He introduced Alondra.

'I couldn't resist the opportunity,' the pathologist told her as they shook hands, 'for a couple of reasons. One to meet someone from my native country, and two, because this is, I believe, unique. It must be the first time Nash has asked me to conduct a test on someone who is still breathing.'

He turned to the detective. 'What's this about?'

'Come through to the bedroom,' Nash said, indicating Daniel in front of the TV.

'Of course, I understand.'

They left the room and Nash explained his theory.

After he finished, Ramirez thought for a while. 'If it had been anyone else I would have dismissed the idea. But experience has taught me never to challenge even the wildest of your notions.' He turned to Alondra and began conversing in Spanish. Nash assumed he was explaining the reason for his visit and putting Alondra at her ease.

Once the pathologist had obtained the sample, Nash showed him out before he asked Alondra what they had discussed.

She smiled. 'The professor said, "Believe me, if anyone is capable of sorting this out for you, Nash is the man. You couldn't be in better hands; as long as you watch those hands carefully." What did he mean about your hands?'

'Err . . . Clara and Mexican Pete have developed an unfortunate habit of taking the Mickey out of me because I've had one or two girlfriends, that's all.'

'One or two?'

He knew she was teasing him, but he felt it was important to tell the truth. That, or close to it . . .

'Well, a few maybe,' he admitted.

Her eyes opened wide with feigned amazement. 'Mike, are you a stud perhaps?'

'No, nothing of the sort.' Suddenly, the room felt unbearably hot. He cursed Ramirez. 'These things get exaggerated.'

'Tell me, Mike, how many is it? Ten? Twenty? More? Do you have a harem somewhere? Will I be sent to join them? Brought out when you fancy me?'

'No, nothing like it. And there hasn't been anyone for a long, long time.' He glanced across the room to where Daniel was still intent on the TV.

She nodded understanding and relaxed her questioning marginally. 'So, why is he nicknamed Mexican Pete?'

Nash explained, as delicately and quietly as possible, *the Ballad of Eskimo Nell.*

'Fascinating,' she murmured. 'What an interesting life you lead.' She took a deep breath, 'Mike, I have decided to go by plane to Zurich. I already owe you so much, and you are going there for my benefit. I don't think I would be able to do this if you were not going with me. It would be selfish of me to risk spoiling Daniel's Christmas.'

There was a world of sadness in her smile as she added wistfully, 'I would have liked to have witnessed that, but it will be so nice if you can celebrate it together in your new home.'

Nash blinked with surprise. 'Don't be silly,' he scolded her. 'When I was talking about Christmas at the cottage, I took it for granted you would be with us, unless you have other plans? I'm sure Daniel would agree that we'd love you to spend Christmas with us.'

She was about to reply when Daniel interrupted. 'Papa, I'm famished.'

Nash laughed. 'You're always hungry. You're almost as bad as Uncle David. We'll order lunch, shall we?'

As the three of them studied the menu, Daniel asked, 'Papa, what's a harem?'

* * *

'I'm in Helmsdale. I missed the woman at the pub. Must have passed her on the road, although I didn't see any sign of her car, and it isn't exactly the M1. Anyway, I spotted the copper's car parked near one of the hotels. So I went inside, I checked at reception and couldn't get any joy so I made my way up the stairs and hung around by the lift. It paid off when I chatted up a waiter pushing a trolley. I guessed he was from room service and he'd know. Turns out they're booked in there as a family unit, so I reckon I'm right, he must be giving her one.'

'Fascinating news, but you're not being paid as a gossip columnist. What are you going to do about snatching the woman?'

'It won't be easy as things are at the minute. I'll keep watching and hope she goes out on her own. That's the best I can do.'

CHAPTER FOURTEEN

Organizing flights to and from Zurich was more problematical than Nash had anticipated. He sought the help of ex Superintendent Pratt, now their civilian clerical officer, who had taken early retirement following a heart attack and found himself unable to stay away. The best Tom Pratt could arrange for Nash was an early morning flight from Heathrow, with a red-eye return three days later, arriving three days before Christmas.

Leaving Daniel with Clara presented no problem. In the absence of his father, Uncle David could be relied on for all sorts of fun things to do. Last time he'd stayed with the couple in August, David had taken him hill walking and turned it into a fascinating nature ramble and survival training course combined.

When not involved in making their travel arrangements, Nash spent time discussing what to do in his absence with Superintendent Jackie Fleming and Clara. 'I need to try and locate any of the detectives from the original investigation,' Nash told his colleagues. 'Some will probably be retired, some possibly pushing up daisies by now, but if I can talk to any of them after we return we might get more insight into the kidnap.'

'Have you learned anything new from the file?' Fleming asked.

'Only that the family fell apart following the abduction. Lottie's father lives in seclusion, her mother became a lush and a druggie, and is now in a rehab clinic somewhere, and her brother has had no end of problems. There are some rumours recorded about rifts in the marriage even before the girl disappeared which I'd like to investigate. Maybe the disintegration was already under way, but whether it had any bearing on the abduction is another matter.'

Jackie frowned. 'You think someone in the family was involved?'

'There was a question scrawled on the file that was probably written by the lead detective. It asked if it had been an inside job. In other words, was it a family member or someone equally close to the parents? They had a lot of friends, which made access to their home simple. However, on the day of the party there was stringent security, so I believe the kidnappers must have had inside help. The abduction might have been achieved without assistance, but detailed information about the layout and people onsite would have made it far simpler.'

'And the motive?'

Nash shrugged. 'I think the motive for the kidnappers was obviously money. My guess is that Mr and Mrs Torres were professional criminals who had been hired to do the job. As to someone from inside, their motive could have been one of several. Jealousy, greed, hatred; take your pick. Paul Davison made a lot of enemies in his ruthless business activities. That's a strong motive to start with. Added to that, he was wealthy; he had a young and beautiful wife, two attractive children. All of which must have sparked a lot of envy. Then there were the rumours that he and his wife had accused each other of serial adultery. Any one of those relationships could have spawned someone with a motive to do them harm through the loss of their child — providing there's any truth in the gossip. Or perhaps someone simply saw this as an opportunity to make a lot of money.'

'I'll try and find out if we can contact some of the inquiry team,' Fleming agreed.

'What do you want me to do, Mike?' Clara asked.

'A couple of things. Try and find out where Lottie's parents are now, and her brother. They've all vanished, it seems. The mother could be dead if she was as seriously addicted as the file indicates. The father seems to have withdrawn from public life and when Lottie's brother was last heard of, was teaching in southern Africa somewhere, so none of that will be easy. Also, I want you to try and locate this woman.' He pulled a sheet of paper from the folder. 'Her name was Yvonne Marcinczak. She's Swedish, but she married an Englishman shortly after the abduction. Prior to her marriage she worked as an au pair for the family and she had one or two interesting things to say about them. I've written her last known address on that paper, see if she still lives there and if you can make contact, ask if I can call on her when we're back from Zurich.'

'I'll do what I can. The chances are they're all still in the London area,' she said as she turned to leave.

When they were alone Fleming asked Nash, 'Where do you think this is going?'

'I have no idea, Jackie. I'm hoping the trip to Zurich might shed some light on it.'

* * *

When Alondra was attempting to finish packing, Nash walked over to the desk and opened a folder on the Lottie Davison kidnap. He flicked through the pages, until he reached a photo that had been taken around the time the girl had disappeared. He stared at the image for a long time. When Alondra came back into the sitting room, he closed the cover quickly. He turned to face her, his smile betraying nothing of what he was feeling. Before she had chance to ask him what he had been looking at, the outer door opened. Clara had arrived to collect Daniel.

The flight departure time meant that travelling to the airport by train was out of the question. Nash's plan to visit the former Davison family au pair on their return gave him no option but to drive. Outside, a bored-looking constable was keeping watch over the Range Rover. The officer reported nothing suspicious and departed, no doubt looking forward to getting back into the warmth. None of them noticed the car that pulled out from the market place seconds after Nash's.

They hadn't been on the road long before the comfortable seat and the warmth of the heater sent Alondra to sleep. Nash hoped she would stay that way until they were close to their destination. The less time she had to dwell on the flight, the better. They were close to the last service area on the motorway when she woke up. They stopped for a quick break and a cup of coffee, which Nash pronounced to be almost as undrinkable as anything Clara could produce.

'It isn't very nice,' Alondra had to admit. 'Can't Clara make coffee?'

'I had to buy a coffee machine for the office. She used to make a brew she claimed to be coffee, but it tasted like something recycled by a sewage works. I didn't realize she's sold the franchise though.'

* * *

'I'm at Heathrow.' He held the mobile away from his ear and grinned at the string of obscenities that came down the line. 'No I'm not winding you up,' he told his colleague. 'I followed Nash and the woman here. They've just checked in for Zurich. No, I've no idea why they're going there. All I do know is that I can't follow them.' He listened again before replying. 'For one thing, there wouldn't be any point. Even if I snatched the woman, what would I do with her? I can't put her in a suitcase to bring her back. Besides which,' he admitted lamely, 'I don't have my passport.'

He waited patiently as his colleague let off steam, before adding, 'One good piece of news. I found out when they're returning. They were last in the queue at the check-in, so after they'd gone through I chatted up the girl on the counter, said I thought I'd spotted a friend of mine, name of Nash. She said that was right, and I asked if he was going away for long. They're due back in a couple of days. All I've to do is make sure I'm here when their return flight lands.'

* * *

When the formalities of check-in and security had been completed and they were strolling through the duty and tax-free shopping area, the enormity of what she had agreed to do struck Alondra.

Nash had been watching her, waiting for this to happen. He took her hand and led her across the terminal. 'You'll be all right,' he reassured her, 'millions of people do this every day, in complete safety.'

She squeezed his hand. 'I'm so glad you're with me. There's no way I could have done this on my own. Just now, I looked out of the window and saw a plane sitting on the tarmac. I've never been that close to one, didn't realize how huge they are.' She turned to face him and let out a juddering sigh. 'Don't worry, I'll manage it,' she said with a forced smile.

'Good for you. We've still plenty of time; let's see if we can find Daniel a souvenir.'

'Sorry. I need the loo first.'

Inside the cubicle Alondra leaned against the wall. She was sweating and felt nauseous. Despite her assurances to Nash, the thought of what was to come terrified her. She paused to inspect herself in the mirror, took a deep breath, and went to find Nash.

No matter how vulnerable the traumas in Alondra's upbringing had left her, there was a core of steel within, as Nash noticed when she was faced with boarding the aircraft. As she walked towards the plane, the covered walkway shielded the view of where she was heading. No problem there, until the point where the terminal section ended. The gap was little more than an inch wide, the gulf it represented enormous. She knew the plane was only a few feet away. She hesitated, and Nash saw the doubt in her body language, louder than a scream. She squared her shoulders and stepped forward, greeting the waiting cabin attendant with a bright smile.

The only minor casualties on take-off were the fingers on Nash's right hand which were crushed almost to breaking point before they reached cruising altitude.

Landing at Zurich presented less of a problem, and after they had cleared security, Alondra remarked, 'That was nowhere near as bad as I feared, I can't understand why I was so worried.'

'Oh good,' Nash retorted. 'With luck the feeling might return to my hand before the flight back.'

When they reached the hotel, a phone call to the bank got Alondra an appointment for that afternoon. With nothing else to do before then, Nash suggested they took a nap.

Once inside their room however, before following his own advice, Nash sent a text message to DS Mironova.

Clara was seated at Nash's desk in Helmsdale when the text arrived. She read the message, intrigued by the contents. 'If not spoken to au pair,' it read, 'don't mention my companion.'

Why didn't Nash want the witness to know that Alondra would be accompanying him? Clara wondered.

* * *

During the taxi ride from the hotel to the bank, Nash could sense Alondra's increasing nervousness. Eventually, she turned to him. 'Mike, I owe you so much already, but I must ask you, please, will you do me another favour?'

'If I can.'

'If there is a deposit box will you open it for me? Will you examine the contents? It's . . . I know this is going to sound silly, but I have this huge foreboding, that it will not be pleasant. Don't ask me to explain, I know it sounds stupid.'

'It's understandable. But a woman who can brave her fear of flying as you did today, need not be afraid of anything that box could reveal.'

Had he known beforehand what was to come, Nash reflected later, he might well have refused Alondra's request.

Their contact met them in the banking hall and conducted them to a small interview room, bare of furnishing apart from a desk, complete with phone, and three chairs. The banker started by asking three further security questions, all concerning events in Alondra's childhood. Nash realized how cleverly they had been conceived. An imposter would have stood no chance. Once satisfied, the man asked her to read out the full account number she possessed and then demanded the key.

He examined the number, comparing it to one in the file before him. Only when he was satisfied did he lift the telephone and issue an instruction before turning to Alondra. 'Your box will be brought to this room. You may open it and inspect the contents here. If you wish I will vacate the room. Alternatively, I will stay with you to answer any questions.'

A second door in the far wall opened silently and a uniformed security guard entered carrying an oblong metal box which he placed on the desk before leaving.

'Please stay,' Alondra told the banker as she passed the key to Nash. He opened the box and glanced inside. His first sensation was of disappointment. He wasn't sure what he'd expected, but the A5 buff coloured envelope hardly seemed just reward for their efforts. He plucked it out, and with a nod of approval from Alondra, slit the envelope open with his finger. He took out a sheet of folded A4 paper, plus yet another key.

The paper was headed with the logo and address of a second Swiss bank. Inscribed on the paper was another number, which was clearly a bank account number. The accompanying key looked so similar to the one still protruding from the deposit box that Nash couldn't believe it served any other purpose.

He and Alondra both stared at the banker, who smiled gently at their obvious consternation. 'I have been instructed to tell you certain facts, Senorita. Your father left orders that I could reveal how he and his wife conducted their banking arrangements. They maintained an account with us for over thirty-five years. During that time, apart from certain exceptional circumstances, their balance has remained in credit by the same sum, which is how it stands today. That sum is five-thousand Swiss Francs.

'Occasionally we would receive special instructions from Senor Torres. A large sum of money would be paid in by a third party. This sum was invariably at least six figures, often more. Once the funds cleared, we transferred an identical amount to another account which was held at a branch of that bank.' He pointed to the letterhead. 'For conducting this transaction we would be allowed to deduct a substantial handling fee.'

The banker phoned someone at the other bank on their behalf. It appeared that they too had been anticipating contact.

As they waited for the taxi, Alondra could not help noticing that Nash was trying hard not to laugh. 'What is so funny?' she asked.

'I was reflecting on what happened in there. It is really ironic, but you wouldn't appreciate it if you hadn't read the abduction file. Following the kidnapping, British detectives and their Swiss counterparts spent two weeks camped out conducting an intensive surveillance operation on this bank.' Nash waved his hand at the building. 'They monitored everyone and checked alibis for the day of the abduction and the period leading up to it. As they were doing that, the kidnappers could walk into a bank only a few streets away, without fear of detection. It's no wonder they weren't caught. The scheme is pure genius.' He shook his head. 'I had a vision of those detectives sitting there, hour after hour, day after day, while Torres or his wife went in and out of the other bank in perfect safety. Then I wondered how big the bill for coffee and doughnuts might have been.'

'Coffee and doughnuts?'

'American movie mythology,' Nash explained. 'Detectives on a stake-out are often portrayed as living on a diet of coffee and doughnuts.'

* * *

The ritual varied little from bank to bank. Up to that point Nash had been a passive observer but as they waited for the second box to be brought to Alondra, he spoke for the first time. 'Perhaps you could tell Miss Torres what the account balance is, and how the account has been conducted?'

The woman nodded. 'At present, the balance is' — she glanced down at the topmost sheet of paper in her file — 'forty-two thousand, seven-hundred and seventy-two Swiss Francs in credit. The account has been open since 1972, and there have been irregular, large credits transferred into it. Withdrawals have been more frequent, but smaller. There has been no credit to the account since 1989, when the balance was the equivalent of nine-million pounds sterling. I cannot equate the amount to euros, given that the single currency didn't exist at the time.'

'At a guess, I'd say they retired to concentrate on your upbringing,' Nash suggested.

Alondra nodded, too overcome with the emotional maelstrom of these revelations to speak. When the box arrived she watched in silence as Nash withdrew a large folder from within. He looked through it, barely seeming to glance at the contents. He hadn't reached the back of the folder when he stopped and looked across at the banker. 'I think the best way would be for us to photocopy this file and leave the originals here. It is already almost time for you to close and going through these papers will take some time.'

The woman nodded. 'If that is what Senorita Torres wishes.'

Alondra nodded, then watched in silence as Nash fed sheet after sheet into the copying machine in an adjoining room. When the originals had been returned to the safe-box, they thanked the woman and left.

As he guided her out of the door, Nash said, 'Much better to read these at the hotel.'

'Whatever you say,' she told him. She had seen his expression change as he was looking at the file. She could tell by the frown that he'd seen something unpleasant. 'Is it about me?'

'I think some of it is, but don't worry, it'll be all right.'

If he'd been hoping to soothe her disquiet, it didn't work. Her feeling that the contents of the folder would prove disturbing had intensified. She was certain there would be something horrid in there, although she couldn't imagine what.

Even Nash, whose imagination was better than most, was unprepared for the revelations the file contained, and for the devastating effects that would follow.

CHAPTER FIFTEEN

The first set of papers they looked at confirmed part of Nash's theory; photocopies of press cuttings from newspapers throughout Europe. Each of these detailed a daring and successful theft of an article of great value. Most were works of art, although some were jewellery collections, and one, a highly valuable piece of antique furniture. Attached to each cutting was a piece of paper bearing an amount and an inscription in English that read 'ransom paid'. There were also handwritten accounts of other robberies, which Nash presumed was because the press had failed to get hold of the story.

'This is astonishing,' Nash said. 'When I was in training school we were given a lot of case studies to report on for our exams. One of mine was a gang that operated across Europe, stealing valuable works of art.' He gestured to the paperwork. 'This is their work. The case fascinated me, much in the way that many people are intrigued by unsolved crimes such as murder. The idea that the criminals had got away with so many thefts without anyone having a clue as to their identity was only part of it. Added to that was the daring ingenuity of some of the raids. As I remember it, the thefts stopped after one of the gang was killed, falling from a rooftop in Vienna,

I think it was. I believe he was a trapeze artist, or a high wire-walker. I wondered if the others were also acrobats or something similar. I certainly never dreamed I might come this close to identifying them.'

It was after they finished reading these that they came across the letter. 'That's my father's writing . . . I mean.'

Nash patted her hand. 'I know.'

She was leaning over now, getting closer so she could decipher the script.

My dearest Alondra,

I know that if you are reading this you have successfully followed the trail I left. This letter will explain why I took such stringent precautions to avoid the contents of the safe-boxes falling into the wrong hands. I hope it will not cause you too much shock and pain.

I must first tell you that we are not your natural parents. Sadly, we were unable to have children, but when you came into our lives, you became so much a part of our existence that very soon it was as if you were truly our own, and we loved you as a daughter because of that.

The next thing I have to confess is that our name is not Torres. Indeed we are not even Spanish. However that pretence was necessary because of our profession. We are, or were, professional criminals, thieves who specialized in removing high-value articles from the wealthy and holding them to ransom.

Before you came along we had decided to retire, but we were tempted to accept one final commission. Our reasons for that were complex, but we never regretted that choice, because we gained a treasure far more valuable than any we had ever stolen.

Events leading to this decision started in 1986 after we pulled off the theft of a sculpture. The details are in one of the press reports you are holding. Afterwards, we received a communication via the bank that processed our ransom payments. The letter contained a proposition. Our potential client wanted us to carry out another theft. We were at first against the idea. We thought it might be an elaborate trap. There had been other attempts to snare us previously. Insurance companies can become very unpleasant when they are coerced into paying out huge sums of money. Equally important, the item we were being asked to steal was one of a type we had never considered before. The client wanted us to abduct you.

Yes, Alondra, that is how you came to us. The amount was enormous and, with the ransom added, the offer was difficult to turn down. Not that we entered into the scheme lightly. Kidnapping, particularly that of a child, is a grave offence. However, the money, and the fact that we would only be at risk by holding you for a short time swayed us to accept.

I won't bore you with the details, but with the inside information provided by our client the scheme worked perfectly, and we were sitting in the farmhouse in Onati celebrating the success of the venture within hours of the abduction. You were upstairs asleep, in that bedroom that became yours. That was because we had to administer a light sedative to ensure you didn't give the game away.

When the time came for the ransom to be paid I travelled to Zurich to ensure the bargain had been fulfilled. Some of the money was there, but along with it there was a letter; the contents horrified me. The instruction it contained was that you were not to be returned. Our client wanted us to kill you and dispose of the body. The method was up to us, but proof would be required that you were dead. Without that proof we wouldn't get the rest of the agreed sum.

We now faced a terrible dilemma. We were unsure of the client's identity. However, we believed it to be someone closely connected to your family. That meant returning you was not an option as it would have put you in grave danger. The client wouldn't baulk at paying someone else to dispose of you. We could not have that on our conscience.

Needless to say, the other option was equally unthinkable. We had done many criminal things, but always without violence, and child murder was going too far. Apart from that, we had already become extremely fond of you.

Instead, I faked a photo that purported to show your dead body. That wasn't difficult, and it worked, we got the rest of the money. We then had to decide what to do with you. Again, that was easy. Your sweet and loving nature made it so. We retired and devoted our lives to bringing you up in the safety and seclusion of our country retreat. We had sufficient money to ensure a comfortable lifestyle. And so we went on, and the light and joy you brought into our lives repaid us. More recently, your artistic ability and growing reputation have also made us proud. Everything went to plan until recently, when the illness that had afflicted my wife many years previously, returned. This time, her only

146

chance was surgery that cost an enormous amount of money, and one she would have to travel to America to undergo.

We no longer had that sort of money. Long years without income had eroded our savings, so in desperation, I was forced to activate what I referred to as our insurance policy. This involved a blackmail approach to our client, informing them that you were alive and well, and offering photos as proof. You remember the ones we took on your birthdays? I am awaiting a reply as I write this, but for once, I am afraid this plan might go wrong, so please read what follows carefully.

Whatever you decide, my advice would be on no account to approach your natural family. It would involve the greatest danger for you, and to be honest, I do not think you would have anything to gain. You are already becoming talked of as a potentially great painter; let that remain the centre of your being. Always remember, it is from within those close to you as a small child that the plot to have you abducted and murdered originated.

However, I will tell you that your real name is Charlotte Alexandra Davison. You were kidnapped from the London home of your parents in 1989. At the same time as we abducted you, we were instructed to steal a painting. I never knew why as it is of little value, so we kept it as my wife liked it. I am telling you this because you will remember it. It hung in the room where we found you, the mountain scene that you loved to look at as a child; the one I believe sparked your interest in landscape painting. The one entitled 'Stark Ghyll'.

At first they thought the letter ended there, but on turning over the last sheet they found another paragraph. Although there had been much to surprise Alondra in what had gone before, Nash had managed to prepare her to some extent with the ideas he had suggested. Reading that final instalment, however, was quite a different matter.

When the order to kill you arrived, I was determined to discover the identity of the person paying us. They had adopted the same means of communication as we used: via a bank. No doubt they thought if it was safe for us, it would be equally secure for them. However, whereas we were but one name among thousands of account holders, and even if that became known there would be no way of finding us, the reverse was not true for them.

I knew the bank, knew the sort code, knew the account number. More to the point, I had familiarized myself with everyone in, and connected to, the Davison family. All I needed was the name of that account holder. I found a bank employee whose gambling habits had put him in a situation the bank would not have tolerated had they known. Although he resisted my bribe when I first approached him, he soon crumbled once I pointed out the alternatives, loss of home, loss of family, loss of job. When I obtained the name, I was immediately able to make the connection.

The paragraph ended with the account details Torres had obtained. Nash and Alondra read it, their expressions mirrors of disappointment. They had achieved much of what they had hoped for in setting out for Zurich. Unfortunately, they had not been able to obtain the most vital piece of information, the name of the person who had ordered Lottie's abduction and murder. The statement from Torres merely narrowed the field. It was some time before Nash spoke. 'That doesn't tell us much we don't already know. There could be quite a few people with access to this account.'

'I hoped we would know for sure.' Alondra's face reflected her continuing stress.

'The fact that the account is in the name of one of the Davison Group companies at least rules out a lot of the friends and anyone unconnected with the business,' Nash pointed out.

Even as he spoke, he was aware that this was scarcely likely to be of much comfort. The knowledge that someone had paid to have her abducted and murdered was bad enough. Not knowing who or why was tearing her apart.

* * *

Alondra decided to take a shower. Nash was reading the letter once more when he was startled by a sudden rattling sound. He'd left his mobile on vibrate mode while they were in the banks.

'What's happening, Clara? Any news?'

'I've spoken to the Swedish woman, Yvonne, who was the au pair. She's happy for you to go along and talk to her. I didn't mention Alondra.'

'Good, anything else?'

'I haven't had any luck tracing the immediate family yet and Mexican Pete has been on the phone jumping up and down, wanting to talk to you. I told him you were in Zurich and he said he believes they have telephones in Switzerland.'

Nash grinned, but his smile faded as Mironova asked, 'What's happening over there? Have you been to the bank yet?'

'Yes, we went this afternoon. Not to one bank, but two.' He explained the device Torres had used to avoid detection.

'That's bloody clever,' Clara agreed. 'What was in the safe?'

He told her, leaving the most sensational revelation until last. When he explained, Clara let out a whistle of disbelief, following which there was a long silence before she said, 'That is one of the most awful things I've ever heard. What on earth can the motive have been?'

'I wish I knew. I have absolutely no idea.'

'Could the kidnap have been used to conceal something else? Child abuse, for instance?'

'I don't think so. If that were the case the emotional scars would still be there, even if the memory was repressed.'

Alondra entered the room and listened intently, aware they were discussing her. Nash put the phone on speaker mode, so she could hear both ends of the conversation. She heard Clara ask, 'And you've seen no evidence of that?'

'No, none at all. She seems to be handling things very well. She was very upset of course, but she seems to be bearing up all right, no matter how hard it was.' Nash ended the call and looked across at her, noting her troubled expression, on the verge of tears.

'Why can't we go back in time?' she asked. 'Everything we discover is worse than before. Why couldn't it have stayed as it was, before we found out such terrible things about horrible people?'

'I'm afraid that's the way life works. I spend most of my time investigating terrible acts, done usually by ordinary people who have taken a wrong turn in life. On this occasion, Torres was concerned at what might happen when he wrote that letter. If he'd realized exactly where the train of events he was setting in motion would lead, I guess he wouldn't have posted the blackmail letter. But he did, and we're left with what *is*, not what we'd *like*. After I phone Mexican Pete, why don't we go for dinner?' Nash suggested.

'I don't much care what we do,' Alondra replied, her tone subdued.

With concern for Alondra uppermost in his mind, he made the call, unaware that he was in for another seismic shock.

Ramirez answered. 'Ah, Nash, I'm glad you haven't fallen off an Alp. I have some news regarding the DNA on Miss Torres.'

'That's come back quickly, I thought it took longer.'

'It does as a rule. There are a number of reasons. For one thing the laboratory closes in a couple of days for Christmas. Once they finish there's only a skeleton staff at work.'

'I assume that's what passes for a pathology joke.'

Ramirez ignored him. 'Apart from that, this is only a partial result, the full analysis won't be available until after the break. However, the reason they were able to feed information back so soon is that they already have a match for the sample. Not an exact match, but close enough to establish a familial link.'

'That is interesting.'

'It's more than interesting. Remember the young woman who fell to her death? Her body was found at the foot of Stark Ghyll.'

'I remember. You couldn't understand how she came to be pregnant.'

'Exactly, but what I also don't understand is that DNA strands recovered from the foetus show a close familial link between the child and Miss Torres, suggesting that the father is a close relative of hers.'

There was a long silence as Nash tried to digest this news. 'How close are we talking?' he asked, eventually.

'No further away than first cousin, I'd say,' Ramirez told him. 'Take your pick, cousin, uncle, father, brother, grandfather even. We would need a sample from them to be absolutely certain.'

Mironova was more than a little surprised when Nash called her back immediately. After repeating what Ramirez had said, Nash told her, 'It's now doubly important that we trace all the living members of Lottie Davison's family. The male ones in particular. Make that your priority, and ask Jackie for extra help, see if she'll lend you Lisa Andrews from Netherdale. Get Viv, and Tom Pratt to work on it too.'

After they had eaten, Nash told Alondra, 'I guess Torres fooled everyone with that fake photo. It must have come as a hell of a shock to the client when years later they received a blackmail demand stating that you were alive. I bet they were less than happy at the idea of shelling out even more money, so they decided to dispose of Torres and you. What I haven't been able to work out is how they knew where to find you and the kidnappers.'

'Couldn't it have been done the same way that Torres discovered the identity of whoever the client was?'

Nash shook his head. I don't think so.'

He stared at her for so long that she stirred uneasily. 'What is it?' she asked. 'What have you thought of?'

'It's just possible that they found out through you. That profile of you in *El País* was in some of the English papers as well.'

'I'd no idea. I wasn't aware that sort of thing happened.'

'My word,' he teased her, 'you have led a sheltered life. Newspapers do that all the time. They syndicate features and articles worldwide if they can. It gives them extra income. Not only that, they post a lot of their content on the internet nowadays. That's how I came across your details, remember?'

'OK, but there's still no reason anyone would connect me from the article to Lottie Davison. Nobody would recognize me after all this time.'

Nash paused before replying. 'Actually, that isn't true. Nobody would recognize you as Lottie, that's for sure. But you bear a striking resemblance to your mother at the same age. Anyone who knew Bev well would stop and wonder when they saw that photo.'

Alondra glanced across at the folder from the bank, which was lying on the dressing table. 'Is that letter conclusive proof of my identity?'

Nash shook his head. 'Not in law. Take what we have to a court and they'd be interested but not convinced. All we have is circumstantial evidence and the statement of a self-confessed criminal. That's why I want Clara to make it her priority to discover where the other members of the Davison family are. Besides which, there's something else I don't understand.'

'Go on,' she urged.

'Something that doesn't make sense. Sometimes the oddest little fact can be the clue we're looking for. In this case it might be unimportant, but there is one strange detail about the kidnapping that everyone seems to have overlooked.'

'Tell me.'

'I read the reports of the abduction, the crime scene inventories, looked at the photos. Nowhere, in any of those, did it mention the painting of Stark Ghyll.'

'Perhaps it got missed in all the confusion?'

'No way. The rest of the investigation was handled with great thoroughness, so there's no chance they would miss it. That implies that the theft of the painting wasn't reported. Which is extremely strange.'

'If the family was upset, they might not have thought to mention it to the police,' Alondra suggested.

'No, that doesn't work either. In his letter Torres mentioned the location of that painting. I remember the crime scene photos. The painting should have been in the room where your brother found you during the game of hide-and-seek. How big was it?'

Alondra thought for a moment. 'Going from memory, I'd say it was a pre-stretched canvas, which would make it one hundred centimetres wide, by seventy-five centimetres deep.'

'There's no way they would have missed something of that size, no matter how traumatized they were. So why wasn't it reported?'

Try as he might, Nash couldn't come up with an answer to his own question.

CHAPTER SIXTEEN

The farmer had been expecting one visitor, not two. He barely glanced at Nash or his warrant card. His attention was fixed on Alondra. Nash noticed his expression change to a puzzled frown of half-recognition, and that alone spoke volumes to the detective. 'Come in,' the farmer told them, 'my wife's upstairs at the moment. Go through to the kitchen and I'll give Yvonne a shout.'

He summoned his wife and seconds later they heard the light patter of footsteps on the stairs. The farmer had barely reached the table when a woman in her late-forties appeared in the doorway. 'Inspector Nash?' She greeted the detective, and was halfway across the room when she stopped dead, her hand still outstretched as she noticed his companion. Nash saw the confusion. 'Bev?' she whispered. 'Bev, what are you . . . ?' She recovered her composure. 'I'm sorry; I thought you were someone else.'

Beneath the table, Nash held Alondra's hand, sensing the tension in every muscle. 'I should apologize for not warning you,' he told the couple, 'but I wanted to see your reaction.'

Yvonne sank into the kitchen chair alongside her husband, her eyes still fixed on Alondra. 'I'm sorry,' she repeated, 'but you look so like someone I knew. The similarity is extraordinary.'

'You thought you were looking at Bev Davison,' Nash suggested. 'Not as she is now, but as she was a quarter of a century ago, before her daughter was kidnapped.'

Yvonne cast Nash a swift glance before looking back at Alondra. 'It really is an uncanny likeness. Who are you?' As she spoke she looked to her husband for support.

'That's right,' he agreed. 'I noticed too, but thought it was coincidence.'

'It isn't coincidence.' Nash put his hand on Alondra's arm. 'Allow me to introduce you. This is Carlota Alejandra Torres. She was brought up from the age of five by a couple who lived in Spain but has no memory prior to that. We have a letter written by Senor Torres shortly before his death in which he claims that he and his wife kidnapped her from the Davison house, and that Alejandra is in fact Lottie Davison.'

'Carlota Alejandra,' Yvonne repeated the names, 'but Lottie was . . .'

'Charlotte Alexandra,' Nash nodded. 'I was almost convinced before I read the letter from Torres. Any remaining doubts were dispelled when I saw your reaction.'

'I don't see how there can be any mistake.' She placed her hand on Alondra's. 'The more I look at you, the greater the resemblance becomes. You are the very image of your mother. My poor child, what happened to you?'

Alondra shook her head. When she replied, it was in little more than a whisper. Yvonne bent forward across the table to hear what she said. 'I have no memory from before Spain, just some confused images that might be true, or may be only dreams. But I know I'm not their child, Mr and Mrs Torres, I mean.' She glanced at the detective, who was watching her with concern. She smiled at him fleetingly. 'Mike figured all the rest out.'

As Yvonne moved closer, Nash saw Alondra's expression change as she lifted her head, her face a mask, and when she spoke again, her voice had altered, 'You smell pretty today, Bonny.' Alondra sat back, her voice returned to normal. 'I'm sorry,' she said, 'I've no idea why I said that.'

The effect on Yvonne was dramatic. She half rose from her chair, then sat down again, all the colour drained from her face, her mouth agape as she stared at Alondra. Nash glanced from Yvonne to her husband. He too looked stunned.

'What is it?' Nash asked.

'Lottie,' Yvonne whispered. 'You *are* Lottie. You couldn't say my name properly. You always called me Bonny. You were the only one who did. And you loved my perfume. You always said I smelt pretty when I was wearing it. I still use that same brand. I put a squirt of it on just before I came downstairs.'

Yvonne turned to Nash. 'I don't know how you did it, but this is definitely Lottie, my poor dear little Lottie who I thought had been murdered all those years ago.' She began to weep, holding Alondra's hand all the while.

Nash felt he should explain. 'According to Torres, they' were instructed to kill her, but couldn't do it, so they kept her and raised her as their own daughter. For which I shall be eternally grateful.'

'I'll put the kettle on,' her husband said. He too looked close to being overcome with emotion.

As he placed a plate of freshly baked mince pies on the table, he asked, 'Is that what you came here today for, Inspector Nash? To try and get confirmation of Lottie's identity?'

'Not entirely,' Nash admitted, 'although it has been very useful. What I really need is for Yvonne to tell me whatever she can about the Davison household. I know it's a long time ago, but I'm afraid the threat to Alondra, Lottie, is still as potent as it was then. What we didn't tell you is that Senor Torres was murdered, and there have been several attempts to kill Alondra recently. Someone has discovered that she is alive, and they are even more desperate to murder her than they were years ago. If I'm to prevent that, I need to learn as much as possible about the family, their friends, regular visitors to the house, anything and everything.'

He looked at Yvonne. 'You gave a statement at the time in which you suggested that the marriage wasn't exactly a bed of roses.'

Yvonne frowned in an effort of concentration, her mind obviously still filled with the shock appearance of her former charge. Eventually, after a struggle that was almost visible, she responded to Nash's request. 'I confess I wasn't surprised when I heard Paul and Bev Davison got divorced. I think that would have happened anyway. In fact it looked as if it was going to end earlier.'

'Why do you say that?'

Yvonne hesitated, aware that Alondra was listening. 'I don't think Paul Davison was suited to married life but as Bev was already expecting Lottie's brother Keith, he didn't have much choice. You have to bear in mind that they were both celebrities, and even then the tabloids were hungry for celebrity muck-raking. Paul was always with one woman or another which made Bev very unhappy. She had been used to the catwalk and the fame that went with it, but after they married she devoted herself to being a housewife and mother and to her charity work. I only joined the household after Lottie was born, but from what I gleaned from staff gossip, Paul could be a nasty piece of work, bullying and taunting Bev. So much so, that she had all but become a recluse a while earlier, drinking too much, taking drugs, and refusing to leave the house. Then things had changed. She began to go out and started taking more care over her appearance and becoming more like the woman who had captivated people at fashion shows, on TV and in magazines. She was always a beauty, but apparently she had let things slide. When I first arrived, it was such a joy, hearing her singing to herself. They seemed to be living separate lives, and she was more in demand than ever. Parties, charity events, they all wanted Bev. And there was a queue of men wanting to escort her, had she been willing to let them. Some did get the chance, but usually . . .' Yvonne stopped, aware that she was about to say something indiscreet.

'Go on,' Nash urged her. 'We need to hear it all.'

'I'm not saying there was anything wrong, because I can't be sure. By that, I mean that I have no evidence one way or the other, but it wouldn't surprise me if she and Luke were having an affair. She was lonely, and Luke was as kind, loving and sweet-natured as Paul was the other way.'

Alondra was mystified. 'Who is Luke?'

Yvonne smiled reminiscently. 'Luke was your uncle. For my mind, Luke was by far the best of the Davison brothers; worth Paul and Matthew put together and then some. He was a gentle person and wasn't at all interested in the family business, or getting involved in the rows between Matthew and Paul. He had a job as a teacher, but that was only to pay the bills. All he was really interested in were his hobbies. And possibly Bev,' she added.

'What were his hobbies?'

'Rock climbing was the main one; it was more of a passion than a hobby and, sadly, it was what killed him. He died in a climbing accident when you were about three years old,' she told Alondra. 'I was only supposed to be with them for two years, but they begged me to stay on. I was happy to' — she looked across the room at her husband, who smiled back — 'because I no longer wished to return to Sweden. I left shortly after you were kidnapped, but by then Bev had reverted to her old ways, drinking more than ever, hardly leaving the house. It was if the last spark of life in her had died with Luke's death and yours — as we believed.'

'What about Matthew Davison? Was he a regular visitor?'

'Yes, he and Paul were two of a kind. Matthew was always chasing women too. And neither of them could bear it if the other had something they didn't; couldn't rest until they had the same or better. What really pissed Matthew off was that Paul could have any woman he wanted then return home to Bev and his family. Matthew hated that, and was insanely jealous because he didn't have children.'

'Did Matthew chase Bev? Was she one of his conquests?'

'He most certainly did, but I'm fairly certain Bev didn't sleep with Matthew. She might have done so, if only to spite Paul when he'd been behaving particularly badly, which happened far too often. But for my money, Matthew was too like

Paul for her to want to jump from the frying pan into the fire with him. That certainly didn't stop Matthew trying, but whether he wanted Bev for his own gratification or simply to get one over on Paul is another matter. Put it this way, Paul would do anything to thwart Matthew, and Matthew would stop at nothing to hurt Paul; far worse things than sleeping with his wife. I'm afraid if you want to know the ins and outs of it, you'll have to ask Bev. If she'll tell you — and if she can remember.'

'Where did all that intense rivalry come from, do you know?'

Yvonne thought for a moment before replying. 'Bev told me once that in order to understand the brothers, you really need to know the Davison family history. Paul hero-worshipped his father, they were very similar in character, and because he was the eldest he got to spend more time with him than the other boys. She said she only knew their father in his latter days and described him as a typical dirty old man. She said he even made a pass at her. Bev's opinion was that Paul's behaviour, and Matthew's too, was due in part to their father's influence.'

Yvonne smiled. 'Whether that's true or not, they both worked hard at trying to outdo one another in the number of women they slept with.'

'Not Luke, though?'

'No, apparently, following Luke's birth, his mother was very ill, so much so that they had to employ a full-time nanny to care for the infant. When their mother died, their father married the nanny. Bev told me she was a very caring, gentle woman, and she believed her character influenced Luke, making him different from the two older brothers.'

'Why not them?'

'I think Paul was too far gone by then, from what I could gather. And of course Matthew wasn't about much.'

'Why not?'

'He was sent away to boarding school soon after his mother died. Paul told Bev about it; and said there were terrible rows and tantrums, with Matthew actually suffering a hysterical fit on one occasion, before they actually got him to the school. Apparently, he was very unhappy there, but whether that was homesickness or because he'd been singled out and sent away, I couldn't say.'

'Do you know where Bev is? She seems to have vanished off the radar.'

'Not offhand, but I could try and find out for you. We still have a few friends from the old days that we keep in contact with. I did hear that she had gone into a very expensive rehab clinic somewhere, but that was a while ago. I haven't heard if she's still alive, even, although I feel sure there would have been something in the press had she died. The case still sparks a lot of interest in the media, even after all these years.'

Although Nash knew the answer, he asked, 'Who paid for the rehab clinic? Do you think it was Paul?'

Yvonne laughed. 'Not likely. If anyone from that side of the family did, it would have been Matthew. I suppose he might have done it simply to spite his brother. Or because your suggestion of an affair with Bev was correct and he felt guilty.'

'What about Paul Davison? There's a note on the file that mentions he too became a recluse a few years after Lottie disappeared, he went to live in Somerset, gave up all his business interests, made a huge donation to help found some religious community or other.'

Yvonne shook her head. 'Whoever wrote that knew very little of Paul Davison's character.' She enumerated Nash's statements on her fingers. 'Paul would never relinquish his connection with DMG. He's far too acquisitive for that. It would be like asking a tiger to become a vegetarian. As for founding a religious order, it would either be one that allowed him to keep the contents of the collection plate, or where the ceremony ended with him deflowering a virgin. That, or he had a very good reason to want something the order could give him. Those are the only reasons he'd get involved with religion.' She paused for a moment before continuing, 'If you want to find Paul Davison, you could do worse than look for that thug he employed as a bodyguard. Head of security at DMG was his official title, but Paul never went anywhere without him along as minder.'

Nash frowned, trying to remember the contents of the file. 'Was his name Dermot something or other?'

'That's right, Dermot Black. As nasty a piece of work as you're likely to meet, even in your job. I suppose that's why he and Paul were thick as thieves. Rumour was that Dermot was ex-army, but whose army, I'm not sure. I'd be more inclined to believe he was ex HM Prisons — as an inmate, not a warder. Whatever his past, he and Paul were inseparable. Find Dermot and you'll find Paul Davison under the next stone.'

She turned to Alondra. 'I'm sorry if I'm not casting your father in a very good light, but I'm afraid it is the truth. What sort of religious order is he supposed to have founded?'

'I don't have any details; I'm only going on what's in the file.'

'Well, when you look into it, I bet you'll find that whatever goes on behind those walls has little or nothing to do with religion as we know it. The true reason will be something Paul doesn't want the public to know about, or even suspect.'

'We've taken up enough of your time,' Nash said as he got to his feet. 'I'll leave you my card in case you find anything of interest. And I'd be obliged if you forget about our visit, for the time being at least, or at least fail to mention it if the subject comes up in conversation.' He saw the couple's surprised expressions. 'I want Alondra's whereabouts kept secret because of the attempts on her life, and the same goes for her identity,' he explained. 'I've no reason to suppose they won't try again. And there's absolutely no way I'm prepared to chance that happening.'

Yvonne saw the implacable expression on Nash's face, then noticed how it softened as he looked at Alondra. Following his gaze, she too looked at her former charge, and was intrigued by the smile the girl gave Nash.

Alondra promised Yvonne whatever the outcome she would keep in touch and thanked her for all she had done to help. As they reached the doorstep, she stopped to repeat her thanks to the farmer and wish them both a happy Christmas.

Nash was a couple of paces behind, and as he paused to say farewell, Yvonne said, 'This is more than merely an investigation for you, isn't it? This is personal. And unless I'm wrong, highly-personal.'

'What makes you think that?'

She smiled. 'The way you speak about Lottie, the way you look at her, and the way you look at one another when you think no one else is watching. If you're not already lovers, my guess is that it's only a matter of time. If that's the case, I think you are a very lucky man, Inspector Nash. And I think Lottie is a very fortunate young woman, having someone like you taking such care of her.'

Nash smiled. 'You're right; she's a very special person.' He was about to move on, but then he stopped as a stray thought struck him. 'You said earlier that Paul's brother Luke was only interested in his hobbies. You mentioned rock climbing, and I was going to ask you about the others, but we got sidetracked.'

'Well, he was fond of music, but his main love was an extension of his work as a teacher.'

She saw Nash's puzzled frown. 'I assumed you knew. Luke was an art teacher. He was also a very gifted artist. There was a painting by him in Paul and Bev's house, a birthday present to Bev I think. Luke hadn't signed it, but I can remember he did give it a title. It was of a mountain called Stark Ghyll. It disappeared when Lottie was kidnapped.'

'We know about the painting being stolen. But there was no mention of it in the file. I read your statement. Why didn't the family tell the police at the time?'

'Those were the instructions. I was told to concentrate on the facts surrounding Lottie's disappearance. A worthless painting didn't matter.'

'Instructions from whom?'

'Paul Davison. He took charge of everything that happened right from the start. He had to. Bev had collapsed and was under sedation. From there she slid back into the addiction she'd been heading for before Lottie was born. Once they received that awful photograph there was no way back for her.'

CHAPTER SEVENTEEN

'They're back. I'm on the M1. Nash and the woman went from the airport to Norfolk, of all places. Spent a couple of hours visiting a farmer and his wife, and now by the looks of things they're heading home.'

He listened. 'No, how should I know why they visited the farm? I couldn't get near enough to put my ear to the keyhole. I can tell you the farmer's name if it helps. It doesn't mean anything to me, but it might do to the bloke who's paying us.'

Again Dermot Black had to face his boss. 'I've had a report from the men following the Torres woman. She's been staying with that detective she met in Spain. Our men followed them to Heathrow a few days ago. Apparently they boarded a flight for Zurich.' As he spoke, Dermot saw the shocked expression on Davison's face.

'Anything else?'

'They're back in the UK now. However, they didn't drive straight back to Yorkshire, where Nash lives. They went to Norfolk first.'

'Norfolk? What's special about Norfolk?'

'I wondered exactly the same, until I heard the name of the people they'd gone to visit.'

'And that was . . . ?'

Black told him.

Davison thought for a moment. 'The au pair! She married a farmer with that surname.'

'Yes. And the place where Nash and the woman went — it was a farm, so I think it's safe to assume she went to visit her old nanny. And that means—'

'That they have worked out her real identity. Shit!'

* * *

The further north they drove, the more concerned Nash became about Alondra's state of mind. Heaping unpleasant facts about the closest members of her family on her might prove the last straw. Nash considered it was up to him to try and prevent that happening. For the meantime, however, he felt it better to allow her to digest the unpalatable facts Yvonne had laid bare. In addition, he wanted time to think over what he had learned.

Much of what had been said about the Davison family was less than flattering, to put it mildly. If the former au pair was to be believed, the father was little less than a megalomaniac, hungry for money and power, taking what he wanted where and when he wanted it, regardless of the effect on others. A man who could not tolerate anyone doing anything that ran counter to his own desires. Nash knew the type and was aware that with the lust for money and power came a strong, overriding sex drive that was often close to uncontrollable. Scruples came very low on the scale of importance for men like that.

It was extremely unlikely that Bev was mixed up in the kidnap. It certainly sounded as if she was mixed up in her own personal life, and much of that might be down to the loss of her beloved daughter, added to the browbeating and casual mental cruelty she had suffered from her husband. In view of what he had learned, Nash was particularly keen to locate Bev Davison. There was one question he was particularly keen for her to answer. Whether she would be willing to, was another matter altogether.

Nash suggested they stop at the next service area. 'I don't know about you, but I could do with a break, and some coffee to keep me awake.'

'Whatever you say.'

Her voice was devoid of expression, not a good sign. After pulling to a halt, Nash switched off the engine and turned towards Alondra. 'Spit it out,' he told her, his tone bracing. 'Whatever's bugging you, tell me about it. Bottling it up will only make it worse — or make it appear worse than it really is.'

As she looked at him, her eyes reflected the emotional turmoil within. 'I can't take much more of this. Everything I learn makes me more ashamed. First it was the couple I thought were my parents who turn out to be criminals and kidnappers. Now, I find out that my own family is apparently no better, possibly even worse. Every one of them is either wicked or weak. I don't think I want to know these people, or meet them, and certainly don't want to be part of their lives.'

'Alondra, you are thirty years old. You have the choice. There is no compulsion for you to have anything to do with your family. You owe them nothing, no duty of care for your upbringing. Fair enough, it might not have been their fault that you were abducted, but I saw little evidence in that file of their having spent years scouring the world for you. They assumed, from a photo we now know to be fake, that you were dead. There's an old saying, "You can pick your friends, but you can't pick your relations." Never was that more appropriate. If you want to, you can tell them all to get lost. I can think of lots of people who would consider being able to do that a blessing.'

Alondra leaned forward and stroked his cheek. 'Thank you, Mike. You put everything into perspective. I'm so glad I have you with me in all this mess.'

She smiled, briefly, although Nash guessed she was closer to tears. 'Good,' he replied, 'and I'll even pay for the coffee. What more could you want?'

This time her laugh contained more genuine amusement.

The silence over coffee was more relaxed, and Nash hoped his pep talk might have lifted her depression slightly. When she had finished her drink, Alondra told him she was going to the ladies' room. Nash glanced round to ensure he had a clear view of the entrance to the facilities. 'While you're away, I'm going to ring Clara, find out how Daniel is and tell her we'll pick him up tomorrow, if that's OK with you.'

Alondra felt more cheerful as she walked away. Being consulted about decisions regarding Daniel made her feel part of Nash's life. For some reason that was important to her. She had never dreamed of being this close to someone else, to sharing their daily routine.

When Clara answered the phone, Nash said, 'I'm going to get the business bit over with first, while Alondra can't hear. I want you to try and trace a bloke who was head of security at DMG, by the name of Dermot Black. His details are in the file. He may well have a record, and it's entirely possible that he's not using that name any longer. I'm also keener than ever to speak to Bev Davison.'

'Any particular reason? Is it something you learned today?'

Nash explained.

'Talk about happy families,' Clara said after a moment, 'makes you wonder what really went on back then, doesn't it?'

Nash knew exactly to what she was referring. 'I take it you're thinking what I am?'

'That Luke was Alondra's father? And that she inherited her artistic ability from him?'

'Exactly, and the fact that Paul wanted there to be no mention of the painting being stolen leads me to believe that he knew or suspected it. However, I reckon it would take a miracle for us to get to the bottom of everything that happened years ago.'

'You never know, Mike, it's Christmas, and they reckon that's a time for miracles.'

'I think you've been watching too many old movies on TV.'

'Is there anything else?'

'Yes. I'd like a complete rundown of all DMG companies. The date they were established, what they do, who the directors and shareholders are now and who was on each board at the time Lottie went missing, plus a summary of their financial position and trading results.'

'Blimey, Mike, are you joining the Serious Fraud Office?'

'No, but I don't want to miss any information that might be pertinent. Somebody employed a hit man to travel to Spain and kill Torres and Alondra. That can't have been cheap, and I'd like to know where the money came from.'

'I'll get working on it. Thankfully, there's so little to occupy us on the crime front at present. Viv's still busy trying to trace Bev Davison.'

'Don't worry too much about that, Yvonne might find her for us.' Nash saw Alondra emerging from the toilets. 'How's Daniel?' he asked hastily changing the subject.

'He's fine. Whether he'll recover from all the chocolate David's been feeding him is another matter. If your son is *Toblerone* shaped when you get him back, you know who to blame.'

Nash laughed. 'I don't suppose there will be any lasting damage. Will tomorrow be OK to collect him?'

'Why, do you want the chance for a last night alone with Alondra?'

'Something of the sort,' Nash agreed calmly.

There was a moment of silence. Clara was confused. She'd expected an indignant denial, or Nash telling her not to be nosy. His deadpan reply left her wondering if he was serious or not, which was pretty much what Nash intended.

'I'll be bringing Alondra into work with me,' he continued, 'I can't let her out of my sight for a second.' He grinned as he heard Clara spluttering at the other end of the phone, and paused, before adding, 'for her safety; in view of the threat to her, I mean.' His smile widened as he glanced across and saw Alondra's blush. 'She wants to go shopping, and I thought you might like to go with her.'

'Very well,' Clara managed at last. 'And you can leave collecting Daniel until after work, because I think David's promised to take him ice skating.'

'That sounds fine.'

'Oh, I almost forgot, Jimmy Johnson came for your house keys the day you left, so you've probably no contents left.'

'I think I can trust Jimmy better than that.'

'He also said to tell you "four zeros" and "pantry"; said you'd understand.'

'I do. And now at least we can go home knowing it's secure.'

As soon as Nash rang off, Alondra asked, 'What was that you were saying about me?'

'Clara was winding me up,' he explained.

'You mentioned someone called Jimmy, who is he?'

Nash explained about Johnson, and his change from burglar to locksmith. 'What interesting friends you have,' Alondra commented.

* * *

When Nash swung the car into the drive of the cottage a powerful PIR light came on, illuminating the front of the house. 'Looks as if Jimmy's been busy,' he said as he switched off the ignition. 'I wonder what other surprises are in store for us.'

He unlocked the door, with Alondra hovering nervously behind him. Immediately, an alarm started belting out its strident tones. Nash quickly headed for the kitchen and opened the pantry door. On the back wall of the larder was a newly-installed control panel. Nash pressed four zeros and the sound ceased. 'Well,' he told Alondra, 'at least I don't have to check the rest of the house. Mind you, I nearly wet myself when the alarm sounded.'

'Me too,' she laughed.

A further sign of Johnson's work was a small stack of empty boxes bearing the name of a well-known electronics manufacturer. Nash picked up a note Johnson had taped to the top of a box. 'Jimmy says the alarm is on the default setting and we haven't to change it until he's finished. He's coming back in the morning, when the last piece of kit has arrived.' Nash read on, a task by no means simplified by the Scotsman's writing, which was little short of illegible. He looked across at Alondra. 'I'd better get busy if we're to eat tonight.'

'Anything I can do to help?'

Nash brandished the note. 'Johnson's installed CCTV cameras, but they're not working yet. He says they will operate via wireless connections to four monitors and a recorder. He wants to know where we want the monitors located. If you could have a walk round while I start dinner and see where you think would be best.'

'Of course I will. I'll take our bags upstairs while I look.'

Although she accepted the task calmly, Alondra felt far less than calm. Her heart was beating faster than normal as she turned to leave the kitchen. What was Mike's intention? What was behind his involvement of her in a decision affecting the house? His house. Was he . . . could he be thinking . . . was he hoping she would stay? And if that was so, what would her answer be?

She returned to the kitchen where Nash had defrosted something that already smelled delicious. 'Savoury mince,' he told her. I'll do some spaghetti and grate cheese over it.' He gave a sly, sidelong smile. 'Sorry, it isn't Manchego,' he teased.

'I'll forgive you, this time,' she responded. 'I suggest the monitors should go in your study, in here, plus the dining room and your bedroom.'

'Great idea,' he agreed, still laughing, 'then we can lie in bed together and watch foxes copulating in the garden.'

Alondra turned away to pick up the wine glass he had filled for her. He'd done it again, suggested a less than temporary presence for her in his house and in his bed.

They retired early. It had been a long, tiring and, for Alondra, extremely emotional day. At the bedroom door she hesitated, but Nash took hold of her arm. He turned her gently to face him. 'If you want to be alone, I shall understand.'

'No, I'd rather not be alone.' She took a deep breath. 'I'd rather be with you.'

'Good, I hope it stays that way. You never answered my question about your plans for Christmas. Apart from the fact that I want you to stay here, we have to think of your safety. It would be much safer here.'

She paused, uncertainty flooding back. 'What about Daniel?'

'I'm sure he won't object. In fact, I think he'll be delighted.'

* * *

Nash was ready to leave for work next morning shortly after Johnson arrived to complete the installation work. The Scotsman explained that the CCTV cameras would protect the house from any angle, and that he would install a further piece of equipment, should Nash want it. 'It's a radio link that connects tae the local polis station if the alarm's triggered. I'd have tae order it in, so it would be a few weeks. It'll cost a fair amount though.'

'I'll have to think about that. Get me an idea of the price first.'

Nash was joined by Alondra. 'Jimmy, we're leaving. If there's a problem, ring me. I'll be in the office most of the day.'

When they reached Helmsdale, Nash told Alondra, 'I want to discuss various bits and pieces with Clara. Other cases we have on the books at the moment. Stay with Viv, he'll make you a cup of coffee.'

After he'd closed the office door, Clara said, 'I take it you've something you don't want Alondra to hear, because covering our outstanding cases will take about five seconds.'

'Exactly, I want to tell you why I'm so anxious to talk to Bev Davison, and it's definitely not for Alondra to hear at the moment. The poor girl's been through enough without this on top.'

'Go on, then. What's it all about?'

'It was the painting that set me off thinking. I was curious about it right from the beginning. Why would a couple who were supposedly Spanish keep a painting of Stark Ghyll in a remote farmhouse in the middle of the Basque Country? And why was that painting singled out to be stolen before the arson attack on the Onati farmhouse? From what Alondra told me, the painting was a good one, but nothing special. Then I learned from the Torres' letter that the painting had been stolen from the Davison house at the time Lottie was abducted and I realized that it must have some significance. I also found it extremely strange that the painting wasn't reported missing. I couldn't work out the reason for that. If our theory about the identity of Alondra's father is correct, what if Paul Davison found out that his wife had been cheating on him with his younger brother, and that he was supporting their love child? Would that not be a possible motive for Paul to want rid of Lottie? Would it explain who paid Torres and his wife to kidnap Lottie?'

'That's impossible.' Clara shook her head vehemently. 'Nobody would sink that low. Would they?'

'If the au pair's reading of Paul Davison's character is correct, anything's possible. From what she told me, I reckon there's very little he wouldn't do to get his own way. She said Luke was the only decent one of the three,' Nash paused before delivering the wildest part of his theory, 'and Luke

Davison just happened to die in a climbing accident a couple of years after Lottie was born.'

Nash saw Clara's mouth open, but it took several attempts before the words came. 'You're not suggesting . . . you can't mean that . . . you believe Paul Davison murdered his own brother?'

'It's happened before, from Cain and Abel onwards. It explains everything. If Paul found out Luke had fathered a bastard on him, he sounds like the sort of bloke who would want revenge. But even killing Luke wouldn't be enough. Lottie would be a permanent reminder of how Bev had cheated on him. If she looked in the slightest like Luke, that would be like a red rag to a bull. Simple solution: have the child kidnapped and murdered. Nasty mess all cleaned up.'

'If that's true it must be close to the most revolting thing I've ever heard. I cannot believe human beings could sink as low as that.'

Clara was to realize later that she'd vastly underrated people's capacity for evil.

Before Nash left for Netherdale to see the superintendent, Pearce told him that the reports on the Davison Group companies he'd asked for would be ready later that day. 'There's a hell of a lot to it,' he told Nash. 'You wanted a full breakdown on all the DMG companies. I'm about to start printing them off, but I should warn you the ink and paper alone will probably use up our stationery budget for the whole year.'

Nash shrugged. 'Can't be helped. You were quick gathering the information.'

'Boredom,' Pearce grinned. 'Let's be fair, there's nothing else going on here at the minute.'

* * *

Jackie Fleming listened intently as Nash related all that had happened in Zurich. She was as horrified as Clara when he outlined his theory about the motive for Lottie's abduction, and the possible murder of Luke. After he'd finished, she asked, 'How do you think those DNA results on the dead woman's baby fit into all this?'

'At present I've no idea,' Nash confessed. 'All we know is that either one of the Davison brothers or Lottie's brother Keith are the baby's father. As Luke is dead and to the best of our knowledge Keith is still in Africa; that would leave either Paul or Matthew as the likeliest candidates. Clara reckons Christmas is a time for miracles, which is possibly our best hope, because I think it would take a miracle for us to work all this out.'

CHAPTER EIGHTEEN

It was midafternoon by the time Nash got back to Helmsdale.
'I've put the folder with the DMG company profiles on your
desk,' Viv told him. 'You should be able to lift it without
giving yourself a hernia, just.'

'I'll take it home and read it there.' As he was speaking
the outer door of the CID suite opened. A mass of carrier
bags entered, camouflaging Clara and Alondra. 'I'm glad they
weren't using my credit card,' Nash told Pearce quietly. 'That
lot must have cost a fortune, judging by some of the shop
names.' He smiled at the two women as they emerged from
cover. 'I take it the shopping went well?'

Clara ignored the sarcasm. 'No problems at all,' she told
him. 'No sign of anyone acting suspiciously. Sorry it took
so long, but there wasn't much selection in Helmsdale, so I
took Alondra through to Netherdale. We didn't even stop for
lunch,' she added virtuously.

'You wouldn't have had time,' Nash responded. 'But it
doesn't matter. I've only just got back myself, but I have been
working of course.'

'It isn't all clothing,' Alondra said defensively. 'I needed
some working tools, and Helmsdale doesn't have a shop

selling artists' materials. That was the main reason we'd to go to Netherdale.'

'That reminds me; I had a call a while back. The hire company is sending a recovery truck to collect the remains of your car now the snow is passable. They want you to fill in an accident report for their insurers. I asked them to send a replacement vehicle. They were a bit reluctant at first, but I managed to persuade them. I told them at the first sign of snow I'd hide your keys.'

'I'll go put the coffee pot on and make us all a drink,' Clara volunteered.

Nash shuddered. 'No, you sit down and have a rest. You must be tired after slogging round all those shops. I'll make the coffee.'

They had barely finished their drinks when David Sutton walked in, accompanied by Daniel. The boy's delight on seeing his father was compounded when he spotted Alondra. When Nash asked if he would mind Alondra joining them for Christmas, the boy's reaction surprised even Mike. He rushed over and hugged her, almost causing her to fall off the typist's chair she was perched on.

'I take it you're OK with that?' Nash asked dryly.

He was acutely aware of the keen interest Clara was taking on the interaction between Daniel and Alondra, who was now asking him how he'd enjoyed his stay with Clara and David.

'We're leaving early,' Nash told the others. 'I have to collect the turkey and other meat from Lee Giles on the way home. No way am I doing that tomorrow. Not on Christmas Eve.'

'That's our butcher,' Daniel told Alondra. 'He's great. His sausage rolls are yummy.'

Nash herded Alondra and Daniel towards the door. 'We need to sort out rotas for Christmas and New Year,' he told his colleagues, 'we'll attend to that tomorrow.'

'It's OK, we've sorted it,' Viv informed him. 'Lianne's on nights over Christmas, so I'll take standby. I can call for help if anything serious crops up, can't I?'

'That's good of you to volunteer.'

'Don't worry; she's got leave after Boxing Day. I'll get my present then,' he added with a big grin.

Clara watched them leave. She turned in time to see the unmistakeable gesture Pearce was making to David. 'I think you're right,' Sutton acknowledged. 'I reckon he's giving her one. I thought so when I was at the house. Not that I blame him. She's not exactly hideous.'

'You've minds like sewers, the pair of you,' Clara chided them.

'You mean you don't think they're sleeping together?' her fiancé asked.

'I don't need to think, I know,' Clara told them smugly. 'Alondra's a lovely girl, and she needed someone to confide in. I happened to be that someone.'

'Go on then,' Pearce encouraged her, 'what did she say. Are they . . . ?'

'And they reckon women gossip! Yes, of course they're lovers. She's obviously very taken with him, and he's well-smitten by the look of things, so let's hope it all works out. The only worry I have is that she might be using him as a rock to cling to. Subconsciously perhaps, but if that is the case it strikes me as a recipe for trouble.'

* * *

Alondra soon learned the simple collection of the Christmas meat order was no quick thing. Despite the fact that it was almost time for the shop to close, there was still a queue waiting to be served. When it came to Nash's turn, the task was completed only when the ritual of enquiry as to health and wellbeing had been observed.

'They must sell good meat,' Alondra said when Nash had placed the large cardboard box in the boot and got back into the car.

Nash looked across at her and smiled. 'They do,' he agreed, 'but what made you say that?'

She pointed at the doorway. 'The queue,' she said, 'people don't queue for bad meat.'

'You're dead right of course,' Nash laughed, 'but Lee's father says it different. He once told me he'd given instructions for the lads to serve slower if the queue dwindled.'

When they reached the cottage, Nash was amused by Daniel's reaction to the newly-installed alarm system. Within minutes he had more or less taken control of the operation of it, mastering with ease the controls that had baffled his father.

* * *

Christmas morning at Smelt Mill Cottage was a relaxed affair. There was none of the last-minute panic associated with so many households. The vegetables had been prepared the night before and the bird went into the oven as soon as he got up. Daniel came downstairs and was sent into the lounge to sort the presents for distribution.

When Alondra appeared, Nash directed her towards the lounge. She had bought gifts for both father and son. Nash's was a small oblong parcel. As he unwrapped it, Alondra said anxiously, 'I hope you like it.'

Nash stared at the contents with delight. 'That's absolutely perfect,' he told her.

'What is it, Papa?'

Nash held up the box, which bore the distinctive roundel of the Sheaffer pen company. Nestling inside was a fountain pen, in black with a gold trim, an ideal match for his roller ball.

Daniel got a book from her, an illustrated guide to birds of the United Kingdom. Much to her surprise, Alondra also got a book. The present was inscribed from Mike and Daniel, but she guessed Nash had chosen it. She flicked through the glossy volume. It was a guide to landscape painting through the ages. The price on the flyleaf made her blink.

Daniel was struggling to unwrap a really oddly-shaped parcel. They watched with interest as he managed to get part of the wrapping paper off. At first, the shape had made him think it was a football. Now, he could see it was a crash helmet. Or so he thought. Closer inspection revealed it to be a batting helmet. The next two parcels, that contained a bat and a pair of pads, completed his delight.

After the present-opening ritual was complete, Nash returned to the kitchen. He was keen to establish a Christmas morning tradition that he had enjoyed as a boy, that of bacon sandwiches. In a sense, although he didn't realize the fact, he was attempting to make up for the long years as a bachelor where he had been either alone on Christmas morning, or on duty. Once the bacon was under the grill, he lifted the turkey out of the oven and set to work moistening it.

Alondra, who had the self-appointed task of tidying up the torn wrapping and gift tags that were strewn around the sitting room, entered the kitchen, her arms filled with paper. She headed for the waste bin but stopped and stared at Nash. He was standing still, his face a mask of concentration, his thoughts with the young woman found at the foot of Stark Ghyll. Alondra looked from him to the turkey baster in his right hand. 'Is something wrong, Mike?'

He turned at the sound of her voice. 'Sorry,' he mumbled, 'I got distracted.'

'We thought you might like to go for a walk after dinner,' she suggested.

Nash glanced out of the window. The low winter sun was flooding the valley with soft afternoon light, reflecting on the last of the snow. It would be cold, but not unpleasantly so. 'Great idea,' he approved, 'but let's make sure we go before we lose the daylight.'

Shortly after dinner, they left the house. As they strode along the lane they were unaware that their progress was being observed from the lower slopes of Black Fell.

The watcher saw they were heading towards the unoccupied farm and guessed this would be but a short walk to counter the effects of their Christmas meal. He had protested the futility of spending Christmas Day in what he considered a fruitless task. This opinion changed briefly when he saw the Torres woman emerge. He was on the point of going to fetch his vehicle when the woman was joined, first by the boy, and then by his father. The watcher merely noted the time and settled back uncomfortably. He looked at his watch, wondering if it had stopped. How many times he had looked at it that day, he couldn't begin to guess. There was still an hour of daylight left. The sandwiches he'd brought were all eaten, as were the chocolate biscuits. The flask was empty, the coffee it had contained, merely a memory. Another long, weary hour before he could bring this, cold, lonely, and boring vigil to an end and return to his cold, lonely and boring lodging. Some bloody Christmas, he thought. Still, the money made it worthwhile.

* * *

All the detectives were able to enjoy Christmas, so when he left for work the day after Boxing Day, Nash wasn't expecting a heavy workload. He had extracted promises that neither Alondra nor Daniel would open the door and should anyone approach the house, they were to telephone him at once.

As he pulled out of the drive, Nash experienced another new and pleasant sensation, as he responded to their farewell waves. As he drove to Helmsdale, Nash reflected about Alondra. She had taken so many shocks in the short time he had known her, but she seemed more settled; less insecure.

His own feelings were also not what he expected. They had met when she was in deep trouble and highly-vulnerable. The need to save and protect her had been paramount. Somewhere along the line, that had changed, and Nash was uncomfortably aware that he was close to being deeply in love with the young woman who had entered his life so unexpectedly.

There was little new on his desk, so once he'd examined the paperwork that awaited him, he was free to make the phone calls he'd planned. Before he could start, however, his phone rang. Sergeant Binns told him the name of the caller. It took a second for the name to register, 'Put her through, will you, and Jack—'

'I know; I'll put the kettle on.'

Nash grinned as he answered the caller. 'Hello, Yvonne, how can I help?'

The former au pair's voice was excited. 'I've found her! Bev, I mean. I've located her for you.'

'That's brilliant.' Nash reached for a pad. 'How did you manage it?'

'After you left, I tried to think of the people Bev was closest to, the ones she might have stayed in touch with, and who might still know where she is. Of course, a lot of them were hangers-on and when the marriage went belly-up, they drifted away. But the few genuine ones tried to help. Someone I'd contacted rang someone else, and they rang me back with the details. Are you ready?'

'Fire away.'

She read out the address. Nash stared at it in dismay. If he had wanted to choose somewhere as far away from Helmsdale as possible, this would be high on the list.

'It's another rehab clinic and the woman who told me said they only deal with the most severe cases of addiction. Apparently, Bev has been there three months or so. When she was admitted she was in a particularly bad way. I got the feeling the long-term prognosis isn't encouraging. She's been in and out of these places for years.'

He thanked her and put the phone down as Binns entered bearing a mug of coffee and a slip of paper on which was written 'ring Mexican Pete'. Nash nodded appreciation to the sergeant, his manner abstracted as he dwelt on Yvonne's final words. 'If you are planning to visit her, I think it might be better to go alone without taking Lottie, or Alondra, or whatever her name is now. The shock might be bad for both of them. Better to break it gently.'

Nash mentally added another name to his list of phone calls. The first of which was the return call to Mexican Pete.

'Professor,' he greeted the pathologist, 'I hope you had a good Christmas?'

'I have, so far,' Ramirez replied cautiously, 'that was before I discovered a problem.'

'Tell me more.'

Although the pathologist's voice was calm, Nash sensed the concern behind it. 'The woman who threw herself off Stark Ghyll; I admit I didn't look at the DNA results in depth. All I saw was the covering note from the laboratory.' He sounded uncharacteristically penitent. 'I am truly sorry. It was careless of me to overlook this. If I have an excuse it's because I couldn't believe this sort of thing could happen. The test shows a single strand DNA. Do you understand the significance of this?'

There was a long silence as Nash took in the horrific implication of what the pathologist had said. Eventually, he replied, 'I think so, although I don't want to believe it. Are you talking about something like Dolly the sheep? Cloning?' Genetic engineering?'

'I am indeed.'

'In that case, Professor, it means we are investigating a crime the likes of which we haven't witnessed before.'

'Sadly,' Ramirez added, 'it also means that there must be someone within the medical profession involved, because there is no way this could have been done by a layperson. I will have to inform the relevant authorities that I believe there to be a rogue specialist operating, presumably in this area.'

'We don't know that,' Nash pointed out. 'The procedure itself could have been carried out anywhere.'

He finished his coffee before making the other calls. Even as he was trying to contact those he needed to speak to, he could not get the horror of what Ramirez had told him out of his mind.

He needed the approval of Jackie Fleming before setting off on two potential wild goose chases. With the distance involved, travel and overnight accommodation would need to be sanctioned. Having paid for the Zurich trip, Nash was reluctant to stand these extra costs, even though Alondra had shared the Swiss expenses.

Getting his superiors' approval wasn't the only difficulty. Arranging the appointments was no simple matter. His call to DMG head office resulted in him listening to a recorded announcement that confirmed the group companies were closed for the holidays. Irritatingly, the message didn't make it clear whether they would remain so until after the New Year or not. That meant not only was he unable to arrange to see Matthew Davison, but if he was to tie in both visits, he couldn't arrange an appointment to see Bev Davison either. Reluctantly, Nash was forced to put all these plans on hold.

As the uniformed officers were dealing with the usual seasonal crimes, mostly drunken scuffles and minor incidents, Nash had little to occupy him and was able to take more days off. It was a happy time for all three, with Daniel able to share the attention and care of two adults for a rare moment in his life. Although the youngster didn't regard Alondra as a surrogate mother, she had become a good pal, someone he could confide in. To the boy's surprise, he found himself telling her things he hadn't even felt able to confess to his father. Alondra, who had little knowledge of the game of rugby, let alone the rules, listened sympathetically as Daniel confessed a sin that had caused him to get in much trouble. She knew enough, however, to appreciate the disgrace of him being sent off and promised not to add to his shame by informing his father.

Her own feelings confused her. Although she had no experience with children, she felt drawn to this motherless boy. Was what had happened to her behind her sudden rush of maternal instinct? Or was it a by-product of what she felt for Mike? And as her relationship with Mike deepened and strengthened daily, what would happen in the future?

Nash had little doubt this was more serious than most of his encounters. He wanted it to become a long-term relationship rather than another casual affair. He tried to analyze what was so special, what made Alondra different? She was very good-looking, that was undeniable, in certain lights, or when her head tilted at a particular angle, she was extremely beautiful. But it went a lot deeper than her looks or the little things about her: her slim fingers, which could create an image of a place or a person in just a few strokes of pencil or brush and excite him with a simple caress.

Nash was unwilling to admit it, unwilling to allow the expression, hook, line and sinker to enter his thoughts at the same time.

CHAPTER NINETEEN

When Nash phoned DMG again the receptionist admitted that Matthew Davison, now group chairman and managing director, was in the building; getting to speak to him was the next hurdle. As a detective inspector from 'somewhere up north', Nash didn't appear to stand much of a chance.

The first person he encountered was a secretary who sounded as if she'd only recently left school. 'What do you want Mr Davison for,' she demanded.

'Kidnapping, murder, arson, attempted murder. How's that for starters?' Nash replied.

There was a long silence and a hint of a nervous gulp in the young woman's voice as she said, 'I think I'd better put you through to his PA.'

One down, one to go, he thought. The PA was easier. 'It's in connection with the disappearance of his niece Charlotte. Fresh evidence has come to light.'

'Oh dear, not a dead body, I hope?'

'No, not a dead body,' Nash reassured her.

'I see, but how can Mr Davison help?'

'I've been unable to speak to either his brother or sister-in-law yet, so I thought he might be able to provide some of the information I need.'

'Please wait, I'll see if he's free.'

Davison was the easiest of all to convince. Nash, who already had a fair idea of the man's character, sold him the idea principally by hinting that once he was in possession of all the information and evidence to back it up, he was of the opinion that Matthew would gain full control of DMG.

'What makes you think I haven't got that already?' Davison sounded torn between arrogance and amusement.

'I've seen the group statistics and figures. You haven't got it when it comes to a shareholders' meeting,' Nash pointed out.

In the silence that followed, Nash could almost hear the man's brain working. 'Very well, make the arrangements with my secretary.'

Staff at the rehab clinic were at first reluctant. Nash pointed out that this was part of an ongoing police investigation and asked to speak to the doctor in charge. He explained the reason for his request. 'Look back at her file, there must be information in there about the trauma she suffered. I feel certain you'll find that the drug abuse only began following the kidnapping and alleged murder of her daughter.'

'Yes, that is the case.'

'What I am about to tell you must be treated in the strictest confidence.'

'Of course.'

'I believe I can prove that her daughter is alive, but for that, I need a DNA sample. I'm more than happy for a member of staff to be present when I speak to her. Do you think it might help Mrs Davison's recovery to discover her daughter is alive and well? If not, I'd be extremely interested to hear the reasons for refusing it.'

Only a fool would have said no, and Nash was certain he wasn't dealing with a fool. Taking a chance on Fleming's approval of his expenditure, Nash arranged both appointments for early the following week.

He told Alondra that he had to go away to interview some witnesses, and that the distance meant he'd probably be absent for one night.

She looked only mildly upset by the news. 'I'll miss you,' she told him.

'I've arranged for an officer to remain here on guard until I return. If you decide to go anywhere, he'll accompany you, OK?'

Alondra smiled. 'I'll be fine. Besides, I'll have Daniel to look after me as well as your officer.'

* * *

Nash's reaction on first seeing Bev Davison was heartrending. Any similarity to the glamorous, beautiful young woman whose photos had graced the covers of almost every fashion magazine in Europe and America was minimal. It was only by close examination of her bone structure that Nash was able to convince himself that staff at the clinic hadn't brought the wrong patient into the visitor's room. The gaunt, haggard-looking woman with wispy, unkempt hair turned grey by nature's stylist, who shuffled down the corridor towards him looked more like an old woman of eighty. Her shoulders were set in a permanent slump, her eyes hollow-rimmed and darkened; their depths reflecting the demons that haunted her. She would not have occasioned a second glance, except perhaps one of pity.

There were other signs as well. The slight tremor in her hands, the occasional twitch of her head, the tic that spasmodically afflicted the muscles below one eye. Worst of all, her teeth. Once, her mouth alone had earned her thousands of pounds a year via commercials for a well-known brand of toothpaste. Now, rotted by years of drug taking and unhealthy diet, they were little more than blackened stumps. Some were missing altogether.

The accompanying therapist guided her gently through the door and into a chair before performing the introduction and reassuring Nash, 'I've been advised that this meeting is being held in confidence. Rest assured, Inspector, anything you say will remain in this room.'

Nash nodded and placed his chair opposite Bev.

Bev looked at the detective, her expression one of wary disinterest.

The less visible signs of the damage her addiction had caused were the state of her heart and liver. The latter, he could do nothing about. Breaking the news gently would alleviate any strain on her heart.

He began by explaining that he hadn't come with bad news. He repeated that statement in various forms during the early part of the meeting, gradually introducing the impression that on the contrary, he was the bearer of good tidings. Speaking clearly and slowly, the tone of his voice gentle and relaxed, he told her, 'I shall want to ask you one or two questions about what happened all those years ago, but I promise to do all I can to avoid causing you any distress. For the time being, however, I want you to concentrate on the present day. Can you do that for me?'

'I suppose so.' Her voice was low, husky, barely above a whisper. 'I don't know what good it will do, though.'

There was a world of desperate sadness in her dejected tone; one that told Nash she was convinced there would never be any news that was good.

'I know that you received a photograph that appeared to show that Lottie was dead.' Nash leaned forward and took hold of her hand; it was skeletal, the veins showing through the parchment-like skin. 'However, I want you to look at two other photos.'

Nash produced the first of them. He laid it on the table in front of her. 'This was a photo taken of you at the same age as Lottie would be today. I chose that one because unlike the others, your hair was short. Do you remember having that photo taken?'

She looked down, and Nash sensed a vague stirring of interest. 'They cut my hair,' she told him. 'They said they wanted a tomboy image. I wasn't happy, but they insisted, and they were prepared to pay a lot of money. In the end I agreed because my hair would grow back. Besides, someone else wanted to see me with short hair.' She smiled faintly, and even that expression conveyed more sadness than pleasure.

'Now, I want you to compare that photo of you with another one.' He held it out and watched her stare intently at it.

'I don't remember that one.' She examined the photo even more closely, then looked up. 'I never wore a top like that,' she told him. 'I would have remembered it. Who took this photo, do you know? I'm sure it's a fake.'

'No, it isn't a fake. But you're quite right; it isn't a photo of you. I took this photo only a week ago. If you look in the top left-hand corner of the photo, you can just see the date it was taken. Only digital cameras offer that facility.'

She nodded her understanding. 'But if this isn't me, who is it?'

'I am absolutely convinced that the young woman in the photo is your daughter Lottie.'

She shook her head. 'No, Lottie's dead. They told me so. My Lottie is dead. That can't be Lottie. Why are you lying to me? What are you trying to do?' she demanded; anger in every word, her eyes piercing through him.

Nash took her hand again and felt it tremble violently. He squeezed it gently, aware of the extreme fragility of her mind as well as her bones. He glanced at the therapist who was also leaning forward in her chair, eager to catch sight of the image. Nash laid the photo of Alondra alongside that of Bev. Side by side, the similarity was astonishing.

Bev stuffed the fingers of her free hand against her mouth, biting back the scream she was struggling to contain. She looked at Nash, her eyes haunted by a hundred unasked questions. He stroked her hand, held it gently between both of his. 'Let me explain. It is a complicated story, but I feel sure you will feel it was worth listening.'

He took her through it, step by patient step, allowing each fact to register before moving on. When he recounted Alondra's reaction to Yvonne's perfume and the name she called the former au pair, Bev was convinced. She lifted her head and he saw her smile, and this time it was a genuine reaction. 'I remember Lottie calling her Bonny because she couldn't get her tongue around the name Yvonne properly.'

When he had finished, Bev was in tears. Tears of joy, tears for all the wasted years, tears of pride at the handsome young woman she had brought into the world, and of what little this stranger had told her about the child. Nash knew full recovery would never come; but at least Bev now had hope.

'She is a lovely young woman, with a kind, sweet and loving nature. If you would like me to, I'll bring her to see you soon. I know waiting will be hard, but after all this time a few weeks will be worthwhile, won't it?'

'Lottie.' She picked up the photo, stared at it for a long time before clutching it tight. 'My poor, darling Lottie.' She looked hard at Nash. 'Please bring her to me.'

'I will bring her as soon as possible, but I have to ensure her safety first. Now, I want to ask you a very personal question. One that may distress you. One you might not be prepared to answer.' Nash didn't add that she might not be able to answer, because she didn't know.

She stared at him suspiciously. 'I will try,' she agreed.

'Very well, but you promise you won't slap my face for asking?'

She shook her head and Nash saw her smile slightly as he continued, 'I want to ask you who Lottie's father is.'

He heard the therapist catch her breath, but his gaze remained fixed on Bev. 'Is it your ex-husband Paul? Or his brother Matthew?' He paused, before adding the million-dollar question, 'Or was it Luke?'

The sob she choked back at the mention of Luke's name told Nash the answer long before she spoke. She clasped her hands over her face as if hiding from the truth. When at last she spoke her voice was dreamy, reminiscent as she recalled a far happier time. 'It wasn't Paul, and it certainly wasn't Matthew. If you knew the Davison family history better, you'd never have asked if Matthew could have been Lottie's father.' She spoke again; it was as if a floodgate had opened, spilling information about the Davison family. She gazed out of the window for a moment as if gathering her thoughts.

'Strange isn't it? Three brothers and all of them wanting you? I sometimes wondered which of the two was more jealous of my friendship with Luke, Paul, or Matthew. But I didn't care what they thought, or how jealous they were.' She looked down and tried to control her emotions; emotions Nash believed had been closeted for years. 'I was in love with Luke, loved him with every fibre of my being. I was so much in love with him that if he'd asked me I would have given up everything, my home, my lifestyle, my children even, simply to be with him. Later, when Luke died, and then after Lottie went missing and we were told she was dead, I believed it was a judgement on me for so much sinful happiness.'

Nash realized repressed feelings were pouring out. He doubted Bev had spoken so much for years.

She stared at Nash. 'Why did you suspect that Paul wasn't Lottie's father?' she asked, suddenly.

He explained about Lottie's artistic ability. 'She has become quite successful and that was the first clue. Then there was the painting.' He told her about the Stark Ghyll landscape that had brought Lottie in contact with him.

The mention of the painting led her to reminisce. 'It was impossible not to love Luke, because he was so different from his brothers, so different from Paul. Luke was gentle and caring, where Paul was hard and callous, brutal even. And Matthew, so filled with spite and envy, so vindictive. Luke was everything I wished for, everything I wanted Paul to be. When I was with Luke, when we were together,' she paused, emotion threatening to get the better of her, 'we had such wonderful times. I didn't care, didn't worry. For the first time since my marriage I didn't think of anything or anybody but Luke. I knew the child I was carrying was Luke's, and I suppose that should have made me feel ashamed. On the contrary, it made me rejoice.

'When Lottie was born, she looked so much like her father, I was surprised nobody noticed. But then all the brothers looked pretty much alike. Now, I had everything I wanted.' She faltered as if seeking the courage to continue. 'But then it all changed. First, Luke died and I thought I would never get over that. Then Lottie was taken and it seemed as if someone was targeting everything precious in my life, punishing me for having been so happy. Suddenly, everything I cared about had gone.'

'When did you last see Paul? Have you seen or spoken to him since the divorce?'

'I haven't seen or spoken to him for over fifteen years.'

There was one more question Nash had to ask. He waited for several seconds before speaking, aware of the shocking nature of it. 'Bev, have you any reason to suppose that Luke's death was anything other than a climbing accident?'

Bev looked up from the photo of Alondra she was still clutching. Nash could see the dawn of realization by the shock and horror in her eyes. 'You think Luke was murdered?' she whispered. 'Is that what you're implying? You think Paul had him killed because he found out about us? Because he knew Lottie was Luke's child, not his?' Horror was etched across her face.

'You have to admit the possibility exists,' Nash said gently.

'I've never been sure whether Paul knew or not. He used to taunt me, accuse me of sleeping around, but I thought that was only a cover for what he was up to. Now, I don't know. I'm fairly certain Matthew knew, though. I was worried he might tell Paul out of spite, because of the way things were between them, but I don't know that he did. That goon of a security man, Dermot Black, was forever snooping around, eavesdropping, following me. He might have found out, and if he had he would certainly have gone running to Paul.'

She paused again. 'I used to believe Paul was capable of almost anything if he wanted it badly enough. But murder? That I can't say, because I honestly don't know.' Bev looked as though she had awoken from a deep sleep, her eyes were wider, her voice becoming stronger.

'It's strange isn't it, the way things work out? When you told me all this started after Lottie wrote to you about the painting, it brought back so many memories. One in particular that sent shivers down my spine. You weren't to know, but to me it was as if the past had returned in a bizarre way. The fact that Lottie wrote to you at Smelt Mill Cottage I find so eerie it's hard to explain. Did you know that it used to be a holiday cottage? Luke rented it. It was there that he did the painting of Stark Ghyll. He was there all summer. Paul was away for most of the time; told me he was negotiating a business deal in California. He didn't mention the Hollywood actress he was sleeping with. I was lonely and miserable after I found out. I needed time away from London to think things out. So I left Keith with the staff and drove up to Yorkshire to pour my troubles out to Luke.'

She shrugged. 'What happened was inevitable, I suppose. Later, I realized I'd been in love with Luke for a long time. The reason I find the things you've just told me so spooky is that it was in that cottage that Lottie was conceived.'

'Are you absolutely certain that Paul didn't find out?'

'I was,' she admitted, 'but not any longer. What you've told me and what you asked about how Luke died; now it all makes sense. Maybe Matthew did tell him, if Paul goaded him enough. Or maybe it was that creep Dermot Black.'

'You said you haven't heard from Paul since the divorce.'

'Not a word.' Bev frowned. 'And that's unlike him. Even when Keith was having problems he didn't attempt to get in touch.' She shrugged. 'Not that I'm aware of anyway. But I wasn't exactly lucid at the time which means, I suppose, that he could have tried to contact me, but I was too far gone to remember.'

'Why were Paul and Matthew always at each other's throats?'

'Paul hated and feared Matthew because he was academically far brighter. Matthew was jealous of Paul because he got to be head of the company and had a talent for making money and attracting beautiful women. Besides, he had other things Matthew could only dream of.'

Nash frowned. 'I don't . . . Oh, you mean what you said earlier?'

Bev nodded, but whether the explanation made matters clearer, or simply muddied the water, Nash couldn't be sure.

When Nash left, besides the required DNA sample, he carried three memories with him. One was of a woman who, having sunk to the very lowest point in her life was suddenly given a reason to carry on, a meaning to the time that was left to her. The second was the realization that the rumours of Bev's mental deterioration had been greatly exaggerated. It wasn't that she didn't understand what was said to her; simply that no one had been telling her anything she found interesting. The final thought resulting from what Bev had confirmed, was that when the time came to interview Paul Davison, the first, the main item on the agenda would be the murder of Luke Davison.

It was too late for Nash to continue on to London, as he had planned. Following the long session, he felt drained. He was sure the local police station would advise him of somewhere to stay, but his presence in the area was sure to raise questions he wasn't prepared to answer. He spotted a local pub advertising bed and breakfast and took the next best option, left his bag in the comfortable room and set out to find something to eat. He thought briefly of phoning home but remembered that Alondra had promised to take Daniel into Netherdale, accompanied by DC Lisa Andrews, to watch the local pantomime. Nash smiled as he recalled them making plans, pleased at this fresh sign of Alondra and his son bonding so well.

Before going to bed, he took his mobile from his coat pocket and looked round for the charger. It was then he discovered he had forgotten to pack it. The mobile was already dangerously low on power. He switched it off, hoping to conserve enough life.

Next morning, Nash tried to call home, but as soon as he got the ringing tone, the mobile cut out. The blank screen told him the battery was now completely dead.

* * *

'What have you got to report? I take it you haven't rung to discuss the weather.'

'Hardly. I rang to suggest we act this morning.'

'About time, I'd say. Our client is getting very fractious. By the way, you've lost your Christmas bonus,' he added sarcastically. 'Any special reason for choosing today?'

'Because Nash isn't there. There's a copper on duty, otherwise she's alone. Apart from Nash's kid and I don't think a snotty little brat will cause us too much trouble, do you?'

'Where's Nash?'

'I don't know. His car wasn't there yesterday evening, and it still isn't there this morning.'

'Right, I'll be with you as soon as I can. What do we need?'

'Depends on what you have available. Two pairs of overalls and a couple of laminated photo IDs and a toolbox. We could pass ourselves off as engineers from the power company. You have the van, don't you?'

'Yes, but it's black. Not exactly the power company's livery.'

'We can say it's a hire vehicle. Blame it on the weather if we're asked.'

'Right, I'll mock the badges up and phone the client to find out where he wants us to take the woman.' He paused. 'Actually, I think that brat of Nash's can come along as insurance for Nash behaving himself. And if things go pear-shaped, we can use him as a bargaining tool.'

'Sounds good to me. As long as I don't have to spend too much time looking after him. I hate kids.'

CHAPTER TWENTY

Nash arrived at the headquarters of DMG with only a few minutes to spare before the scheduled time of the meeting. Having complied with the stringent checks required by the security man at the reception counter, a guard escorted him to the lift. The second he stepped out on to the top floor he was greeted by Davison's PA.

After being ushered into the plush office he was neither greeted, asked to sit down, nor offered a handshake. Nash stood in front of Davison's large, crescent-shaped desk waiting for the man to speak. Matthew Davison was exactly as Yvonne and Bev had described him. His attitude, one of pompous arrogance, was the sort that Nash particularly disliked. He knew the only way to achieve a satisfactory outcome to the interview would be to break down that barrier. Shock and sarcasm were Nash's weapons of choice.

Davison looked him up and down as if some trivial thought had amused him. 'The reason you gave for wanting this meeting was to speak to me about my niece Lottie. I contacted the Metropolitan Police after your call, and they are unaware of any new developments in the case, so would you care to explain exactly what it is that you appear to know that they don't?'

'If you spoke to the officers heading up the original investigation you would have needed a Ouija board,' Nash retorted.

'What leads you to the belief that after all this time officers from North Yorkshire Police, so far distant from events a quarter of a century ago, will have any more success than the Met, with their detailed knowledge of the case and infinitely greater resources? What special brand of magic can you bring to the case after all this time? Please enlighten me, for I am most anxious to know.'

'That's an operational judgement that I decide on, together with my superior officers. If you're wondering how or why we became involved, the reason is that at least one of the crimes was committed in our area.'

Davison frowned. 'One of the crimes? I thought there was only one. My niece's kidnap and murder here in London?'

'I am investigating one case of abduction, two murders, and several attempted murders. Depending on what I discover there may be other charges as well.'

Davison stared at him for a second, before spluttering in disbelief. 'Two murders? I understand Lottie was killed. Have you found her body? Is it in Yorkshire? Is that how you got involved? And who's the other victim?'

Nash's voice was casual, giving no warning that he was about to deliver his first bombshell. 'Lottie isn't one of the victims. She isn't dead. She's alive and well.'

He reached into his folder and produced two copies of the photos he'd shown Bev. He placed them on Davison's desk. 'As you can see, the resemblance to her mother at the same age is uncanny. And you can also see that she's remarkably fit and well.'

Matthew stared at the photograph of his niece. Alondra was smiling at the camera. He glanced from her image to that of Bev. They looked more like twins than mother and daughter. He gasped, the only sound he seemed capable of for some time. Eventually, he looked up at the detective. 'If . . . if that really is Lottie, who are the murder victims you mentioned?'

'Lottie was abducted by a couple of professional criminals, a husband and wife team who went by the name of Torres. The wife died last year from natural causes. Her husband's death was anything but natural. According to eyewitnesses, his car was deliberately forced off the road into a ravine, killing him instantly. That makes it murder.' Nash paused to allow Davison to absorb this and to give greater impact to his second bombshell. 'The second murder victim was your brother Luke.'

There was no mistaking the power of Davison's intelligence. Once he'd recovered from this fresh shock, Nash watched the changing emotions on the man's face, from incredulity to a kind of acceptance, and calculation of the implications of Nash's statement.

'You'd better sit down,' he waved to a chair, 'and tell me what you know — and what you suspect. I take it you don't believe that I am implicated in any of this?'

'Not now,' Nash conceded, 'although until a short while ago you were in pole position. However, certain facts have come to light as a result of a talk I had with your sister-in-law that have changed all that.'

'Bev? You've spoken to Bev? What has she said?'

'I'm afraid I'm not at liberty to tell you that. Are you paying her bills at the clinic?'

Davison nodded. 'Not me personally, but DMG has a fund for deserving causes. Bev's care package comes out of that.'

'Is your brother still involved with DMG?'

Nash wasn't sure if the pause before Davison replied was the natural result of the change in his line of questioning, or whether the man was framing his response carefully. 'No,' Matthew told him, 'Paul no longer has anything to do with the day-to-day running of the companies.'

Which wasn't quite what Nash had asked. 'But he is still a shareholder, the largest shareholder?'

'Yes, he is.'

'Do you keep in touch with him? Consult him perhaps?'

This time there was no hesitation. 'No, definitely not.'

'But you do know where he is?'

'I haven't the remotest idea.'

'How do you pay his dividends? Given the massive profits the group makes, there must be dividends for the shareholders.'

'Paul's dividends are paid electronically into a bank account he nominated several years ago. When I authorize that payment, it is the closest I come to direct contact with my brother. Other than that, I haven't seen or spoken to Paul for many years. I've no problem with that,' he admitted. 'It's no secret that Paul and I never got on well. Apart from the fact that we didn't like one another, I disapproved of the way he treated his wife. That's only one of the reasons. My dislike of Paul goes back way beyond that, to the time when my father was dying. Paul tried to get him to change his will, to have Paul as sole beneficiary. In other words, to disinherit me. That would have given him sole control over DMG.'

'You realize what you've just told me could be construed as a strong motive for wishing to harm Paul, either directly or through his family?'

Davison's smile was cold, humourless. 'But you've already admitted I'm no longer a suspect.'

'That's true — now, but others may not believe it. Not unless they had access to the same information I have. One thing strikes me as odd in what you said, your comment about Paul's behaviour. From what I've heard, you weren't exactly a saint yourself.'

'I never said I was, and I never pretended to be. The difference is I was single. I didn't have a wife and family to consider. My misdeeds didn't hurt anyone.' Davison paused. 'Well, not in that way, at least. The way Paul carried on caused Bev immense distress. And it wasn't a few isolated incidents, bear in mind. It went on continually, almost from the time they returned from honeymoon. With Paul, it seemed he only had to see an attractive woman to want her.'

Davison shook his head. He looked down at Bev's photo. 'I still don't understand it. Don't understand Paul.

Never have done. It's a shame you only met Bev as she now is, Inspector Nash. I have to say, if I had a woman like Bev was in those days, warming my bed, I wouldn't even think about straying. It'd be all I could do to get up in a morning and go to work. This photo doesn't do her justice. Bev was a stunning, sexy, exciting woman when she was young.'

'Did you . . . ?'

Matthew smiled ruefully. 'Sleep with Bev? I assume that's what you're asking.' He gave Nash a cunning glance. 'What did Bev say? Or didn't you ask her?' His gaze switched to Alondra's photo. 'I'll tell you something, Inspector, if this is Bev's daughter, and I can't believe she isn't, then it might do her mother more good than all the expensive therapy I'm paying for.'

'We need to establish her identity beyond question. We have a DNA sample from Bev, which will establish that she is her mother, but I also need one from Paul.'

'If you have one from Bev, why do you need . . . ?' Davison's voice tailed off as he realized the implications of Nash's request.

'Good God! You don't think Paul is Lottie's father, do you?' Matthew started to laugh. 'Now that would be funny. Talk about poetic justice.' His laughter died away. 'Hang on, if you believe Paul wasn't the father, why do you want his . . . ?' He gulped. 'Of course, you think it was Luke. So by getting Paul's DNA you'll be able to disprove his paternity, and thus provide a motive, correct?'

Nash nodded.

'Very clever, Inspector Nash.'

Nash waited for the last penny to drop. He saw Davison's eyes widen, the memory of what Nash had said at the start of the interview returning. 'Oh, dear God, no. If you think Luke was Lottie's father, and you think Luke was murdered, that means you think Paul had him killed. Possibly also had Lottie kidnapped. That's it isn't it?'

'I'm trying to keep an open mind at the moment.'

Davison's expression told Nash he didn't believe him.

'Tell me,' Nash went on, 'do you think Paul capable of doing something like that?'

Davison's reply was instantaneous. 'Yes, without a doubt. I saw the way he acted in business. If anyone thwarted him, or tried to pull a fast one, his reaction was extreme. I had to spend a fair amount of time going around mending fences with people he'd upset because of his temper. To be perfectly honest, Inspector Nash, the business hasn't suffered at all since Paul retired.'

Matthew's expression reminded Nash of a magician about to perform his best trick. 'Since I took control, DMG has gone from strength to strength. Before Paul retired we were losing market share, losing the goodwill of suppliers and customers alike. Much of that was down to Paul's ruthlessness and corner-cutting ways. I rebuilt trust with all our trading partners, but it was a long, hard battle. Now we're a household name worldwide, but it's in spite of Paul, not because of him. And if he behaved like that in business, I suppose he'd be even more capable of it in his private life. But if he did, then he certainly reckoned without the effect on everyone around him.'

'How do you mean?'

'Well, you've seen Bev, for one. Lottie, if this is her, has only just reappeared. Paul's great hope was for Keith to take over at DMG. But Keith didn't want to know.'

'Why was that?'

'Why do you think Keith is working in the depths of Africa? Because he believed Paul was to blame for his mother's addiction. As soon as he could rid himself of Paul he was away. Couldn't settle here in Britain, because it was too close to his father. That's not speculation. It's fact. Keith told me so.'

'You wouldn't be funding the place where he's teaching, would you?'

Matthew smiled. 'Old habits die hard. I told you I used to run around after Paul picking up the pieces. What puzzles me is why it's all kicked off after so many years.'

'I was fairly sure I knew the reason for it. What you've told me about Paul's character pretty much confirms it.'

'I don't see how you're going to prove any of this.'

Nash smiled. 'Neither do I at present, but with a bit of luck I hope to do so.'

Matthew Davison remained seated, staring at the door, long after Nash had left his office.

* * *

Nash set off on his journey home. Leaving the capital was a trial for motorists, he felt as though every red traffic light knew he was coming. Desperate for a hot drink and something to eat, he stopped at a small town where he searched in vain for a public telephone that was in working order. Those that hadn't been vandalized hadn't been maintained either. Frustrated by this, he opted for something to eat. The fish and chips were not the best. The batter tasted floury, the chips greasy. He was edgy, anxious to get home. It wasn't that he was worried about Alondra or Daniel. Although he had been absent less than two days, he was keenly aware how much he missed them.

The outskirts of Netherdale resembled a ghost town from an old Western, or a scene from the opening of a horror movie. The roads dimly lit. The cold weather keeping most people indoors. Fortunately, the weather and the roads were clear and he was able to travel faster than he would normally have considered. He knew the roads well and at that time of night there was little traffic to delay him. Oncoming vehicles gave plenty of advance warning via their headlights. Nevertheless, it seemed an age before he swung the steering wheel to turn into the lane leading to Smelt Mill Cottage.

He was well short of the house when he felt the first twinge of alarm. At this range, he felt sure he should have been able to make out some light coming from the building. There was no moon, and no other buildings to mask it. Yet, apart from his car headlights, there was nothing. He was certain something was wrong.

As he pulled to a halt, the PIR light, spurred to action by the motion of the car, sprang to life, startling him. Apart from the beam illuminating the drive the building was in total darkness. Before he turned off the headlights he noticed Alondra's replacement hire car on the drive, alongside it the police car. If they weren't out, why were there no lights on?

Panic caused him to fumble to unlock the door, a feeling he wasn't used to. Panic turned momentarily into terror as he realized there was no alarm sounding.

Once inside he entered the kitchen and looked around, hoping to see a note on the worktop. He moved into the lounge. The room felt cold. The log fire in the huge grate was dead, the fire basket filled with grey ash. He walked over and felt the wrought iron rungs. They were cold to the touch. The fire had been out a long time. He entered the study. Again, nothing. He walked over to the desk and looked at the display on the phone. There had been no calls, no messages.

As a last resort he went upstairs. The bedrooms were empty, the beds neatly made. If it wasn't for the clothes hanging in the wardrobes, or in Daniel's case, strewn around the room, he might have suspected that they'd gone away. Perhaps they had gone to the Golden Bear after all and had forgotten to set the alarm — but they wouldn't do that.

Perhaps they were at Clara's house and hadn't been able to reach him — but there would have been a note. His whole being now told him that something was dreadfully wrong.

He returned to the study and rang Clara's home phone number. The fact that he was phoning at this late hour would tell her how worried he was. For once, he felt unable to think clearly and needed someone else to help him make sense of what had happened. However, when the phone was answered, it wasn't Clara's voice but that of David.

'No, Mike,' Sutton told him, 'Clara isn't here. She's been called out to a domestic in Bishopton. Some bloke's holding a twelve bore to his wife's throat, and with you being away, Clara got the call. She rang me a while back, Jackie Fleming's with her and they've got an ARU team there, but they're waiting for a trained negotiator to arrive from York. Is it urgent?'

Nash explained the situation.

Sutton whistled. 'I agree, it doesn't sound good. No sign of your officer?'

'No sign of anyone.'

'Listen, would it help if I come out there? Until the rest of them are available? Viv's with Clara, so he won't be free either.'

Nash accepted the offer, grateful of the company. 'Before I set off,' Sutton told him, 'I'll send Clara a text, let her know what's happened.'

CHAPTER TWENTY-ONE

'The bloke surrendered after the negotiator talked to him. When we checked the shotgun, it wasn't even loaded. Jackie had him taken to the cells at Netherdale. Viv's processing the paperwork. According to what his partner told us, the gunman is being treated for a mental disorder and has medication, but she thinks he hasn't been taking it. I brought a couple of the ARU team along with me in case we need more bodies,' Clara explained, glancing at Nash as she finished. She wasn't sure if he'd heard anything of what she'd said. 'Mike, tell me exactly what happened.'

Nash's story took less than a minute.

'I can organize a search locally but that will have to wait until daylight.' As she spoke, Clara had a dreadful thought. She hesitated before mentioning it, but knew she had to raise the possibility. 'Mike, you don't suppose they might have gone anywhere near the old workings, do you?' She gestured down the valley in the direction of the disused lead mine.

Nash shook his head. 'One of the conditions of buying this house was that I made Daniel promise never to go near the mine. I don't think he'd break that promise. Besides which, Alondra knew not to leave the house unaccompanied.'

'Just a thought,' Sutton suggested, 'but why don't I check the CCTV tapes? I assume the equipment is up and running?'

'Yes, have a look, I'd forgotten about that.' Nash didn't sound over-optimistic.

When Sutton re-entered the room a few minutes later, they could tell he had something to report and one look at his face told Clara the news wasn't going to be good. 'They've been taken. Alondra, Daniel, and the police officer.' Sutton's voice was flat; totally lacking in emotion.

'The tape shows a black van on the drive. The officer confronted two men and was overpowered. They came into the house, and then the tape shows them emerging with Alondra and Daniel. She wasn't resisting, but Daniel was squirming like an eel. The three of them were thrust into the back of the van. There are no markings on the vehicle and the registration plate is covered in mud. At a guess I'd say that was deliberate, so I doubt whether the image can be enhanced. The blokes had overalls on, so I guess they got in by pretending to be telephone or power engineers, or something of the sort.'

'I'd better have a look,' Clara said. She nodded towards Nash, a clear message for Sutton to stay with him.

After she left the room, Nash looked at the army officer. Despite the expression of desperation on his face, Sutton saw kindling interest in his eyes. 'Was there anything to identify the van?' Nash asked him.

Sutton shook his head. 'Nothing, unless you count one of those Come-To-Jesus stickers in the back window.'

He looked across at Nash, witnessing for the first time what Clara had described on several previous occasions. 'Mike goes into a sort of deep thought, almost trance-like,' she'd told him. 'He drifts off and re-enacts the crime. When he comes out of it, he usually has a load of pertinent questions, or the answers to some of the things that have had us baffled.'

Nash struggled with the elusive memory. Someone had mentioned those stickers before. Who had it been? The image of the old man outside Good Buys supermarket came back to him. Of course: Jonas Turner had used the phrase in connection with the religious sect at Ghyll Head Manor. What had he said about them? Nothing good, that was for sure.

His memory came bounding back. Turner had mentioned the leader of the oddball religious sect in less than flattering terms, as Nash recalled. What had he called him? A name from the Old Testament. Ezra? Joshua? Elisha? No, Malachi; that was it, Malachi. Nash had been struck by the incongruity of that and the man's surname. Malachi Entwistle As he fought for recall, Nash realized he'd seen or heard that surname somewhere else but couldn't for the moment remember.

Clara re-entered the room and was about to speak, when she saw Sutton raise his hand to warn her. She looked across at Nash and nodded imperceptibly.

'What do we know about that religious sect at the other side of Stark Ghyll? Somebody was talking about them only recently.' Nash was looking at Clara as he spoke, but it was Sutton who answered.

'The ones the snowplough driver was talking about, you mean? He reckoned there was something odd going on there.'

'That's it! Can you remember what he said?'

'Something to do with his brother-in-law. He delivers there, if I remember rightly. Didn't he say the place used more medical supplies than the cottage hospital?'

'You're right,' Nash agreed, 'and when Jonas Turner was talking about them, he mentioned that the senior Brother, or whatever his fancy title is, has a degree in chemistry or biology, or some such thing. That's more suitable for a medicine man than a prophet.'

'What's brought all this on?' Clara asked.

'The van had one of those religious stickers on the back,' Sutton explained.

'You really think this might be significant?' Clara was dubious.

'Not on its own, but there's something else, something at the back of my mind about that character Entwistle, but I just can't place it at the minute.' Nash paced up and down the study. His gaze strayed to his desk, and the file that was on the blotter.

That wasn't the file he wanted, but it was sufficient to prompt his memory. He walked over and opened his desk drawer. He took out the folder Pearce had given him. It contained details of the DMG companies. He explained the contents to the others; took out the top summary sheet and passed it to Sutton. 'There are so many companies in the group; we'd better take half each, Clara.' He passed her a sheaf of papers.

'David, if you read out each of the names on that list, Clara and I will check their directors and shareholders. I think somewhere in this lot, we'll find what we're looking for. Matthew Davison said Paul has no connection with the group now, except as a shareholder. I'm still not convinced that's true.'

'You think Matthew lied to you?'

'Possibly, but I'm more inclined to think he isn't aware of what Paul is up to. There was no love lost between them according to Matthew's own admission, so if he saw a way to drop Paul in the mire, he'd take it. Apart from anything else he detests Paul for what happened to Bev. He thinks her addiction is down to Paul's behaviour as much as Lottie's abduction.'

'What exactly are we looking for, if Paul isn't a director?'

'I seem to recall that one of the companies had a director named Entwistle. I may be wrong, but if not, it might be the link we're looking for.'

'I don't know if you spotted this, Mike, but the original company was DCG, manufacturing chemicals, but they changed it to DMG. The M is for medical supplies,' Sutton told him.

Nash looked up, though for a moment then nodded. 'OK, let's start checking.'

'Davison Pharmaceutical Supplies Ltd,' Sutton began. He read out company after company, while Nash and Clara checked their details. He'd gone through Davison Medical Equipment, Davison Orthopaedic Supplies, Davison Paper Products, Davison Hygiene & Sanitary Supplies before he reached Davison Research & Development Ltd.

'Got it!' Clara exclaimed. 'The directors of Davison R and D are listed as JM Entwistle, Paul Davison and Dr A Nixon,'

'What else does it tell us?' Nash asked.

'Clara read out the details, date of incorporation, nominal and issued share capital, shareholders, trading results, and when she turned the page, found a final entry. 'Davison Research and Development has a subsidiary,' she told them. She frowned. 'That's odd.'

'What is?' they asked in unison.

'All the other companies are given their full titles. This one only has initials. I wonder why?'

'What are the initials?' Nash asked.

'DGE,' she told him. 'That's all it says, apart from it being a non-trading subsidiary.'

'DGE? So if all the other companies are pharmaceutical related, what does the GE stand for?'

'Electronics?' Sutton suggested.

'David, Mike said pharmaceutical. You might as well have suggested engineering,' Clara pointed out.

Sutton was watching Nash and saw his expression change to one of dawning horror. 'Oh no!' They heard him mutter. 'Oh, dear God, no! They can't be . . . Surely not.'

'I don't understand.' Sutton frowned.

Nash glanced from the army officer to Clara. She understood. Only too well. The look of revulsion on her face told him so. 'Davison Genetic Engineering.' She whispered the title as if it was an obscenity.

'Genetic Engineering? That's cloning isn't it?' Sutton asked.

'Yes,' Nash agreed. 'I believe the work being carried out at Ghyll Head Manor is a series of attempts to clone a human being. We've suspected something like this was going on ever since Mexican Pete got the DNA results from the woman who was found dead at the foot of Stark Ghyll. The baby she was carrying had only one strand of genes, the father's. And when he compared Alondra's DNA, he found it to have a close familial relationship to that of the foetus.'

'That's revolting,' Sutton said. 'Can they really do that? In human beings, I mean. I know they succeeded with a sheep.'

'It has been tried elsewhere,' Nash pointed out. 'I read an article a while back.'

'That's right,' Clara added. 'I remember. There was a heck of a row about it. The man who tried it was an American scientist with a Greek sounding name. Dr Zavos, or something like that. He claimed to have attempted it several years ago, although I believe he failed. It's clear he was well on the way to completing the cloning process, which got all the pro-life groups very agitated.'

'It's highly illegal here,' Nash told Sutton. 'But what they're doing makes sense now, in a mad sort of way. Paul Davison is trying to reproduce an exact copy of himself. He must see it as the only way to achieve the result he so desperately wants. His son Keith was a bitter disappointment. The daughter he believed to be his turned out to be someone else's child. If Paul needed someone to succeed him, he'd not be prepared to see his own genes watered down, or chance having to raise a child that wasn't even his, so he set about trying to create an identical match, one that hasn't been polluted by cells from elsewhere.'

'But if Alondra's not his daughter then why does he need her?' Sutton asked.

'Because she's his niece. She carries familial DNA from his brother, Luke. Who better than her?'

Clara looked down at the paper she was still holding. 'Bloody Hell, you're right, Mike!' she exclaimed. 'Right at the bottom of this sheet, tucked away in tiny print. The registered office of DGE is Ghyll Head Manor.'

'Which is where the experiments have been taking place — right under our noses. And that will be where they'll have taken Alondra and Daniel, I'm sure.'

'We'll need a search warrant. I'd better get onto Jackie and start organizing it.' Clara fell silent, her expression thoughtful.

Sutton saw his fiancée look towards him, and nodded agreement to the unspoken question. 'You will have someone expert in hostage extraction on hand,' he said quietly.

'You won't get authorization for that, will you?' Nash asked.

'Very rare that we'd be called in, certainly in this country,' Sutton agreed. 'Not unless there was real fear for the lives of the hostages. But remember, I'm already involved. This just adds to the training.'

'Given what we know, I don't think we can afford to wait for official sanction,' Clara looked to Sutton for support, but he shook his head. 'Not up to me to decide, thank God. But I was given authorization before Christmas. All I will say is, the longer you wait, the more chance of them doing what they have in mind or moving their hostages where we can't find them. If I had to sell it to a superior officer I'd say that they've already committed one serious crime. You need to go in as fast as possible.'

The phone rang, startling all of them. Nash was about to pick it up, when Sutton put a hand on his arm. 'Check the number on the caller display. If you don't recognize it, let it go to voice mail. It might be the kidnappers.' Sutton pointed to the clock. 'Who else would be calling at this hour?'

Nash glanced at the number. 'It's nobody I know otherwise it would display the name. All my contacts are in the memory.'

The answering machine kicked in. They listened to the recorded message, following which there was a short pause. Then a voice spoke. 'Nash, by the time you hear this you'll have realized that there are a couple of items missing from your house. The woman and that kid of yours. Before you go

211

ringing any of your friends and colleagues, let me make you a promise. Any trouble from you and I'll post your son back to you,' there was a short silence, 'in several parcels. Remember, we know exactly where you are, but you don't know where we are. More to the point, you don't know where they are.' They heard the click as the caller cut the connection.

'I think that answers your question,' Sutton told Clara. 'Now you know you have to act fast. Before they realize what you're up to. How many of your lot can you raise by daybreak? More to the point, can you get more of them with hardware? We'll need more than the two you brought with you. I'll phone my CO and get clearance to act as liaison, shall I?' He took his mobile from his pocket and left the room.

'Do you want me to get hold of the chief, Mike?' Clara asked.

Nash nodded, unable to speak. He swallowed a couple of times. When he did manage to say something, the stress was clear in his voice.

Clara got through immediately and explained the situation.

'Right, get off the phone, leave everything to me,' Gloria O'Donnell told her. 'I need to make some phone calls. Tell Mike I'll be with you inside the hour. Charlie can drive me while I'm ringing round.'

'She's on her way,' Clara told Nash, who was hovering by the phone. 'She didn't say exactly what she has planned, but she's making phone calls while her husband drives. Sounds as if she's hitting lots of panic buttons.'

The first evidence of this came shortly before the chief constable arrived. A vehicle pulled up by the end of the drive. Clara went to the door, believing it to be the chief. Instead she saw two uniformed men emerge from a Land Rover that was painted in camouflage. They walked briskly up the drive. 'Is Major Sutton here, ma'am?' one of them asked.

Clara stood to one side as David emerged from the kitchen. 'These are the other members of my team,' he explained. 'This is John.' He pointed to one of the men, then gestured to the other. 'And so is this.'

'The CO says we've to put ourselves at Chief Constable O'Donnell's disposal,' one of the soldiers reported. 'He said she'd obtained MOD and Home Office sanction for us to act.'

'Good, come through and have a look at the CCTV tape,' Sutton gestured to them. 'I want you to memorize the faces; you may need to identify them fast.'

CHAPTER TWENTY-TWO

Brother J. Malachi Entwistle, known to Doctor Anna Nixon as Malcolm, stared at his assistant in dismay. 'You're joking, Anna.'

She looked tired, having been working all night. She shook her head. It wasn't the sort of subject she'd joke about, as he well knew. 'I've done the blood tests; you'll have to make do with that for now. I don't know how you expect me to work in such conditions. I've one more test to do this morning. There's one thing that disturbs me. Is the subject violent or mentally unstable? I'm asking because of the fact that she was bound and gagged. I've had to sedate her before I could start. If she is unbalanced I think it would be dangerous to continue anyway. I take it she isn't a volunteer?'

'Don't let that worry you. And don't ask too many questions. Just remember what you stressed about the DNA and get on with your work. I shall have to tell the boss though. He's hoping for positive news. I'll delay until we know something definite.'

She could see the disappointment in his face. He'd hoped that today would mark the beginning of the achievement many considered impossible. Now, it looked as if that might have to be delayed.

Entwistle's office was illuminated by a desk lamp and fluorescent light overhead. As he was about to speak again the room was plunged into near darkness. 'What the—? Damn! Not another power cut.'

They waited, hoping that the lights would come back on, but after several minutes when power still hadn't been restored, he reached for the phone. 'Stay put and you won't bump into anything. I'd better ring the supplier.' Before he could dial, the door opened. 'What do you want?' he demanded of the intruder.

Anna could tell from Entwistle's tone that he disliked Dermot Black almost as much as she did. The man they knew as head of security was forever snooping round, often appearing as if out of nowhere.

'What's going on?' Black demanded.

'Power cut, I think.'

'Are you certain?'

'What else could it be?'

'I'll get my man to check the fuse board. It might be something's activated the trip switches.'

Black marched up to Entwistle's desk and snatched up the internal phone. He growled instructions into the receiver. After a few minutes he had his reply. He turned to Entwistle. 'Ring the power company. Tell them we want it dealt with immediately. I'll wait.'

The woman on the power company help desk checked her screen. 'There's nothing showing for your area,' she told them. 'Nobody else has reported a fault. Are you certain the problem isn't within your building?'

'The reason nobody has reported a fault is there are no other properties close by,' Entwistle told her, his tone abrupt. As the woman was based in Johannesburg she could hardly be expected to know that.

She promised to send engineers to investigate but could give no guarantee when they would be able to do this, or how long they would be without power. 'It depends on their workload,' she explained, 'and the nature of the fault when they locate it.' And with that he had to be content.

He replaced the receiver and relayed the conversation to Black, who didn't seem particularly happy with the news. He stared at Entwistle for a few seconds before turning abruptly and marching out. As the door slammed behind him, Entwistle looked at Anna, 'What else he expects me to do, I've no idea.'

She sympathized. She detested Black. The way he looked at her sometimes made her flesh crawl. She'd have left a long time ago but for the challenge of what they were hoping to achieve. That, and the nature of her relationship with Entwistle.

Outside the door Black listened to what they were saying. When he decided it was uninteresting, he strode off down the corridor and entered another room. The sole occupant was sitting in front of a bank of TV monitors, staring at the blank screens. 'Did anything happen before the power cut?' Black asked him. As he spoke, he looked round for evidence that the man might not have been paying close enough attention to his work, a book, a newspaper, a magazine, an iPod, anything that might have distracted him.

'Anything, such as?'

'I don't know. Even the smallest, least significant thing.'

'There was nothing. Not since dawn when I saw a fox cross over to that woodland,' he pointed towards the front of the building. 'But he goes that way every morning. I think his lair is in the woods.'

'If I want a fucking nature programme I'll put David Attenborough on,' Black growled. 'As you've fuck all to do here you can make yourself useful elsewhere. You're not being paid to shine your britches staring at nothing. Go check the grounds and the perimeter. I want to know of anything suspicious, anything out of the ordinary. It's called security, and it's your job.'

'What if the power comes back on?'

'Then I'll stand in for you until you get back, dickhead.'

* * *

The engineers at the power company weren't overstretched. It was a welcome respite after the traumatic time they had endured in the run-up to Christmas. Now that the weather had eased they'd been able to catch up on all the emergencies and return to routine maintenance. Even that was hardly taxing them so that when an early morning e-mail came in detailing a potential problem at Ghyll Head Manor, the duty manager was able to despatch a two-man team straightaway.

Having checked that all was well at the substation the engineers set out for the property. As they neared the junction that would take them towards Stark Ghyll they saw that their exit was blocked by large orange plastic barriers. Alongside these was an estate car bearing the distinctive yellow and blue panelling of the local police force. They pulled up as an officer approached. The van driver was surprised to see a woman emerge from the passenger side. She wasn't in uniform but was wearing a charcoal-grey trouser suit beneath a parka jacket and woollen scarf, muffled against the cold. She joined her colleague by the driver's door of the van. 'What's the problem?' the engineer asked.

The woman answered his question with one of her own. 'Have you had a fault reported by Ghyll Head Manor?'

'Yes, why? How do you know?'

'I'm afraid I can't tell you that. Here's what I want you to do. Call your office. Explain that you believe the power lines over Black Fell are down and that it will take several hours to reach the spot and rectify the problem.'

The driver glanced at his colleague, who shook his head. 'I can't do that,' he protested. 'Not without authority. What's this all about?'

The woman produced her warrant card. He read the name, Detective Constable Lisa Andrews. 'That's your authority. My orders are for you to comply with the instructions I've given you to the letter, failing which I shall have to arrest you for obstruction.'

For one moment the engineer wondered if this was some form of elaborate practical joke and that TV cameras were recording what was going on. 'I need some justification, something to explain this to our boss.'

'There is a major police operation ongoing,' Andrews told him, remembering the script she had been given. 'Taking out the power supply to Ghyll Head Manor is part of it. You need to be on hand to restore that power as soon as the operation is over. It won't take long, but until further notice, once you've contacted your office you won't be allowed any other communication. Sorry, but security is vital.'

'What's behind all this secrecy?' The driver had no expectation of receiving a reply, but Andrews surprised him.

'It's part of a large anti-terrorism operation. Similar raids are taking place elsewhere.'

Her instructions to reveal this had been issued in the safe knowledge that it would be the one explanation that no one would challenge. As she was speaking, her colleague was reporting over his radio. 'The engineers have arrived. Andrews is sorting them out now.'

'Thank you,' came the reply.

At a nearby location, Clara looked at the chief constable. 'All systems go. We can send in the troops now.'

* * *

The long hours of waiting through the night had been agonizing. Nash kept telling himself this was necessary if they were to achieve the safe release of both Alondra and Daniel. It didn't help. Around 8 a.m. Clara received the report from Andrews. He listened as she informed the chief constable, and the operation began. Any hope that the move from waiting to action would reduce his stress levels was unfounded.

Back at the roadblock the service engineers had complied and reported to their office. Now, deprived of their radios and mobile phones, they were sitting in their van watched over by Andrews and her colleague. They were surprised to see a camouflaged army Land Rover approaching. The vehicle drew up alongside and three tough-looking men got out. They were all dressed identically, from head to toe in black. One of the men approached their van. 'Out,' he gestured with his thumb.

'What?'

Andrews approached. 'Do as he says. Your van's being requisitioned. You're in the police car for the duration.'

'Bollocks! No way will we do that. No way can you take our—'

He looked down. Braced against the sill of his window was the barrel of a very efficient-looking machine pistol. The driver's immediate priority changed from righteous indignation to bowel control.

His terror was augmented as his colleague pleaded, 'Do as they say.' A glance to his left confirmed his fear. One of the others was in identical pose. The engineers trudged towards the police car. 'Jackets,' said the third man, offering a blanket to each of them. They complied.

Several minutes later DC Andrews installed them in the back seat of the police car. They watched helplessly as the tail lights of their van disappeared along the road leading to Ghyll Head Manor. Their bewilderment increased when a small procession of unmarked vehicles sped past. The final one paused by the barrier to allow Andrews to get in. Once it had gone, the police officer replaced the barrier and strolled back to the car. He wasn't worried that either of the engineers would try to escape. Even if they'd wanted to they wouldn't be able to open the rear doors. At that moment an ambulance drew to a halt alongside, the paramedic driver signalled to the officer, killed the engine and picked up his morning newspaper. The officer got into the front of the police car and smiled at his two guests. 'Now we have to sit and wait. Either of you got a pack of cards?'

* * *

Entwistle was in shock. He didn't believe what he was hearing. 'You're certain? Absolutely certain? No chance of a mistake? You've not got much light to work by.'

Dr Nixon's scornful expression told him the answer before she spoke. 'I'm not in the habit of making mistakes.'

'Shit! I've got to go tell him this. He'll hit the roof. Ever get the feeling this is turning out to be one of those days when nothing goes right?' With the benefit of hindsight, that was probably the understatement of the year. 'I'll go now. Pointless putting it off any longer.'

'Good luck.' Rather you than me, she thought.

As Entwistle was crossing the Minstrel's Gallery on the first floor he heard a loud knock at the front door. This was unusual to say the least. He frowned and paused, waiting until the security officer hurried to the door. He heard the caller identify himself, heard him tell their security man that they were from the power company. Listened as he explained that a power line had come down over on Black Fell and that it would take some time to fix; that they'd brought a standby generator which they would need access to the premises to install. That was good news. He wished he could say the same for what he was about to tell his employer.

* * *

Overpowering the security guard was simple enough. Two members of the team moved forward to search the ground floor. Sutton remained in the hall, watchful, even as he spoke quietly into his radio, 'We're in.'

He waited until his colleagues reported back. One returned with a second prisoner, a woman in her mid-thirties, who looked both scared and confused. As she was being led across the hall, the front door opened. Clara signalled the ARU team and her men to enter. The first of them accepted the prisoner, handcuffed her, and took her outside.

The second soldier was standing in the doorway of what appeared to be a refectory. Inside were at least a dozen men and women who until a moment ago had been enjoying their breakfast. As their bacon and eggs congealed on the plates, they were now sitting at the long tables in total silence with their hands clasped on top of their heads staring at the man in black with the ominous weapon in his hand.

The search party made their way quietly upstairs, with Clara at the head of the police contingent. At the top of the stairs they split up, with half the police team following Sutton's man, while Clara went with her fiancé and the remaining officers. In the first room they found a man sitting behind a desk, peering at a blank computer screen. He would have spoken, but the gesture from Sutton with his finger to his lips dissuaded him; that, and the gun pointing directly at his heart.

Their way into another wing of the building was blocked by a locked door which was quickly opened by Sutton. The rooms beyond were no longer bedrooms and offices, but a laboratory and what seemed to be individual cells; the first of which was occupied by a young woman, barely out of her teens. She looked terrified as one of the officers led her away.

* * *

Alondra was lying on an examination couch. The tape used to secure her wrists had chafed and her head ached from the sedatives that had been forced down her. That was nothing compared to the misery she felt. She was afraid for herself; more afraid for Daniel. She hadn't seen the boy since they had arrived at this place. She had been threatened that any failure to comply meant a risk to Daniel. She hadn't seen anyone apart from that horrid woman who had taken blood from her arm, examined her, both physically and intimately, and demanded information. What she was up to, Alondra couldn't begin to imagine, and the woman wasn't about to tell her. Wasn't about to say anything.

Alondra felt ashamed. She had let Mike down. She ought to have been capable of protecting his son. Instead she had put him in danger. That small boy she had come to love was now in peril because of her. Where was Mike? She desperately wanted to believe he would come to her rescue. He had rescued her twice already, but how could he do it again if he didn't know where she or Daniel were?

Her miserable solitude was rudely interrupted. The door to her room was thrust open with such violence that it crashed against the wall, dislodging flakes of plaster. A man she'd never seen before strode into the room, every step denoting anger. Alondra stared at him. He had a vaguely familiar air about him. His face was purple with rage.

'You slut! You filthy whore! You disgusting, evil slag. You're as much of a nympho as your drug-ridden mother. Any man that comes near you, it's legs open time, isn't it? Doesn't matter who it is, anyone will do.'

He slapped her once, then a second time. Before she had chance to recover he aimed a punch that hit her on the bridge of her nose. As her eyes filled with tears she heard the crunch of a bone breaking. The next punch hit the side of her head, and another closed one eye, the next broke her jaw. She tried to scream as he tipped the couch sideways to the floor and kicked her head and body repeatedly where she lay.

Through the mixture of pain and distress, Alondra heard dim sounds, of the door again crashing open, of voices, as she felt the impact of a final kick, before consciousness left her.

* * *

In the confusion that followed nobody noticed the figure creep stealthily from a door at the end of the corridor and down the rear fire escape. The man reached a black van parked behind a disused stable block and dived in.

Clara spoke urgently into her radio. 'We've missed one! There's a van racing down the drive.'

The van approached the gates and a car pulled to a halt across them, effectively blocking the escape route. The tyres screeched in protest and the driver darted round to the back of the van almost before the vehicle stopped moving. He opened the rear door and dragged a small boy out. Daniel, although held firm by his captor, was wriggling and kicking in a desperate attempt to free himself.

Nash stood by the chief constable's car, along with O'Donnell and DC Andrews. 'Move that car,' the escaper ordered. He pointed a pistol at Daniel who became stock still. 'I'll shoot the brat if you don't.' His attention and the gun were then fixed on Nash. In turn, Nash, Andrews, and O'Donnell had eyes only for the weapon.

Nobody took any notice of Daniel, who was now standing two feet in front and slightly to one side of the man, staring with pleading eyes at his father. He was scared, had been frightened since he was captured, afraid for himself, for Alondra and now for his father. He had endured a lot since his kidnap. His wrists were tied with tape; he had been given only water to drink. Shut in the dark interior of the van, he had not been allowed to use a toilet. He was soiled, hungry, weary, terrified, but suddenly, above all else, he was very, very angry. Anger such as he had never felt in his young life, coupled with the humiliation he had been forced to endure. But what could he do? A puny, small child faced with a grown man holding a gun he was now pointing at his beloved father.

Two months earlier, Daniel had been in trouble at school. Sent off from the rugby pitch and been told to report to the headmaster. As he stood dejectedly in the teacher's study, he had received the sternest of lectures. 'You must never, ever do that again, Daniel. You can have no idea of the pain it creates and of the damage you could have caused. Do you appreciate that you could kill someone by doing what you did? Anyone, even a grown man, let alone another boy of your age. In view of the seriousness of this, I shall require you to spend two hours in detention next Saturday afternoon in the hope that it teaches you never to do so foolish a thing again, ever.'

Daniel offered his headmaster a silent apology as in one movement he spun round and struck. Once, twice, three times. Swift kicks, delivered with every last ounce of power his small frame could summon. His captor's eyes glazed over and he fell forward on to his knees, squealing in pain, the gun dangling uselessly from his fingers as he clutched at his bruised testicles. A stream of hot vomit splashed onto the tarmac surface of the drive, narrowly missing Nash as he dived forward to retrieve the weapon. Lisa's foot went directly into the small of the man's back sending him sprawling, before she tugged the weeping prisoner's arms behind him and cuffed his wrists.

Nash passed O'Donnell the pistol as he clutched Daniel tightly. The chief constable smiled affectionately at the reunion. Daniel was trembling, tears coursed down his grimy cheeks as Nash freed his bound hands. 'Daniel, are you OK? That was very, very brave,' he said, as he kissed the top of the boy's head. He hugged him again. 'It could have been dangerous though. What made you think to do it?'

'I know it's dangerous, the head told me. I got sent off at rugby for doing it.'

Nash laughed aloud with relief. 'I didn't mean dangerous for him, what I meant was that you could have been shot. But you did very well, my brave little hero.'

Lisa pointed to the prisoner. 'What shall I do with this?'

'Hand him over to our men. Tell them to charge him with kidnapping and false imprisonment. Under the name Dermot Black. We also need to find our officer — if he's still alive.'

'He's tied up in the van, Papa.'

As Daniel was speaking, Andrews' radio crackled. She listened to the message. 'Mike, we're needed inside. It sounds urgent.

CHAPTER TWENTY-THREE

The trio sitting in the sister's office at the accident and emergency department waited anxiously for news. Seeing the desperate unhappiness on Nash's face, O'Donnell attempted to distract him. 'That place was kitted out like a hospital. What exactly were they doing in there?'

'They were attempting to clone human beings,' Nash told her. 'Well, one human being to be exact.'

'And that young woman who committed suicide,' Clara added, 'she must have been carrying the result of one of their ghastly experiments. Apparently, from what little I could glean from Entwistle they tried several more times without success.'

'But why did they need Miss Torres? What made her so special?' The chief was having difficulty coming to terms with such crimes on her patch. 'I thought they wanted her dead, or was it someone else that was trying to kill her?'

'Originally, she was to be killed because she had survived as a child. The reason they kidnapped her this time was they realized they had to have someone with a similar genetic structure to the original, to avoid yet another failure. Apparently, their theory was that it needed to be a bit like organ transplants where the risk of rejection is reduced by tissue matching,' Clara explained.

'It all sounds bloody sick and totally abnormal.' O'Donnell looked disgusted. 'It's like something out of a horror movie. I still can't believe any man could be degenerate enough to do something like that to his own daughter. Surely that's tantamount to incest?'

'Alondra isn't Paul Davison's daughter,' Nash said quietly, 'her father was Luke Davison. But I think you've—'

He was interrupted by the arrival of a harassed looking doctor. 'Mr Nash, your son is fine, just a couple of bruises and slight dehydration, he'll be with you shortly. Moreover, you'll be glad to know that Miss Torres is out of danger. Our main concern now is that her nose and jaw set correctly.' He paused, fidgeting uncomfortably. 'I'm afraid that although we tried as hard as possible, we were unable to save the baby after the beating she received. However, I think you should be aware that given the injuries she has sustained, the damage could well be permanent; and it is possible that she may never be able to have children.'

Nash closed his eyes. His head dropped into his hands as he took a deep breath before he controlled his emotions. 'Thank you, Doctor. I'm sure you did everything you could. May I see her?'

'I'm afraid not. I've given her a sedative. She's asleep now. She did indicate that she didn't want to see anyone.'

The others looked thunderstruck at the news, but O'Donnell recognized Nash's acceptance of the facts. 'Mike, you knew she was pregnant, didn't you?'

Nash's expression was bleak. 'I wasn't certain, but I suspected. She'd been sick a few times. I don't think she'd realized though, so it must have come as a worse shock for her on top of everything else.'

'Oh, Mike, I'm so very sorry.'

Nash shrugged. 'As long as Alondra's OK, that's what matters. Anyway,' he smiled briefly. 'I still have Daniel.'

'You were about to tell me something about Paul Davison,' the chief constable reminded him, 'when that doctor interrupted you.' She looked up. 'Drat! The man's back again.'

'Sorry, I forgot to say the other young lady you brought in can be discharged.'

Clara glanced at O'Donnell. 'Another of their experiments,' she said by way of explanation.

O'Donnell nodded acceptance and looked back to the doctor as he continued, 'We've checked her over and she doesn't appear to have any injuries. The other patient is also going to recover,' the doctor told them. 'However, he isn't being very cooperative. In fact he won't say a word, which makes it very difficult as I have to write up his notes. I wondered if you could supply any details. If nothing else, his name and address would be a bonus.'

'I'll tell you what I can,' Nash agreed. 'His name is Matthew Davison. The address,' he reeled off the DMG London headquarters.'

As the doctor was writing the details on his form, Clara leaned across. 'Mike, are you sure you're OK? It's just that I think you're getting a bit muddled up. Just now, you meant to say Paul, surely. You actually said Matthew.'

'No, I'm not a bit muddled.' He waited until the doctor had left, then continued, 'You forget; I've met Matthew Davison. I thought for a long time that it was Paul who was responsible for all this, I was almost one hundred per cent convinced until after I interviewed Bev Davison. Bev told me that Matthew was insanely jealous. "Consumed by jealousy" were the words she used. She said Matthew envied Paul because Paul had a wife and children, while he had neither. She also told me that Matthew had tried to get her to sleep with him and was furious when she refused. When she rejected his advances and started her affair with Luke, that must have rubbed salt into the wound, and when he found out that Bev was carrying Luke's child, his jealousy must have gone right off the scale. Bev said she didn't think Paul knew that he wasn't Lottie's father. But Matthew certainly did. Matthew desperately wanted other things in life that Paul had, things he could only dream of. One was the international recognition Paul had achieved through the company's pioneering work in new drugs. What galled Matthew most was that many of them were drugs he had helped to develop.

'The second thing Matthew wanted was overall control of the group, answerable to no one. But no matter how much he might desire it, he knew he would never stand the remotest chance of achieving it, not with Paul around. How that must have festered. Matthew knew that there was no way Paul Davison would have considered relinquishing even a small part of the control he had over the group. Paul simply wasn't the type. I should have realized that, and I should have seen all along that the story about Paul vanishing, going into seclusion, retiring from the business and living the life of a hermit couldn't be true.

'Finally, and above all other considerations, Matthew was frantic to found a dynasty, an injury he suffered as a boy meant that he was sterile, so he would never be able to become a father, not by the orthodox method. He had sought out all sorts of remedies, therapies, spent a small fortune over the years trying to reverse the damage. And all the time, there were his brothers, procreating like rabbits. At least, I guess that's how he saw it. As soon as I knew what was going on at that ghastly house I should have realized it had to be Matthew who was responsible. But I wasn't thinking too clearly at the time.

'I'd say Matthew originally planned the kidnap and murder of Lottie partly out of spite. Only partly, though, along with it, I think his long-term intention was to destroy Paul and gain control of the DMG empire, perhaps hoping he'd acquire Bev as a trophy along the way. I assume he thought Paul would crumble, but Paul was made of sterner stuff and stayed on as head of DMG for a further five years after Lottie's disappearance. By then, Matthew must have realized he was never going to get rid of Paul as he'd hoped, so he would need to try other methods. Or maybe it took him that long to pluck up the courage to do what he had to. And perhaps by that time, with scientific developments to provide inspiration, he'd formulated the idea that perhaps he could establish that dynasty after all. Moreover, it would be one that was uncorrupted by any outside genetic influence. Along with that, once the moral and ethical issues had been thrashed out, he would at last receive that international recognition denied him for so long.'

'What other methods? If that isn't Paul Davison in there, where is he?'

'That's the question nobody seems able or willing to answer.'

'I still don't see how you can be sure it was Matthew, not Paul who did those dreadful things. I know you've met Matthew, but didn't Bev tell you the brothers looked very much alike?'

'True, and I might have gone on believing it was all down to Paul, but for one big lie Matthew told me, and the things Bev said. And once I got to thinking about it, a lot of other things didn't add up. It was when we were looking through the DMG company information, looking for Entwistle, remember?'

Clara nodded. 'What did you spot that I didn't?'

'Something that clashed with what Matthew Davison told me and what I discovered when I visited DMG headquarters. He said that Paul had divorced himself completely from anything to do with DMG, and that he had not been in communication with Paul by any means whatsoever for the last twenty years. Matthew said even Paul's dividends were paid into an account Paul had set up.'

'I still don't get it.'

'The company that Entwistle and that other scientist were directors of was Davison Genetic Engineering. The third director was listed as Paul Davison. However, the company secretary was Matthew Davison, and the date of incorporation was seven years after Paul left the group, seven years after Matthew said he was last in communication with Paul. That had to be a lie. You can't appoint someone as a company director without their knowledge. Not legitimately, anyway.

'Add to that what Matthew said about the dividends being paid into an account and Paul not being in touch. I took that at face value at the time, but the more I thought about it the more it didn't ring true. Paul wasn't the type to let go of everything he'd created and built up. If he was so overcome with grief for his murdered daughter as everyone made out, he'd have gone much earlier. Having survived that, given that he'd made DMG into the huge concern it had become, he wasn't the type to retreat to a celibate existence. A celibate existence didn't ring true for a man with a reputation for sleeping around that was second to none.'

Present company excepted, Clara thought but decided it was hardly appropriate to say so in the circumstances.

'Anything else you found suspicious?' O'Donnell asked.

'Paul enjoyed the limelight, the chance of being seen with glamorous women, of being photographed, being on TV. The unlikeliest thing would be for his retirement to be announced in a discreet little statement from DMG. Not even issued by Paul himself in a blaze of glory.

'Then there was the matter of the universities. Jonas Turner told me Entwistle went to Bristol. Fortunately, the detectives looking into Lottie's disappearance were extremely thorough. In the background information, it states that Paul didn't go to university. However, Matthew attended Bristol as did Entwistle. I feel pretty sure they would have been there at the same time, probably studying the same subjects. Then, above all else, what they were trying to do at Ghyll Head Manor tallied with what Bev Davison told me.'

'And that was?'

'That Matthew Davison was unable to have children. A groin injury left him infertile.' Nash smiled, mirthlessly. 'Ironic, isn't it? This whole nasty business started because of that and ended because Daniel kicked Dermot Black in the balls.'

'Why choose Ghyll Head Manor for their ghastly experiments?'

'I'd say they needed somewhere remote, away from prying eyes. Entwistle hails from round here, he'd be sure to know the area.'

'I'm still struggling to believe it,' Clara confessed.

'If you still have doubts, I think when we interview Dermot Black the truth will come out.'

'Hang on, Mike. You've said all along he was Paul's man?'

'Black's a hired gun. He's not devoted to one man, or to a cause. At a guess I'd say there could be plenty of dirt in his murky past. All it would take would be for Matthew to uncover something Black wanted to remain secret, and guess what, instant conversion from Paul's team to Matthew's. I think if we accuse him of the murder of Luke and Paul Davison he'll tell us everything, including the identity of the two men who kidnapped Daniel and Alondra.'

'There's one snag, Mike,' O'Donnell pointed out. 'You can't interview any of the suspects. Given your personal involvement that would be inappropriate. I can imagine what a defence barrister would say on that subject.' She shuddered. 'On second thoughts, I prefer not to. However, I'm sure you can trust your colleagues to handle the interviews, especially if they know what questions to ask. And there's nothing to stop you briefing them beforehand or listening to the interview tapes afterwards. I gave instructions for them all to be housed at Netherdale. There are more cells, far better than Helmsdale.'

'Thank you, ma'am. I'm sure Sergeant Binns will be grateful,' Clara added.

'Yes, I'm sure he will, but he can come across and assist us. I asked Jackie to get the forensic boys in and she and Viv are currently eliminating genuine sect members from Davison's science team. It seems few of them knew what was going on in the second wing. The door was always locked and they were told it was to keep the weirdoes out!' She shook her head in disbelief. 'By the way, why did Davison require hospital treatment?'

'Resisting arrest, ma'am, so I was informed,' Nash replied vaguely.

* * *

DC Viv Pearce was detailed to take notes. As such, he thought it resembled more of a script conference than a planning meeting. Along with DC Lisa Andrews he had been assigned the job of interviewing and taking statements from the two scientists, Entwistle and Nixon. The drift of their questions would be not only to confirm the purpose of the experiments at Ghyll Head Manor, but the involvement of Davison and Black, plus the fate of the woman found at the foot of Stark Ghyll.

Jackie Fleming thought for a moment. 'I suggest we wait until we hear what the scientists tell Viv and Lisa, then Clara and I will talk to Black, leaving Davison until last. If it all goes to plan the first two statements will tie Davison and Black into the experiments, then we can start questioning them about the abduction of Miss Torres and Daniel. That should lead nicely into the kidnapping of Lottie Davison, ending up with the alleged murders.

'And before we start, I've some good news. Ballistics tests on Black's gun show a clear match to bullets recovered from a corpse found in the motorway service area a few months back. We'll be able to use that as leverage to get Black to talk.'

'What will you do, Mike, while we're in with the prisoners?' Clara asked.

'I want to hear what Black's got to say, so Viv's going to set up a link to the CCTV inside the interview room. I'll watch it from the next room. That will be much easier than playing it back later. If anything occurs to me I can get word to you.'

* * *

To begin with, Dermot Black was proving obdurate. Apart from confirming his name and address he hadn't spoken a word. Every question Fleming fired at him was followed by a long silence. It was the ballistics evidence from Black's gun that broke him. And once he began talking, they had difficulty stopping him.

The first part of his confession settled one matter that had been bothering Nash. Black admitted that he had tampered with Luke's climbing gear on Matthew's orders.

'What about Lottie Davison's abduction?' Fleming asked. 'What part did you play in that?'

'I found out how to make contact with the kidnappers through one of my associates.'

'Why Lottie?' Clara asked. 'Why not Keith?'

'She was younger, smaller, easier to handle for one thing. Also, Matthew was frightened of her. Knew how bright the kid was, far more so than the boy. And above all, he was furious because he knew Lottie was Luke's bastard. Matthew was desperate to shag Bev, he'd been after her for years, and when Luke got in there before him it sent him crazy.'

Fleming and Mironova exchanged glances, before Clara leaned forward and asked the only question still bothering them. 'Do you know where Paul Davison is?'

Black shifted uneasily in his seat but shook his head. 'I haven't seen him for years.'

The silence was interrupted by a knock at the door. Mironova announced for the tape, 'Sergeant Binns has entered the room.'

'Sorry to interrupt, ma'am.'

In the next room, Nash had hastily scribbled a note and handed it to Jack Binns instructing him to take it to Jackie. 'I've just had a message for you from Detective Inspector Nash.' He handed her the slip of paper and left.

Jackie read the note and looked up. 'You said you hadn't seen Paul Davison in years, and yet we've just learned that someone withdrew cash from his bank account yesterday over in Helmsdale. CCTV footage seen by Inspector Nash suggests that it looks very much like Matthew Davison, and yet we know he was in custody at the time.'

Black was unable to check the outburst. 'That's impossible, Paul's . . .'

Clara leant forward. 'Paul's what? Dead?' she demanded. 'Is that what you were going to say? Is that why it's impossible for him to take money out of his own account?'

They tried various questions, but Black refused to answer. Jackie suspended the interview and Black was returned to his cell after being charged with the murders of both the car victim and Luke Davison.

Nash was with Viv Pearce waiting in Fleming's office. 'I take it that message was a fake?' Jackie asked.

'It was,' Nash answered grimly. 'And if Black hadn't stopped himself in time he would have said "Paul's dead".'

'How do we prove it without a body?'

Nash had a sudden vision of the unkempt grounds at Ghyll Head Manor. 'I'm going back to the manor, and I'm going to take an expert with me.'

'An expert? Who's that?' Clara asked.

'Your boyfriend, Jonas Turner.'

Clara smiled at the reference. Turner had a soft spot for the detective sergeant, always referring to her as Sergeant Miniver. 'Why Jonas?'

'Our budget won't stretch to a full forensic search of the grounds. All that sophisticated equipment costs a fortune. So, unless you're able to get one of the prisoners to confess, which is fairly unlikely, I want an expert gardener to inspect the grounds. I hope Jonas might find a clue as to where Paul Davison's body is hidden. Unless we can find that, we've no chance of getting a murder charge to stick. And with no evidence in the case of Luke Davison, only Dermot Back's statement, and as yet no provable connection to the death of Juan Torres, we have little more than kidnapping, assault, and the illegal medical procedures to hit them with.'

'You're convinced Paul Davison's body is there, aren't you?'

'It seems the logical place. Once I was sure Matthew was involved, it stood to reason Paul was dead.'

'Good luck with that,' Fleming approved.

Viv Pearce was staring into his coffee mug. 'I still can't believe Davison intended to use his own niece to clone an embryo of himself.' He shook his head and sighed; appalled by the thought. 'He must have known the risks of creating something monstrous. I mean, it's almost like incest, surely.'

'I think Davison was beyond rational thought,' Fleming told him. 'Apparently, when the experiments weren't working, someone suggested he needed a subject with similar genetic makeup for it to succeed, and he saw Miss Torres, sorry, I mean Lottie Davison, as the logical solution.'

'We still need to discover who actually snatched Daniel and Alondra,' Nash reminded them. 'I've seen the enhanced CCTV footage and we have clear images of them, it would be nice to have names to go along with them. They could be amongst those we rounded up.'

'That reminds me,' Clara said. 'How come the CCTV at your house was working? I thought it only came on when the alarm was set.'

'That's normally the case, but there's a manual override button. Daniel told me he saw the men attack the officer. He managed to activate the override but didn't get to the door in time to lock and bolt it before they got in.'

'Lucky for everyone he did. But for that sticker on the van we might not have found them in time. He's a bright, intelligent, and brave little lad,' Fleming said.

Clara couldn't resist adding, 'He must get it from his mother.'

Once the meeting was over, Clara followed Nash out into the corridor. 'Any news from the hospital?'

Nash saw the concern in her eyes. He shook his head. 'Alondra still won't see anyone. I believe you managed to speak to her brother Keith?'

'Yes, he's coming home from Africa as soon as he can book a flight. I also spoke to the clinic where Bev is being looked after. The plan is that when Keith lands, he'll go and visit Alondra, if all goes well, then he'll collect Bev and bring her to Netherdale. I'm surprised she hasn't asked you to visit her though.'

'She sent me a note,' Nash said. Clara saw the pain in his eyes as he added, 'She said she was sorry and will write to me.' He shrugged. 'What that means, I've no idea.'

CHAPTER TWENTY-FOUR

The weather was grey and overcast, fitting enough for the sombre task. Jonas Turner was waiting by the entrance to his allotment. Nearby, his small terrier was investigating the possible scenting of a rat near the shed. 'Would it be OK if I bring Pip along?' Turner asked. 'He's about all t' company I get these days. And mebbe he'll come in useful.'

'Why not,' Nash agreed, 'you never know, he might do our job for us.'

Turner pointed to one side. 'I got them ready, just in case.' Leaning against the fence was an array of tools that might be needed for the macabre business of unearthing a body, should they be able to find a likely site. Having loaded the tools into the back of the Range Rover, they set off for Stark Ghyll. Pip perched on his master's knee, staring arrogantly out of the window at lesser canines that had to walk or travel in inferior vehicles.

Nash's first task was to unlock the padlocks on the front gates. As the estate was technically a crime scene, the whole area had been secured. Once they arrived in front of the house both men put on waterproof over-trousers and wellingtons. The gardens had not been well tended, and the once neatly clipped lawns were almost knee deep in grass.

The flower beds were overrun with weeds and the hedges were an unkempt profusion.

'Bloody hell, Mr Nash, you were reet when you said this place were a mess.' Turner watched his dog as he spoke. Pip was in his element, with a thousand new scents to check out. The dog was invisible for much of the time in the long grass, but reminders of his presence occurred from time to time via the alarm calls of various birds whose habitat had been suddenly invaded.

'I dunno what some folks are thinking of,' Turner's voice was filled with disdain. 'It used to be a grand spot this, but the buggers 'ave let it go to rack and ruin. That's a crime in its sen in my book.' Turner shook his head, his expression a mixture of sadness and disgust. 'A pal of mine, Ezra, was gardener 'ere. That were a long time back. I used to pop in and see 'im now and then. We swapped seedlings; that sort o' thing. It hasn't changed much, 'cept fer weeds. I reckon Ezra would be spinning in 'is grave now if 'e saw this place; God rest the poor bugger.'

Nash suggested they took the front of the house first, starting with the outer perimeter and working inwards, finishing off with the small area of woodland to the western edge of the property. It was a long job, made harder by having to struggle through masses of bramble and briar.

By the time they'd finished, both men were hot, hungry, and thirsty. Nash had provided sandwiches, a thermos of coffee, and some bottles of beer. Turner accepted a sandwich, declined a coffee, but his eyes lit up when he saw the beer. 'Theakston's an' all. By 'eck, Mr Nash, tha'd make a reet good boss. I could work fer you.'

'Funny you should mention that. I was going to have a word with you about my new place.'

'Tell you what, let's get this job out of t' road an' then we can talk about owt else.'

They had only just begun their sandwiches when Pip reappeared. Neither of them had seen the terrier for the past half hour, but obviously Pip's keen ears had detected a sound he associated with food. 'Looks like he'd been busy some-where,' Turner laughed as he pointed to Pip's nose, which had been decorated with an incongruous looking lump of clay. 'Mebbe he's teken up modelling or become a potter.'

Nash noticed that the dog got almost as much of the sandwiches as Turner.

'Right, let's look at the back garden, and see if Master Pip can earn his pay.'

They stood on the flagged terrace that ran the width of the building. 'Garden?' Turner spat the word out with disdain. 'Wilderness more like. What a bloody shambles.'

Nash could see nothing immediately suspicious from their vantage point, but then his was an untrained eye, and Turner had the advantage of having visited before. 'That's rum,' the old man said after a while.

'What is?'

'See yon summerhouse.' Turner pointed away to his left.

Nash looked. In the shade of a giant weeping willow was what had once been an elegant summerhouse. Given the same lack of care as the gardens it was now little more than a dilapidated shack. 'Yes, I see it. What about it?'

'There used to be a path ran across from this 'ere terrace. Somebody's dug it all up. Put that raised bed there.'

'Maybe they thought it would be nice to look at the roses from the summerhouse, catch the scent of them on a warm summer evening.'

'Aye, well, they'd need ruddy good eyesight, that's all I can say. Yon bed's in t' wrong place. It ought ter be further over — yon direction.' Turner indicated with his finger.

'So they dug the path up and put the bed in the wrong place. Anything else different?'

'Aye, and I know why they stuck that bed there. Right under where t' rose bed is, where Pip's digging, there were a fishpond.'

'A fishpond?'

'Aye, about half t' size of that bed, and about three foot wide.'

'If you drain a fishpond, what are you left with?'

Suddenly, the purpose of their visit hit home. Turner shuddered and scratched his head. 'I reckon pond were about four-foot deep.'

'Six-feet long, three-feet wide and four-feet deep,' Nash concluded. 'The makings of a grave.'

'Aye, and that's why Pip's diggin' there I reckon.'

'I'll go get the tools,' Nash said. 'We can't expect the poor little chap to do it all on his own.'

* * *

The detectives brought Dermot Black back to the interview room and were in the process of trying to obtain more information from him when Jack Binns once more interrupted their interrogation. 'I've had a phone call from Inspector Nash,' he said.

'Do you want me to come outside?' Fleming asked.

Binns shook his head. 'No, that's not necessary. He said he's at Ghyll Head Manor. They were searching the back garden and they've found a body.'

Fleming and Mironova were looking at Black. His hands trembled slightly; they could see panic in his eyes as the colour drained from his face. 'Interview suspended,' Fleming snapped.

She waited until Clara had stated the time and switched the tape machine off. As she got up to leave, she leaned forward. 'You refused the offer of a solicitor earlier. I suggest you reconsider.'

She glanced at Binns. 'Take him back to his cell. We'll head off for the manor. Has the pathologist been informed?'

'I believe Inspector Nash was attending to that.'

'Good. By the sound of things, I think you might need to check the supply of charge sheets.'

* * *

Following his March wedding, Viv Pearce strolled into the CID suite on his first day back at work. Clara was the only occupant. After a brief chat about his and Lianne's honeymoon, Viv asked about Nash and Daniel.

'Oh, Daniel's fine. Mike was concerned about the effect all this would have on him. The experts don't think there'll be any problems. He hasn't even had a nightmare from what Mike said. Daniel seems to think it was a great adventure and is enjoying telling the tale of his heroics at school.'

'That must be a great relief for Mike. Where is he?'

'He's gone to court today. It's the preliminary hearing for Black and the two scientists, so he's likely to be out all day. Did you want to see him about something in particular?'

'No, just wondered how he was, and what's happened since I went away.'

'Not good. Alondra's out of hospital but still refuses to see him.'

'What about her evidence statement?'

'We had to wait until she was able to speak. I took the statement. While I was there, I met her brother, he seems really concerned, and I think she'll be OK, despite her reservations about the family. None of this was to do with him, or Bev, for that matter. She said that she and Keith have got on well and with his help, she's beginning to remember little things from her childhood. Keith brought Bev to the hospital and that's provoked more memory. Once all the family matters have been sorted out, they plan to move to Spain to renovate the farmhouse and care for Bev there. Keith intends to sell all his shares in the business and use it to help the African village he taught in. As Alondra put it, they want the money to do some good instead of the evil it has caused in the past. I tried to persuade her to see Mike, but she just burst into tears and said she couldn't face him.' Clara's face saddened. 'He eventually got a letter from her last week.'

'What did it say?'

'She apologized for not seeing him, said she felt ashamed of who she is, of belonging to a family that's rotten all the way through, she was disgusted with herself that she had let him down, that she was unable to protect Daniel. She believes there's no future for her in a relationship that would be unfulfilled.'

'Unfulfilled?'

'Because she's unable to have Mike's children, I think she meant.'

'That sounds a right load of bollocks to me.'

'You really have a way with words, sometimes, do you know that? Mind you, in this case, you might be right. She'd already told me that if she couldn't make a relationship with Mike work, she couldn't do it with anyone, and that it was better to break it off now. She realized it would hurt him but thought that was better than them both being unhappy for years on end as her parents had been.'

'That sounds weird.'

'Mike had spoken to her doctors. They reckoned it wasn't at all surprising. Added to what she'd been through recently, together with her past history and the emotional turmoil of losing the baby and the knowledge she will never have a family, they reckoned her hormones are all over the place.'

'Hormones, as in brains?'

'Something like that. After all she's endured these past months I'm not surprised she's struggling with everything. It may be that she just needs some time. Then, who knows?'

'You reckon she might change her mind?'

'Viv, she's a woman!'

'What was Mike's reaction?'

Clara frowned. 'I can usually gauge what he's feeling, but in this case he just seemed to, well, accept it. I know he phoned her several times and wrote to her. He even offered to go out to Spain to talk to her once they're all settled, but she's adamant. Ever since he gave up trying, he's been quiet, polite, with none of his usual bounce. No chat, no humour, nothing. I've gone into his office a few times and seen him sitting there, staring at the wall. He hasn't even been rude about my coffee.'

'Phew, that really is bad.' Pearce nodded. 'I reckon he's well rid of her. Sounds to me like she had it right, and that he'd be buying into trouble. What he needs now is a really juicy murder case and a sexy female bouncing on his balls, to take his mind off things.'

Clara winced. 'Don't say that! You know Mike's superstition about Sod's Law. I'm talking about the murder, not the woman. As he is at the moment, though, women are the last thing he needs.'

* * *

Nash was about to set off for Helmsdale. It was Monday morning, and he had been freed from the necessity of attending court, following the remand for trial of all three of the accused. It would be another month before Matthew Davison's hearing came up, but even that was sure to be little more than a formality. According to psychiatrists who had examined Davison, it would be extremely unlikely that he would ever be in a fit mental state to answer the charges read out to him. Committal to a secure institution for the rest of his life seemed to be the only way to deal with him.

How are the mighty fallen, Nash brooded, and what a pitiful end to the ambitions of both brothers. One had lain unmissed and un-mourned in a makeshift grave for over twenty years. The other was bereft of sanity and would finish his life in an institution for the criminally insane, denied access to sharp objects and locked in a cell with soft walls. The mental health experts put Matthew Davison's behaviour down to something they referred to as Narcissistic Personality Disorder. They had cited character traits such as jealousy, exploitation; the need for admiration, his preoccupation with power and overriding all, his fixation with his sister-in-law.

The causes of Davison's behaviour, the rejection felt by a middle child, whose siblings got the love and attention he craved, the accident that had left him sterile, might make his crimes understandable. Forgiveness — that was another matter entirely.

If Nash had been more detached he might have felt some sympathy for either of them but, having witnessed the evil they had spread like a cancer around them, he felt nothing but anger. Their actions had ended several people's lives, and ruined a whole lot more. His blossoming relationship with Alondra, the baby she was carrying and the future he had hoped they would share, were the final casualties.

Nash took his coffee through to the lounge and stood in front of the window. The view of Black Fell with the peak of Stark Ghyll behind had been one of the main reasons for buying the house.

As he sipped the drink, he stared at the scene, which was much as it must have been when Luke Davison painted it all those years ago. Nash turned and looked at the wall opposite the fireplace. As if a mirror had been put there, the framed picture reflected that view. The landscape had arrived only a week ago, along with the letter. As a peace offering the painting took some beating. Even as a parting gift it was stupendous. The size had obviously been chosen with that wall in mind, for it was far larger than usual. The artist had captured the light and shade that chased each other down the valley when the sun shone through broken cloud. Nash's attention moved to the left corner of the painting. Instead of a signature, there was the distinctive silhouette of a cat. He raised his coffee cup in a silent gesture, a farewell toast.

Nash was aware that the painting was worth a six-figure sum like the one he'd seen in the Madrid bar. He would have given far more than that to have the artist here with him. But it seemed that was not to be.

Glancing back out of the window, the sunlight that had flooded the valley moments ago was gone, replaced by a curtain of rain that swept across the slopes of Black Fell. As if to match Nash's mood, the radio in the kitchen was playing a mournful ballad. Nash recognized the tune, the clear tones of Whitney Houston's voice carrying the poignant message of the verse. As the strains of *I Will Always Love You* died away, Nash felt tears prick the corners of his eyes. The sorrow he felt and the longing for the woman he'd lost was like a physical sickness that stayed in the pit of his stomach through every waking moment.

THE END

AUTHOR'S NOTE

It is a sobering fact that in striving for credibility, all too often the fiction we create is mirrored by more terrible events in real life. The concept of this book pre-dated several tragic and notorious cases. In researching the background to the plot of *Hide & Seek* I came across some truly horrifying statistics.

The first of these was that in Britain, 275,000 people disappear every year. A mind-boggling figure, and although many of these return within a short time, many choose or are constrained to stay out of touch with friends and family.

I'm not suggesting all these are victims of crime — but some are — and it is often only after the passage of many years, if at all, that the truth comes out. At any one time, Britain's mortuaries contain approximately 1,000 unidentified corpses, some of which have remained unclaimed for years. And if those statistics aren't sufficiently frightening, the next one certainly is. It has been calculated that every three minutes, a child goes missing in the United Kingdom.

Once, genetic engineering was solely the province of science fiction. However, advances in research and experimentation have now rendered this perfectly possible. The first test tube baby was born in 1978; from that point the next stage became not only possible but probable. The possibility raised many moral and ethical, not to mention religious, objections, following which many countries banned the practice. Others, less rigidly tied to such moral codes, may already have succeeded in going to that next stage.

Sometime soon, as you sit on a bus, in your train compartment, or in the theatre, it might well be feasible to wonder if the passenger sitting opposite or next to you was conceived in a bed — or a laboratory!

ABOUT THE AUTHOR

Having taken early retirement from the finance industry, prolific writer Bill Kitson enjoys the challenge of writing both crime and general fiction, often with a twist of humour. Both his series, the DI Mike Nash crime thrillers and his Eden House Mysteries, are set in North Yorkshire, the county of his birth.

He also writes his Greek Island Romances under the pseudonym William Gordon.

Living and working throughout most of the North of England he is now settled on the east coast of England, along with his wife.

His writing never stops, and when he isn't seeking inspiration from the surrounding countryside he can be found in a small fishing village on one of the Greek Islands, staring out to sea — laptop at the ready!

For further details, go to:
www.billkitson.com
www.billkitsonblog.wordpress.com

ALSO BY BILL KITSON

THE DI MIKE NASH SERIES
Book 1: WHAT LIES BENEATH
Book 2: VANISH WITHOUT TRACE
Book 3: PLAYING WITH FIRE
Book 4: KILLING CHRISTMAS
Book 5: SLASH KILLER
Book 6: ALONE WITH A KILLER
Book 7: BLOOD DIAMOND
Book 8: DEAD & GONE
Book 9: HIDE & SEEK

**Join our mailing list to be the first to hear
about the next book in the series:**
www.joffebooks.com/contact/

FREE KINDLE BOOKS

Please join our mailing list for free Kindle books
and new releases, including crime thrillers, mysteries,
romance and more!

www.joffebooks.com

DO YOU LOVE FREE AND BARGAIN BOOKS?

Follow us on Facebook, Twitter and Instagram
@joffebooks

Thank you for reading this book. If you enjoyed it
please leave feedback on Amazon, and if there is anything
we missed or you have a question about then please get in
touch. The author and publishing team appreciate your
feedback and time reading this book.

We're very grateful to eagle-eyed readers who take the
time to contact us. Please send any errors you find to
corrections@joffebooks.com